Defenders of the Light
The Battle Begins

By Keith Gunnell

Acknowledgements

Everyone knows that when someone does something outside the norm, there are almost always one or more people who influenced it or helped make it happen. This is my first book. I wasn't contemplating writing any of this until after completing a course on human consciousness at The Monroe Institute (TMI) in Faber, Virginia, which was the first major influencing factor.

During one of the TMI exercises, I had an "event" that turned into an in-depth lecture on something a small group of Spirit Guides (aka Guardian Angel or however you personally relate to as being the unseen guides influencing your life) gave me. They focused on something they called "Order Effect Theory" which we would understand as systemic effect. In other words, they wanted me to understand the importance of what one person does in their life and how it can affect others.

In this case, I was reminded of things that had happened in my earlier life. I was a young man who entered the US Air Force in 1971 trying to find a way to remain connected to my intuitive life through aviation. Instead, I found myself on a path that would take me to my first love and losing her in a violent act committed by someone devoid of any moral character. And then, a second love who had been sent, I believe, to help me deal with the earlier loss, but found herself the victim of the same immoral villain.

This is a book of fiction. But, it is loosely based on certain events that occurred around these women. With that in mind, this book is dedicated to these two souls who helped me through some of the most difficult times of my life. They will remain private and cherished for many reasons.

There are others, though, who also deserve credit. These are the people that helped get this all out and put me on a path that I hope will lead to more books in the future.

An endless debt of gratitude is owed to Jean Jackson, the founder and leader of the writers critique group that accepted me into their fold and helped me begin the process of improving my writing. Along the way, Valerie Pearce volunteered to act as a sounding board for ideas. But, one person I owe a lot to is Joanne S. McGowan. She is a skilled author with a depth of feeling that helped me write the most difficult chapter of this book.

The original version of Linda's death described the scene as it was discovered. Bringing those images back from the distant past and then write about them was more than challenging. It was even more difficult to read this chapter for the critique group. But, Joanne supported me and got me through it. John Nelson, my editor, educated me on how to improve this chapter to make it readable for others who would not be able to deal with the "horror" of Linda's death.

There are two other groups of people that I owe my thanks to for their patience and encouragement. They are the bartenders at the JW Marriott San Antonio Hill Country Resort and the employees of the Starbuck's located within the hotel. These people volunteered to read different chapters, continued to encourage me, offered their opinion, and continued to share their positive energy which moved me forward.

And finally, my wife, Rosalie Manley, stepped up to the plate in the end and read the entire manuscript offering her edits in our attempt to take it easy on Mr. Nelson. But, like most authors, I needed someone like him to bring this project up to professional standards, educate me further on the art of writing, and make the story and the messages flow. My hope is that there will be other projects that I will be able to work with John in the near future.

Also, Candice Meriwether Sanderson, friend and fellow author, deserves a lot of credit for being the person who stepped in at the last moment to do the proof-editing prior to submitting this work to Create Space. She worked into the night to insure all of the small oversights were corrected.

Prologue

The vision began as I found myself walking through a field surrounded with the natural elegance of tall ancient trees. A fresh spring breeze blowing through this open valley would be the perfect setting for lovers to enjoy secret moments as they looked forward to a life together.

As I crested the next hill, I heard what seemed like the crush of battle, perhaps an ancient battle. The awareness of it felt as if I had known this before but could not readily recall. Guttural screams of men battling each other to the death mixed with the terror-driven cries of women and children filled the valley before me. I stood there trying to understand what was happening when I realized that a large group of marauders were attacking a village. They were armed with swords and shields; some had battle axes and were cleaving their victims mercilessly.

The villagers were defending themselves fighting swords with wooden clubs and farm tools. Some of the older children stood by their parents' side fighting back. Despite the greater number of attackers, the villagers were holding their ground at first, but soon the battle turned and they were being killed and their numbers slowly dwindled.

Then my vision shifted, I saw what appeared to be the spirits of the combatants mirroring these physical exchanges. When a villager killed a marauder, I saw a dark energy leave their lifeless remains and move to another dimension. Yet, when one of the villagers died, a scintillating light energy left them heading skyward as if going home.

I then heard a voice say, "All of life is a spiritual battle, and you must choose to defend the Light or the Darkness."

"But why kill these villagers who had nothing of any worth?"

"They had their souls and would be called today, soothsayers and seers, like you David. Defenders of the Light."

As the battle ground to a halt with the last of the villagers and marauders dying, the air was filled with their dark and light energies. A green mist began to form at the edge of this death field. When the cloud was fully formed, I saw a powerful being walk from it. He stood taller than most men. His body was extraordinarily muscular, the glow around him dark and malignant. The shield and sword that he carried were ornate. While his shield was obviously stained with the blood of his victims, his chain mail was different. The red colored steel, I knew without asking, had been dyed with innocent blood as well and not from battle.

As he walked towards me, the darkness of his presence was oppressive. There was no place to run and nothing with which to defend myself, but I stood my ground like the villagers ready to defend my psychic gifts with my life.

He was about thirty feet from me when he was stopped by some invisible barrier. Out of frustration, the entity screamed, "You belong to me. Release this power that separates us." I watched him struggle trying to force his way forward before he finally gave up. "You will regret this interference. One day I will have you and I will spread your entrails across this entire field. Do you hear me?"

When he stopped struggling, I began to feel a kind of heavy velum descend and wrap itself around my body pressing hard against me. This had to be another way this dark being was attempting to attack me, and I began to resist the only way I knew how. I had been attacked before during visions; however, those attacks were nothing compared to this onslaught. As the pressure increased, it strangled me making it difficult to breathe with the battlefield stench continuing to waft through the air.

Then I noticed a fresh breeze surround me like a protective shell. The evil foulness had been pushed away, and its oppression dissipated. My attention was drawn upward to the horizon on my left. And there, an approaching presence appeared first as a brilliant ball of undulating light, which descended to the field of death and separated me from the being who had attacked me.

The light hovered above the bodies and began to take on recognizable shapes. What appeared to be a man and a woman took form, both beautiful and perfect. They smiled lovingly, calming my unnerved psyche. I could feel a kind of warmth radiating all around them. I also noticed that their energy was affecting me in a way that was surprisingly pleasant. Everything the monster used to press his attack had been removed.

The demonic creature screamed his complaint as he left the field, "I am the one who controls your future. You live or die at my behest, not theirs."

The woman spoke first. "He is deluded, David. All of this will pass. It is you who controls your destiny, not him or us." I recognized her voice as the one I had heard earlier telling me of the defenders.

I stood there having no idea why all of this was happening, exhausted from my attack and all that I had seen. Regardless, I knew there was a reason that I had been brought to this place. I exist solely to learn, but what would that lesson be here? Or, was I supposed to do something? And now, what did these two want from me?

"Do you sense a meaning to your experience?" the man asked as he motioned with his outstretched arms to all that was around us.

Gathering strength from somewhere, I asked in a demanding tone, "Why was this done and who are they?"

"The people from the village are part of your clan, dear one. This happened because the person they needed to defend them was not here," the woman said calmly.

"Who might that person be and what does it have to do with me? I've never seen these people before, let alone walked among them," I said.

"Oh, but you have. You are one of them. Like all of us light bearers," the man said.

"These people come from the same soul colony as you. The entity that just attacked you has always been dangerous to our people and our kind. His skills will continue to increase and threaten your people who will need your protection soon," the woman said.

They moved closer to me. Both placed their translucent hands upon my shoulders and the top and base of my skull. I felt their energy move around and through me. Incredibly vivid images began to fill my consciousness. I could see and feel everything as if I had experienced them in the physical. Suddenly, I began to realize that I had known these two at some point in my distant past, though I knew not when or where.

The longer they touched me, the more I began to discern a veil thinning that allowed me to see into this past. "You will have this and similar dreams, and you will begin to see more with each occurrence. Be patient, but know you must act when you are called upon. Everything will depend on you and others like you," said the man.

"And know that this entity, Maridon, is aware of you and sees you as a threat. He will do anything to destroy what threatens him if he cannot persuade you to join his dark clan," the woman added, as the two of them faded away.

I was thrown back into the present, which left me in a cold sweat that enveloped my body like a thick glove. Breathing heavily, I realized I had been exploring again in an out-of-body experience, cloaked as a dream. I sat up trying to reorient myself to my bedroom. Most of my dreams occur once, maybe twice. But they are mostly for teaching something that I should at least try to adapt into my life.

This was one of a few that I knew was precognitive, or predictive of the future. The question remained: what was I supposed to do? Who was I supposedly meant to protect? If there were others like me, then who were they and what are we together, and why are we separated now? In time, I was certain, all of this and more would become known.

Her final words haunted me for years after this dream, "This entity, Maridon, is aware of you and sees you as a threat." I was merely fourteen at the time. My preacher would probably call him Lucifer. I had never bought into this Christian mythology, but evil; yes I believe in that.

I had no understanding of when this would become my reality. And I certainly had no idea if I could intervene and save those who were thought to be, "my people." But either way, my first task was to know who she was talking about.

All of these questions did not diminish my belief that those who came to my consciousness during dreams or visions, such as this man and woman, should not be discounted or worse, ignored. I learned early in life they were sent to teach and protect. I had decided to learn from them and act when it was time.

Chapter 1

Seeing my young body sleeping below me in a small bed was relaxing and it felt safe. It wasn't always that way, but it was tonight. Then a dark shadow caught my attention as it slowly appeared in the doorway of the bedroom I had shared with my older brother before he left home for the Navy. From my position above, I watched the shadow step across the room and stare at me, the night light illuminating my face.

"You son of bitch," I heard my father's voice scream as he pulled me violently from my bed. My consciousness was instantaneously pulled back into my body. I could feel his maniacal grip around my throat as he jerked me out of bed and threw me a short distance into the kitchen of our small house.

"You're still have'n those dreams aren't you? I can tell just by look'n at you," he continued to scream his condemnations. Trying to talk him out of these insane attacks was pointless.

"Come here you demonic seed. I'll teach you to disobey me," he screamed.

My back had landed against the small kitchen counter as I quickly got to my feet. My hand reached back and found a drawer behind me. Had I been guided to find the butcher knife that lay within, the one mom used to cleave meat for our meals? Was this what I would use to defend myself? At age fifteen, I had had enough of these attacks. My body and mind had been abused by him since my early youth. When he was like this, he became a beast whose anger demanded to be sated.

"I'm warning you. Stay away from me," I said through clenched teeth, almost spitting out the words.

He moved forward obviously preparing to beat me yet again. Resolved to take no more of this mindless bloodletting, I reached for the knife and raised it. I was determined to thrust the blade deep into his heartless chest when my mother suddenly forced herself between us.

She attempted to calm him from yet another one of his psychotic attacks. I think she suspected that I was about to kill him, and I would have had she not stepped in between us. Suddenly the gravity of my intent hit me. I dropped the knife and shrank to the floor in tears.

"How many times do we have to go through this, Paul? Leave your son alone," she said firmly.

"But you know what he is. He's not normal. He's possessed. How do I know he won't sacrifice one of us in our sleep?" he asked angrily.

"You heard what Carfon said. Don't you believe what a preacher tells you? If you did, you might have stronger faith," she said, as she pushed him back into their bedroom next to mine.

"But you think he's possessed too," he argued. Their voices began to fade, but I could still hear them arguing.

"Outside . . . I have to go outside," my inner voice told me.

Finally, enough strength returned, and I stood up and ran from the house still in my pajamas. It was a fall evening; a cool breeze blew through the dark trees. Finding a clump of evergreens that offered sanctuary, I slumped to the wet ground and curled up into a ball. I doubted anybody would come looking for me.

"What have I done to deserve this abuse," I cried out to no one. Since I was rarely permitted to express my thoughts, I had become accustomed to talking to myself, or conducting internal dialogues.

As I shook in the cool air, I felt the presence of another being lying next to me. Uncurling and turning around, I found the neighborhood dog that I had befriended years ago, Magregor. Why I named her that is something that only God knows. It just came out of my mouth the first day I saw her.

She had been dead a few years, yet when she appeared to me now, I knew that I would be safe at least for a while. Losing her had been horrible for a ten-year-old who loved animals. She was the only living creature who seemed to know and understand me. We had played together and napped under the trees in the summer. I even dug what some would call a grave so that she and I would have a place to hide.

Then, one day we were discovered. My brother was plowing the field where our private grave was located. Magregor and I scrambled out of our sanctum just before my brother ran over it with the John Deere D tractor and the single-bottom plow he was pulling.

His tractor seat was attached to a spring-tension steel arm. So, when the tractor dipped down into our sanctum, the seat became a catapult that launched him over the front of the moving workhorse onto the ground. Though he survived relatively unscathed, he was determined to "rip me a new one" after he remounted the moving tractor and stopped the engine.

"Come here you little piece of shit. You did that deliberately, didn't you," he yelled as he ran after me.

And, once again, mom saved me from yet another savage beating, but this time from my elder brother.

Shortly after that, Magregor bled to death on our front porch. Someone had cut deep into her shoulder, and she had come to me for help. I found her the next morning and broke down crying. I didn't know who killed her, yet another painful reality for a young boy to accept.

Our love for each other in life had been so deep that I was not surprised that her spirit body would occasionally appear to me when I needed her most. Sometimes, like tonight, she would come in a way that I could feel her presence. With her next to me, I felt safe. Feeling all the pain and stress of what had just transpired in our house, which was supposed to be my home—by definition, a sanctuary—I slipped back into guarded sleep. I didn't dream per se, but when I awoke the decision had been made for me to leave home, if I were to survive my warped childhood.

My family was poor and by extension, so was I. We lived on the south side of a large field that bordered the Flint, Michigan Municipal Airport. I always enjoyed watching the planes land and take off. I could just imagine the freedom that I would experience if I could learn to fly someday.

During the summer months, I spent most of my time at the airport sneaking into the cockpits of old planes that sat in the tie-down areas. Many of them were no longer flyable, yet their history spoke to me.

There was an old Cessna bamboo bomber that I always felt drawn to for some reason. Every time I sat in the cockpit of this one, Magregor would appear and lay down in the small aisle between the pilot and co-pilot seats. One day, someone else began to appear next to me. She was attractive, lithesome, dressed in a loose, long-sleeved blouse and a kind of jean pantsuit that I had not seen before.

At first, she didn't say anything to me. She would motion for me to sit in the pilot's seat while she just looked at me and smiled from the co-pilot's side. Her short close-cropped hairdo seemed appropriate for a woman who loved flying. Her eyes were inviting, and they drew me into her in a way that I did not understand though it made me feel comfortable. The connection with her was so easy I wondered if I had known her in life. At that point, the only person I knew who had died was my grandfather.

After several visitations, she asked a question, "Would you like to fly an airplane, David?"

I had spoken with spirits before so hearing her ask a question did not surprise me. Besides, I was wondering when she was going to do something besides just stare at me.

"Yes, I would. Are you someone I'm supposed to know?" I asked.

"Maybe, but for now go up the ramp and look for American Aviation. When you find it, ask Art, he's the owner, if he'd do me a favor. That'll get his attention, David. When he finally says yes, tell him that Sara wants you to go flying with him."

I did as she asked. Magregor and I walked along the ramp until we found the right office. There was only one person sitting at a desk in the large one room office.

"Hi, are you Art?" I asked the middle-aged man. He had short dark wavy hair and was wearing an old flight jacket and jeans.

"Yeah, who are you?" he asked.

"David Lussier. This might sound odd, but Sara wanted me to ask you if you'd like to do her a favor."

The look on his face was one of total amazement. "Sara? Which Sara," he asked hesitantly.

"I dunno. She and I have been spending time together in that old bamboo bomber in the tie-down area. You know the one I mean?" I asked.

"Yeah, I know it. Damn! What did she look like?" he asked nervously.

I answered his question, and then I said, "Her favor was to see if you'd take me flying. Will you do that?" I asked.

"Geez, she's back. Do you know anything about Sara?" he asked.

"No, she's usually quiet when I see her. But, you know she's a spirit, that's how I'm able to see her," I said deciding to take a leap of faith and hurry past the usual disbelief of me seeing things that aren't there.

"Yeah, I know. I knew her when she was alive. Gawd, I miss her. You know she died in an aircraft accident a few years ago. She must really like you."

"I enjoy being around her. It feels as if I've known her before."

Art Walker explained to me that his small business flew hot freight for the big three auto manufacturers, and Sara flew for him before the accident. She had lost an engine with a fully loaded aircraft. When that happens on takeoff, it's usually curtains for the pilot. The older aircraft he used were maintenance hogs, but they got the job done, except in Sara's case that day. Art was getting ready to fly some freight to Ypsilanti Willow Run Airport near Ann Arbor, Michigan.

"Hey, why don't you ride along, and we'll talk some more," he said.

Everything about Art felt good. Even Magregor was encouraging me to say yes to everything Art asked, including if I wanted to learn how to fly. We flew out that day and talked up a storm. It wasn't long before I was spending most of my summer days at American Aviation. Art and the work I did for him would fill the hole that had been created in my heart by abuse and disrespect for my unorthodox spiritual bend.

Chapter 2

In the summer of 1969, I was sleeping in Art's office off-and-on when the freight business was at peak demand. My parents didn't seem to mind me disappearing for days at a time, and I certainly liked avoiding any further confrontations with them.

Art arranged to share my labor with a small flight school next door in exchange for flying lessons. So I was flying a lot, completing the needed ground school training, and passed the written exams necessary to take my Private Pilot's Checkride. One of Art's friends, Robert Gentry, helped with the flight instruction which accelerated my progress. I was ready by December 24, 1970 for a simulated version of the checkride that he wanted to put me through.

Robert was an accountant full time. He loved flying as much as Art, but he only did flight instruction. He was a devoted Catholic with nine children, which I would kid him about. How many more had he and his wife plan to have? Art was Jewish yet these two were close friends, devoted to their families and to their faith.

"Good thing your wife is as willing as you are," I once said with a grin.

"Really, why do you say that?" Robert asked.

"Doesn't she ever tire of being so 'devoted'?" I snickered.

Robert stared at me as if trying to think of how to answer his smart-ass student. "David, I'm beginning to wonder just how old you really are."

"Well, obviously not old enough to know any better," I said apologetically.

"Okay then, let's get this checkride going."

We took off and went through all of the flying maneuvers leaving the most important one last—the simulated emergency where the engine fails. We were flying over snow-covered farmland when Robert pulled the throttle and said, "The engine has just failed. What do you do?"

"Checklist: declare an emergency with ATC on 121.5, and if the engine fails to restart, find a suitable field to land," I said.

"The engine has failed to restart," Robert added.

"Isn't that oddly convenient," I thought as I looked to the left and noticed a single north-south runway barely visible through the snow with aircraft parked near the landing threshold. As I set up the glide path at the optimum indicated airspeed, Robert said, "We have smooth air and very little wind. Let's land and then we'll taxi back and depart. Be careful of the large tree to the left of the runway and the parked aircraft."

We were flying a small Mooney Alon that I had flown a lot. At this point she felt more like an extension of my mind than a machine. Besides, every once in a while, Sara would show up and give me pointers.

Today was no different. I could feel the Alon moving through the crisp winter air as we found the slot that all pilots talk about when maneuvering for that perfect landing. I could feel Sara close behind me. Had she been physical, I would have felt her breathing next to my right ear. *Be careful, David. Don't panic.*

"Don't panic!" I thought out loud, which got Robert's attention. He was probably wondering what I could be referring to during this critical flight phase. Suddenly, a single, thin dark electrical power line appeared low across our flight path. I could feel the nose wheel skip over the object. The main struts caught the line causing the horrendous sound of high-pitched metallic screeching, as Robert's hand crushed mine pushing the throttle into the instrument panel. The engine roared, which seemed to have little effect, on the indicated airspeed as it dropped precipitously.

"I've got control," Robert said firmly.

I released the controls and wondered what was about to happen. Sara was still next to me and quietly said, *Don't worry, Sweetie. This will be an interesting experience for you.*

Just as she said that, I heard a loud snap and the Alon began twisting to the left. Then another loud snap and she straightened out. We were about the same altitude as the large tree Robert had pointed out earlier. Surprisingly, the Alon cooperated with him and continued to fly. I noticed the pitot system instruments weren't working as we began to climb. Obviously, the wire had destroyed the pitot tube, which was attached to the underside of the left wing. We were now flying literally by the seat of our pants with no airspeed indicator or altimeter.

The decision was made not to fly back to Flint because of a number of factors. Instead, Robert headed for a small uncontrolled airport north of town to avoid messing up the traffic at Flint with our emergency.

As we circled the small airport, I saw someone run to an aerobatic airplane, a 7EC Champ. He didn't bother using the runway and just took off; within seconds he was alongside us, and the pilot was talking with Robert on the radio.

He told us that we were pulling about 300 feet of electrical wire behind us. The choices were now limited to one: land at Flint. The challenge landing there was that we had to fly over major high-voltage transmission lines. The other pilot told us not to worry about it.

"Just fly the airplane and I'll take care of the rest," he said.

Robert declared the emergency with the control tower, set up the approach, and landed. That's when we discovered the brakes didn't work. The responding crash, fire, and rescue crews figured that out and began running over the trailing wire with their trucks, which jerked us to a stop. We were then towed to the ramp along with our wire.

The next day, the Federal Aviation Administration safety inspector met us at the office. He couldn't believe we lived through the accident. Every aircraft that had hit electrical lines in his experience had either exploded, or flipped over and crashed upside down killing everyone onboard.

Then he had to talk about our landing.

"I need to locate the pilot that kept you guys from vaporizing on final approach. You know where I can find him?" the inspector asked.

"We picked him up at the airport in Flushing. Have you gone out there yet?" Robert asked.

"The tower mentioned that, but when I went out there the owner didn't know who I was talking about. No one was there on Christmas Eve, he claimed."

"The tower saw the aircraft, didn't they?"

"Yeah, and they had the call sign too, but I can't trace it to anyone."

That was odd because all the aircraft in the country were registered with the FAA.

"Let me tell you what he did, though. When you guys were on final, the tower controllers said they saw him maneuver his 'non-existent aircraft' behind yours and placed his wings under the wire you were dragging. As you approached those high-tension lines west of the airport, he elevated the wire enough so it wouldn't touch them. Had he not done that, you two wouldn't be here right now. But then again, I don't know how the hell you managed to keep from flipping over in that farmer's field in the first place. This has never happened before. I hope you know just how lucky you've been with this one."

That's when I heard Sara say, *It pays to have friends, doesn't David?*

The inspector had a few more things to say and then left. Robert went home to be with his wife and children. I never saw him after that. He must've been really "spooked." About a month later, I passed the checkride and got my license.

My relationship with Art continued to get stronger, especially when unusual things would happen, like my miraculous near-death landing escape. He knew that I had visions at night and that some of them were difficult for me to handle. He would coach me back from the really bad ones.

"Dave, are you all right?" he asked one summer morning, while shaking me gently and waking me up from the recurring dream that I had been having since I was fourteen. When I opened my eyes, I found him sitting next to my cot with Sara standing behind him. Art could now see Sara on occasion and realized that she was here to help us.

"I'm good," I said haltingly. "Was I screaming again?"

"No, but you were agitated. Your fists were clenched, and it looked like you were about to deck someone. What happened this time?" Art asked. He and Sara looked at each other with concern.

"Nothing new. Just the same old carnage."

"I hope you don't mind, but I've been talking with someone about you at the synagogue. I thought my rabbi could help you deal with the dreams you've been having," he said.

This brought back how my uncles, who were circuit-riding ministers, reacted to my visions years ago. And then the beatings from my father and the arguments my parents had about this "gift." These were traditional believers with a limited perspective about psychic abilities. None of them understood that a person with this gift has no choice. It's not something you go down to the corner store and buy. It's something you're born with for some reason.

I had my first vision-like dream when I was three. Trying to explain that to a Christian traditionalist is like talking to a brick wall. In their minds, if your gift doesn't involve speaking in tongues at church services, then how could the source be anything but the dark side?

Reluctantly, I responded to Art's offer, "I'm not so sure that's a good idea. They wouldn't have any interest in these things."

"Oh, yes they would," Art insisted. Sara was shaking her head encouraging me to agree. "Some of the congregants believe in the mystics of ancient times, especially Rabbi Hoffman. I already told him about your dreams and that you helped me see Sara. He would like to meet you."

I really didn't want to be subjected to the kind of grilling my uncles put me through when I was a youngster. Their goal wasn't to understand my ability; they just wanted to scare the crap out of me and destroy my gift.

"Come on Dave, you'll like these guys. They've got a lot of knowledge about all this sort of stuff and might be able to help you."

"All right, all right. I'll go if you want me to. But you need to understand something. It wasn't me that helped you see Sara. That was my teacher."

The next week Art took me to a small office deep inside his synagogue. We edged our way through barely passable hallways filled with books stacked everywhere. I glanced at some of the titles in this maze and all of them were spiritual in nature; I figured that this was a form of entity self-defense. You confuse the malevolent spirit, and they'll forget what they came for. I was beginning to feel the importance of my being here. It was as if all of these books were alive and emanating some kind of multilateral energy—arcane knowledge for safety. And, as I progressed further along, the stronger the sense of ordered knowledge became.

We finally made it through this labyrinth and entered the hovel of Rabbi Adam Hoffman.

"Shalom, my friends," Rabbi said, as he cleared our seats of various materials.

"This is the young man we've spoken about, Adam." He smiled at me. "I think David would benefit greatly from your guidance about his recurring visions," Art said.

Adam was now studying me. And then I felt something energetic connect deep within me, what you would expect if someone plugged a USB line into your head. "I have given this much thought, David. Do you mind if I ask you some questions?" Adam said, as he continued to study me.

I felt comfortable in these surroundings. While some would say Adam's office was a total disaster, I was seeing a kind of unique order or logic. These books appeared to be focused on alternative realities, human consciousness, and even remote viewing—the ability to see details of objects or events thousands of miles away. Most of the books in this area were authored by Russian parapsychologists, and some of the others by Hindu mystics. My attention was drawn back to the rabbi.

"Ask away," I said tentatively.

"Good, I'd like to ask about your visions and these dreams you've been having." I nodded my head. "Art tells me you have a Spirit Guide or teacher, is that true?"

"Yes, I have had an ongoing relationship with several Spirit Guides all of my life."

The Rabbi leaned back in his chair with the smile of someone who just found what he had been looking for. "And you helped Art 'see' someone that had passed about two years ago whom he dearly loved?

"Yes sir, with my guide's help."

"Would you describe how you did that?" he asked.

It was a phenomenal experience, and I had no idea how to explain it. But then my teacher began speaking through me. The deepening of my voice surprised the Rabbi.

"We placed our hands on Art's crown chakra and suffused our loving energy through him. When he accepted the process, our energy opened his heart and then moved through his third eye to allow him to see Sara."

The rabbi sat there amazed by this description.

After I grounded myself, I added, "It was the first time we did that, and the voice you heard was my teacher."

The Rabbi leaned forward in his chair intensely interested in what just happened. He then began to share his background including how he had become a member of a little-known group known as the Jewish Mystics. There are several forms of Jewish Mysticism, but Rabbi Hoffman was studying one of the oldest known forms called, Meditative Kabbalah. "My studies have links back to earlier periods taking us to the time of the Sufi Piety between the 11th and 15th century. It helps us to understand why some are better able to connect with spirits, while most just see this as a perversion of the true intent of our dreaming," Adam explained.

"So what are you saying?" I asked.

He paused to marshal his reply. "That, young man, you are not the only one with this ability, as rare as it is. Traditional religious dogma would have us believe that none of this is possible. But, the sole purpose of these experiences is to help us to evolve. If we do not learn the lesson, we return to do this one over again until we do learn. You, David, are further along than many others."

"So there is such a thing as reincarnation?" I asked.

"Yes, but the subsequent embodiment is dependent upon what one needs to learn," Adam responded.

"Well, it's not like being in school where the teacher explains every detail of the problem and then how to solve it," I said.

"True, but in school, you do not have free will. In life, you must make decisions based on what you think you know.

Your guides are called that for good reason. They do not instruct you; they guide or influence you. Your free-will trumps anything they could do."

"But, in this recurrent dream, I don't see any way other than to fight a demonic spirit who loves to destroy innocent people," I said in frustration.

"David, this involves far more than just you. It will take the help of others to defeat the beast that you're facing. Why do you suppose your guides make reference to others like you?" Adam asked.

I thought for a moment. "But I don't know how to find others like me. I'm young and would likely be drafted to fight in Viet Nam before long."

"David, you already know there are no accidents in life. You continue on the path of being a good spiritual student, and your teacher will guide you to the answers you'll need. The experiences will be challenging, but that's how you will advance. Anybody can jump over a low hurdle."

We talked further about what demonic creatures do to win a person over to their side and draw them into servitude, and even take you to your death. I needed to be aware of their tricks, their schemes, and the idea they will stop at nothing to defeat you. Adam and his ancient research was very helpful in this regard. With his final words of encouragement and warnings, I thanked him and left his office more prepared to move on with my life.

I had a lot to think about, but the dreams I had been having began to recede into the background. I sensed that the battle arena would soon shift from the dreamworld to the real world. Art and Sara continued to offer great support as I made my transition from a troubled youth to a determined adult ready to take on the challenges ahead.

I graduated from high school with little hope of attending college and became eligible for the draft. Concerned for my well-being, Art encouraged me to enlist into the US Air Force instead waiting to be drafted into the Army or Marines. At least there I'd have a chance of being educated in something more useful than the art of war. Little did I know that my real education would be training for a war of another kind.

Chapter 3

The letter I opened from the local Draft Board announced that I was their lucky winner given that my draft number was 31. It was understood that any male with a number less than 75 was guaranteed an all-expense paid trip to Viet Nam. Art and Sara encouraged me again to take some semblance of control and enlist in the Air Force.

The recruiters for the armed forces were all located in the same government building. An Army recruiter tried to talk me into becoming a helicopter pilot. This sounded attractive, but I had read that helicopter pilots had a guaranteed, non-revocable invitation to the front lines in Viet Nam as did their happy little support family. It also helped to learn that the average Army pilot lasted about 100 flight hours before being shot down. Needless to say, I kept walking down the hall.

The Air Force recruiter, Technical Sergeant Timmons, listened patiently, tested me thoroughly, and made me an offer. "I can't sign you up for anything in aviation except maybe an air traffic controller's job. But, I need you to do me a favor, if I'm going to get you that position."

"What's that Sarge?"I asked having never negotiated anything in my life.

"I need you to first become a Law Enforcement Specialist in the Security Police. Then once you've served some time there, I could see about getting you cross-trained."

I thought about the proposal. Unlike the other recruiters, he didn't sound like a used car salesmen. There was an air of believability in his deportment, and my intuitive sense was gently pushing me to trust him, so I accepted. It wasn't long before I had battled my way through boot camp and found myself in the Law Enforcement Technical Training School at Lackland Air Force Base, San Antonio, Texas.

I was good at pushing my way through the physical challenges. And, I excelled on the firing range with everything from handguns to grenade launchers. Seeing a small object propelled along an arc into a small, almost indiscernible hole a few hundred feet down range and then explode was somewhat startling. Since I was not inclined toward any form of violence, I had not realized that in combat another person would be on the receiving end of that arc. My instructor must've sensed as much and downplayed his delight with my proficiency in these skills.

Imagine my surprise when I was selected by a senior noncommissioned officer who was collecting promising recruits like me. His end goal was to establish SWAT teams at yet to be identified Air Force bases. So, we spent our days learning law enforcement skills, but it was then lengthened by some specialized night training.

On one such occasion, we were transported to Camp Bullis on the north side of San Antonio. This was where the Army and the Air Force trained their snipers. The targets we fired on were so far away that we had to use a specialized targeting scope. For us to pass, we had to hit the center ring 100% of the time within a narrow pattern. I was one of the few recruits who passed the test.

Then, I noticed that during this training, my vision-dreams changed and became less frequent. It was almost as if my very soul was hardening, closing down. When I'd had troubling moments in my life, I would ask for guidance. Sounds like praying, but it isn't. The agreement I had with my spirit guides was that I could always ask questions of them, and they would always answer provided it didn't affect more important outcomes.

So one night lying in my bunk, I drifted into a relaxed altered state and asked. It was a cool spring night, and most of the others were out having fun. It took a while, but I began to feel myself being lifted out of my body and taken to a place faraway. I couldn't see who held me by the arms, but there were two of them and we were moving fast.

They took me to a small grassy knoll surrounded by old hard woods that swayed in the gentle breath of nature. There were two flat stones in this small opening. I felt myself settling onto one of them and facing an opening in the tree line. Once seated, my invisible escorts moved away, and I saw a tall male in a long, shimmering silver robe walking toward me. The closer he came, the more I could feel his incredibly strong but loving energy. He sat on the stone next to me and held one of my hands in his as he leaned toward me.

"You have questions, David?" he asked.

"Who are you?" I asked curiously.

"Oh, that's not important. Just know I'm here to help you."

"Okay, I'm not sure what to do about my training to kill someone from a distance. I really don't want anything to do with it. And, it feels like everyone on this side is drifting away from me the longer I stay involved. Is that true?" I asked.

"You've made a choice, and the longer you stay involved the more your heart hardens. It has to for you to be successful in this arena. We're not moving away from you. You are moving away from us."

That shocked me. I was losing the only relationship I'd ever known that loved and accepted me without condition. But, I was taught to always do my best at whatever I was tasked. I almost pleaded, "How can I keep this from happening? I just can't walk away. They'll court martial me."

His smile widened as if he was surprised yet happy to hear the question. "You know that there are no accidents, David. The dreams you've been having are harbingers of what's coming. You need to work on how to defend what you believe. Do you understand?"

I pulled away, suddenly exasperated with this apparent conflict. How do you keep your heart, your soul open, while you're learning to kill another human being? I finally looked back at him and asked, "I need your help. I want to leave this training and move on, but I can't do that unless you set something in motion that will allow it."

"David, you know we can't do that. Have faith that everything will work out as we prepare you for the future."

This made me nervous. I never understood what was coming other than it was incredibly horrible, and I wanted nothing to do with it. "Look, those ugly dreams have subsided, and I'm thankful for that. But, are you telling me that I'm still going to have to deal with all of that ugliness at some point?"

"Yes, but we're giving you a break right now. Some of those dreams were manipulations by Maridon. We decided to shield you from those, too. He knows that you're being prepared and will do anything to convince you that you cannot win."

"What I see in those dreams doesn't look like anything I'll be able to handle. I'm not a violent person. So why pick me for something like this?" I asked bewildered.

"David, part of what you'll go through will be extraordinarily difficult, but you'll meet others who can help you. You're never alone."

"I know, it's all about learning from the experience and you have to be careful not to bias the outcome."

"Exactly, so be patient, continue your meditation, pay attention to your intuitive sensing, and everything will work out. You'll see."

And with that, he stood bringing me up with him, and placed his hands on my shoulders. I could feel his energy running through me. I swear that could cure anything that ails a person. When he was done, I thanked him. The next thing I knew, I was opening my eyes and looking out the window of my barracks as the sun rose. It was time to start moving and prepare for whatever was to come.

At this point in our training, all of us were allowed off base on the weekends. Exploring religious historical sites had been an interest of mine for several years. In this case, San Antonio was perfect for someone who felt drawn to this kind of discovery. It is one of few places that I knew where you could find sites that had profound historical importance in both the religious and military realms.

The Alamo and Catholic missions were places that I needed to visit. As time passed, the need grew stronger in me. This particular weekend I had taken the base transport to the center of town near the corner of Houston and Losoya. After touring the Alamo, I heard another airman talk about the new River Walk that was close by. It was in its early development as a tourist attraction, and one of the challenges the city faced was the area had a high crime rate. Having been warned about that, I didn't feel it was much of a concern for me. Then my attention was drawn to a fiesta parade making its way down Houston Street.

There were competing drum and bugle teams marching alongside more colorful performers. The children were amazing, dressed in bright blouses, skirts and beautiful sombreros. I had never seen anything like this, and it brought up what I had missed in my own childhood. Suddenly, I experienced a quickening of my spirit and realized there was a reason for me to be here and that I needed to follow the crowd.

The fiesta parade crossed a bridge where the San Antonio River ran alongside the River Walk. For some reason my attention was drawn to a young lady who was staring at me standing in a stairway leading down to the river. *Why do I have the feeling that she knows me?* I asked myself. She wasn't dressed like the rest of the crowd. Her appearance was more suited to an earlier period.

As the crowd continued down the street, I slowly walked to the opposite side where she stood, wondering what she would do next. The lady turned and hurried down the stairs to the River Walk, motioning for me to follow her. There was no warning from Sara, so I walked over thinking I'd see her again when I reached the first step, but she wasn't on the sidewalk directly below me.

When I reached the river's edge, I saw her walking slowly toward Commerce Street. Occasionally, she would look over her shoulder to make sure I was still following her. As I was wondering what this was about, I saw a misty fog form over the river. This was unusual for San Antonio for this time of day. Normally, the area stays quite humid given its proximity to the Gulf of Mexico's warm waters and the flow of moisture from it. This kind of foggy mist would normally form in the early-morning hours, not in the evening.

As I carefully approached this phenomenon, I suddenly felt a drop in temperature and knew what was happening. A portal was forming, and I knew that I had to walk through it. On the other side, I saw that I had stepped back in time, but how far back was anyone's guess. Except for the gas-lit street lights, it was dark. I saw my mysterious escort ahead. She motioned for me to continue following her back down Houston Street, which was now dirt-packed with far fewer buildings. I followed her until we reached the Alamo and then turned south.

What I had seen earlier was a restored version of the fort, but here was The Alamo still ravaged by Santa Anna's attack in 1835. I felt a weight begin to settle upon me the closer we came to the site. The lives lost here were numerous as were those who suffered greatly in the defense of Texas. Eventually, we came to a small two-story building that was a hotel. It looked familiar, but I couldn't place it. My escort stepped into the doorway and motioned for me to follow her inside.

It must have been late because the bar was relatively quiet. She led me upstairs and disappeared into one of the rooms. As I approached the door, I thought it wise to be cautious. I slowly positioned myself to check the room before entering. Up close I could see that the woman was dressed in what appeared to be a Victorian-era long dress. I now realized that I had been in the modern version of this building during my time, and had heard stories of a chambermaid that haunted the hotel.

She was sitting on a divan and looked frightened. "Are you okay?" I asked, concerned that a spirit would go to this length to bring me here.

She didn't respond right away. She looked worried as she stared at the floor.

I knelt down in front of her and said, "I'm here to help. You know that or you wouldn't have brought me here. What's bothering you?"

She began crying. "I'm scared because I'm going to die here tonight," she said, as she looked up at me.

Without thinking, I reached out and laid my hand upon hers. I was surprised that I felt them, as if we were in physical reality. This was one of those parts of my gift I didn't understand.

She looked at me and then wrapped her arms around my neck, crying as she said, "I heard you could do things. Will you help me, please? I don't want to die like this."

"Die like what?" I asked in alarm.

"I know I'm going to be murdered tonight by someone I know."

This was another nebulous area for me. What I did know was that no one was supposed to tamper with past events. If someone were to do that, the risks of creating a catastrophic event in the future would greatly increase. Yet, I knew I was given this gift to help others, and it didn't matter if they were alive in my physical reality or in the spirit world.

"What's your name?" I asked softly, as she still held me tight.

"Sallie Mayfield. I work here, but I also live here as part of my pay."

"Well, Sallie, I'm not sure what I can do to help. Would you like me to stay with you for a while? Would it help you to feel safer?"

"Would you? No one pays any attention to me here. It's like they don't see me at all."

"They probably don't, Sallie. I'll stay with you as long as you like."

She released me leaving my uniform shirt soaked with her tears. It really broke my heart that someone would feel this abandoned. "Sallie, would you mind if I told you what I'm thinking?"

She nodded, and so I continued. "I think you've already crossed over and you're stuck here. This is the place and time of your death, isn't it?"

Sallie looked even more confused having to deal with two wildly conflicted situations. "I . . . I'm not sure. How would I know?" she asked.

"Where do you think you will be murdered?"

"In the next room. This is a suite, and I was cleaning it for the next guest," she said.

I helped her to her feet, and we walked into the bedroom. On the bed, we saw her body lying there with a knife in her chest. It had apparently penetrated her heart and she had died quickly. I closed my eyes and allowed myself to relax and open to see what I could see from earlier in the night.

A man appeared at the entrance to the room while Sallie was straightening the bed covers. I could see him standing there watching her, and behind him I could also see dark shadowy figures moving around and through him. They were obviously controlling his thinking and his emotions. As he quietly walked across the room, I recognized who his dark spirits were, or who had sent them.

It was the work of Maridon doing what he enjoys most. His first approach is trying to convince an ego-centered soul that he will give them power and wealth as long as they allow him to use them to do his bidding. What he wasn't counting on was me showing up here.

The assailant pushed Sallie down on the bed and pulled a Bowie knife from underneath his coat. All it took was one thrust of the cold blade into her innocent heart and another life was taken. I could feel the brazen steel enter her as it took my breath away. This sudden realization, the shock, and panic of what she knew was about to happen washed through me.

As the man withdrew from the room, I saw his possessors detach from him and take recognizable forms. "Why are you here?" they screamed at me.

"To protect Sallie. Why did you take her life? She has done nothing to you," I said firmly, standing my ground.

"This is none of your business. Leave or we'll deal with you, too," they said in unison.

"And you'll do what to me? You have no power over my kind," I insisted.

As I said that, I felt another presence in the room. I turned to find Sara and one of my oldest guides standing there, and they weren't pleased with the situation.

"Go back to your lord. Your work is done here, and you will do nothing more unless you want to deal with me," the guide said. And, as he was threatening them, a ball of intense white light began to form around his hands. Our dark, unwanted friends noticed this celestial weapon and became noticeably upset. They left without saying anything further. I thanked my guide and mentioned that I needed to get back to Sallie.

My guide said, "You're doing quite well in this lesson, David. Be with Sallie and help her finish her journey. She has suffered enough."

Back with Sallie, I could see that she was still concerned about what might happen next.

"Sallie, do you know where I was just now?"

"No, you just disappeared and then reappeared. But, I felt something bad pass through me just a few moments ago."

I told her what I had done and what I had seen. Then I explained how these darks spirits had possessed the man who took her life. Suddenly, a look of awareness came to her.

"I know who that was. That was my husband," she said in shock and began to cry again. I comforted her and tried to convince her that everything would be all right now.

But, I knew it would be better if one of my guides would help, and Sara immediately responded.

"Honey, my name is Sara. May I hold you for just a moment?" she said.

Sallie didn't hesitate to allow Sara to embrace her.

"Honey, you don't have a reason to be afraid or worried any longer. I'm here to take you home, to where your entire family is waiting. They love and miss you so much."

Sallie looked at Sara and said, "But, they've been dead for years."

"There is no past or future here, only now. And it's time to go home. Are you ready?"

Another portal opened near the door to the room. It was overflowing with intense white undulating light. As it eclipsed the door, I saw two spirits walk toward her with their arms open, as if waiting for Sallie to recognize them.

Looking in their direction, Sallie joyfully said, "Mommy, Daddy! You're here!" She ran to them, and all three held each other as they slowly stepped back through the portal. When it was closed, Sara turned to me.

"Well, how was that for a rescue?"

"Different, but I wonder what Maridon had intended for Sallie. Somehow, I don't think he was just going to let her remain here wandering around aimlessly and reliving the moment of her death."

"Perhaps, but I think what was more important, is that you just proved to him that he has competition. Where he wants to destroy souls, you want them to thrive in love. And, you're becoming pretty good at that."

With Sara's last word resonating in my mind, I suddenly found myself standing on the edge of the River Walk underneath the bridge for Houston Street. Off in the distance, I could hear the faint music and cheers of the fiesta celebration. Graduation from Law Enforcement Tech School was tomorrow, and then I was being assigned to a small island in the Azores called Terceira; Lajes Field was located there and was the only NATO base in the Atlantic Ocean.

Chapter 4

To reach Lajes Field in the Azores, it takes a C-141, a four-engine turbo jet aircraft also known as the Lockheed Super Starlifter, about four and half hours flying out of Maguire Air Force Base, New Jersey. As luck would have it, our turbo jet ride had broken down, and we were put onto an old four-engine piston-driven, bloated-looking cargo hauler that could redefine the terms slow and cumbersome. While a C-141 cruises at 39,000 feet at mach .75, the C-124 Douglas Globemaster would struggle to reach 300 knots on a good day and rarely had a reason to go above 10,000 feet.

The staff Sergeant managing Base Operations began leading us around, pointing to our original ride, the now broken C-141, and explained that they didn't know when it would be ready. So, he walked down the ramp and turned to allow his audience to get a clear view, as he told us, "Gentlemen, we at Maguire believe in getting our boys to their destination. If you'll look over here (pointing to an object hidden in the night shadows of a distant hanger), you'll see the time-honored warrior of the U.S. Air Force. This C-124, also affectionately known as 'Shakey' in her day, is your new mode of transportation. She'll get you to Lajes around 10:00 a.m. local time tomorrow morning. And, you will be departing as soon as the crew finishes their OPS briefing which should be in a few minutes," he said proudly.

"But Sarge, that means we'll be flying all night," one of the airmen said.

"True, but let's not whine about the small stuff. Think of it as an opportunity to see what it was like for your fathers and uncles to get from one base to another during the Korean War."

To understand what this really meant, you need to recognize the differences between these aircraft. One is jet driven, the other piston. One flies quietly in the upper stratosphere just under the speed of sound. The other chugs like a race car when idling and intensely vibrates from takeoff to its destination's final approach, so much so, that at the end of the trip it's not likely any of the passengers will be able to hear anything clearly for at least a day.

I spent much of the night wide awake. The rhythmic vibration of the four Pratt-Whitney engines can act as a kind of intense undulating energy massage and cause an otherwise very tired person to relax just enough to pass out only for a few minutes. I did so without realizing it. The next thing I knew one of my Spirit Guides, Ed, was standing next to me. I thought I felt a hand rest on my shoulder and opened my eyes to see his smiling face. A little shocked, I looked around and discovered that no one noticed him. He communicated by thought instead of the spoken word. The experience was amazing the first time he tried it on me.

"Don't worry, son. They can't see me. Are you enjoying your ride on a piece of history?" he asked.

"Sort of," I said. "This is taking a long time. Was there some reason you wanted me on this antique rather than putting me on the C-141?"

"We know how much you loved the older airplanes you flew for Art and thought you'd like this ride more. Besides David, there is something to be learned when you can experience the old with the new," Ed said with one his trademark grins.

"And what exactly is that, Ed? I'll be so tired when we land that I won't be able to process anything."

He laughed and said, "Oh, we'll see what you'll learn, young man. What happens at Lajes Field is key to your future."

"Let's hope I avoid getting myself into trouble. You know I have difficulty dealing with people who abuse others."

"Yes, well, there's a lot to be learned here. Have you read up on the history of the island?" he asked.

"Not really, I haven't had time."

"Well, this should be interesting for you. The Knights Templar escaped to the islands after King Phillip of France convinced the Pope to denounce them. Some of their direct

51

descendants still live here and have their own spiritual practice. You may need to call on them at some point for support."

I was about to ask him, "What kind of support?" when he laid one hand on the crown of my head and the other touched my heart. I felt something move through me that took my breath away and with that, he smiled and vanished.

The old girl found her way back to terra firma early around 9:00 a.m. local time the following morning. We taxied off the runway and rolled into our spot on the ramp and stopped. The next challenge was to make my way down the fuselage ladder in some sort of manly way, despite having had little sleep the previous twenty-four hours. Instead, I ended up providing some comic relief for the others as I slipped and fell backwards going down the ladder. A firm set of hands helped steady my fall, but I still managed to land on the tarmac backwards. Embarrassed, I looked up at the person who had softened my clumsy arrival to thank them. At least I didn't have to be picked up by an ambulance with the hospital being the first stop at my new duty station.

Standing there waiting for me to rectify this poor first impression was a rather well-chiseled and well-shaped woman of moderate height dressed in what was called a class "B" uniform. Her tightly braided blonde hair was held captive by the traditional white security police hat perfectly positioned on her head. As I gazed up at her, I had the distinct impression she was anything but a happy girl.

"Sergeant Lussier, are you through?" she asked in a strong commanding voice.

"Yes, ma'am, uh . . . through with what?"

"Are you through with whatever it is you do when deplaning and showing off?"

"Well, not my intention, ma'am. I've been up for more than twenty-four hours. It's impossible to sleep on these old planes that shake the hell out of you."

"Sergeant Lussier," she leaned into me almost nose-to-nose to enhance the effect. "I'm your supervisor, Staff Sergeant Linda Cross, and I don't like lame excuses or showoffs."

I looked her in the eyes and nodded my head. I got it, lady.

"While you're assigned to Lajes Field, it will be my responsibility to ensure you are trained and certified to perform your duties as quickly as we can get you up to speed. Judging from the way you arrived on the tarmac and your attitude, I'm beginning to wonder just how much work that's going to require."

"Ah, I see, so you're already worried about me and we don't know each other. Look Sarge, I was told in Tech School by a rather demanding drill instructor that it was my job to always look after the ass of my supervisor. But, it would appear that if I made that kind of commitment to you, I could expect to have my face ripped off and stuffed someplace that I might find most uncomfortable."

Oh, the heat shooting through those very dark sunglasses would melt iron. She continued to glare at me with her fists braced on those shapely, but firm hips while leaning over me. The tension in her face was palpable. You'd think she'd at least offer to help me up. But, no, that wasn't going to happen.

"Watch yourself, Sergeant Lussier. I don't put up with shit from anyone, especially wise-ass males. You'll do what you're told and you'll do it right, or you'll think your time onboard that old rattle trap you flew in on was the best time you've ever had in the military."

And so our relationship started out on familiar ground. Having grown up in a household where I was the target of the family's abuse, defending myself in every way known to humankind, her admonishment didn't faze me. Sergeant Cross seemed to enjoy the same tired routine as my less aggressive family members, except the consequences of irritating her would be far more uncomfortable. Obviously, this was going to require some adjustment on my part and hers as it turned out.

Sergeant Cross began her educational tour of the base as we left the flight line. This was a joint military installation. The Navy had a submarine pen on one side that they loved to deny existed. It was kind of hard to miss since there was a large detachment of battle-hardened Marines guarding the damn hole, and few of them had a sense of humor. Then there was the occasional periscope that would pop out of the water on their side of the island and disappear as it cruised toward the shear mountain wall that supported the high-security area the Marines guarded. No one would admit it, but it just seemed too obvious that the U.S. was storing munitions there and servicing our subs. Besides, it added a little excitement to our duties as we chased Russian assets that would wander around the area snooping on us.

The real fun was when the Navy scrambled aircraft from our local VP squadron, whose pilots loved to act crazy in so many delightful ways. They would go out on their missions flying the Lockheed Electra, P-3 Orion to chase down ships. Navy pilots almost always had creative ways to harass their targets, but their favorite were the Russian trawlers that were actually intelligence-gathering vessels.

On one occasion, a crew led by a Navy Lieutenant nick-named Chicken Little provided an afternoon air show. One day Sergeant Cross and I were patrolling the blast pad on the north end of the island which provided an excellent ocean view. A Russian trawler was lazily floating past the island like fishing trawlers normally do.

But, Chicken Little and his little gaggle of intrepid, bored guys thought they might want to convince the captain of the ship to move far, far away . . . from the sub pen that didn't exist. He started out with some low passes parallel to the ship and flying in the same direction. From my vantage point, it looked like they were flying close enough to take down the ship's antennas.

Well, that didn't work so he started dropping red flares across the bow. *Yeah, that's gotta be real scary. That'll convince them to move . . . right?* I thought to myself. But, no, it had the opposite effect. What could Chicken Little do next? Why not something obvious like a high speed pass, and I mean really high speed—like fast enough that it was a challenge to keep a visual lock on the aircraft. All he had to do was come so close to cause the captain and his sailors to piss their pants, thinking that crazy P-3 crew was going to collide with their ship. I had the sense that Chicken Little would do a hard-to-forget risky maneuver, and I could hardly wait.

The P-3 flew out a few miles to position the aircraft for the finale run. At an unbelievable closing speed, the pilot in command flew his government-issued weapon directly at the bow of the ship at the same height above the water as the helm. The aircraft appeared to jump ever-so-slightly as it crossed the target just barely clearing all but one antenna. The pilot popped the top of that puppy and rocked the boat, literally. But then there was the turbulence that could be seen from the rotating swirls of ocean spray that wrapped around the deck of the ship as the aircraft blasted past them. Still drenched from the event, the Russian crew finally decided it was time to leave. I would imagine that there were probably a few crew members on deck that were still coughing from the kerosene and ocean vapor trail left by Chicken Little's influential flyby.

Later that evening, I heard that Chicken Little's squadron was being rotated out to Rota, Spain as a replacement squadron arrived on the island from Jacksonville, Florida. These were important and traditional transition times for them because it would give the crews a chance to party and swap war stories. Certainly, this Russian trawler would be the topic of the evening.

While walking to our unit, Sergeant Cross felt it necessary to add a few pointers. "Okay, Sergeant Lussier, I want you to pay close attention tonight. We have two major events happening, and they almost always result in fights or disturbances. We'll probably have to deal with at least three of these calls. The main one is the VP squadrons being swapped out. The sailors usually party too hard their last night in port and get in trouble."

"What kind of events, Sarge. Just curious 'cause I'm still so new at all of this," I said with a smirk on my face.

She saw that and stopped in front of our patrol truck. She knew my thoughts on the subject and didn't like my attitude about the patrol units. "Look, my little asshole friend, you better fix your attitude or you're going to pay a heavy price some day. This is serious work out here and at times, dangerous."

"Okay Sarge. I know that. Just trying to lighten things up. You don't have to be so serious all the time either. Tell you what; I'll be serious more often, if you'll at least try sharing a joke once an hour. How's that?"

"Oh God in heaven, what did I do to deserve this?" she said in exasperation, rolling her eyes skyward. And, with that, we crawled into our nifty faded dark blue patrol truck and began our evening shift.

As she drove to our on-base patrol area, I continued to think about what she had said. I wondered about the sort of issues she had to deal with that she wasn't talking about. There was a full moon tonight along with it being payday. Our Tech School training touched on unexplainable influences. For instance the instructor said that criminals and crazy people usually did a lot of what they do when there's a full moon.

I closed my eyes for some reason. I wasn't tired, but it was like a natural reaction to the questions I had.

"David, you need to learn when it's better to use force in physical reality and when it's not. As you know already, sometimes your spiritual enemies will use those they can influence to do things that will require your intervention," said Sara.

"Is there anyone I should be careful with?" I asked.

"No, just be patient with Sergeant Cross. She'll provide an example of how to use physical force."

I assumed we'd be responding to out-of-control wild parties. If so, no telling what I'd see there. While I had a better idea what was about to happen, I still had no idea what she meant. But I was about to find out.

Chapter 5

"Lima 2, Dispatch."

"Lima 2, go ahead," Sergeant Cross responded.

"Lima 2, Sergeant at Arms at the NCO Club requests assistance in handling a disturbance at his facility. Respond and report."

"Lima 2, 10-4. Is Eagle 5 en route?"

"10-4, but he's off base. ETA thirty minutes."

"Lima-2, 10-4. Will report on scene. Request Lima-1 be prepared to assist if this is a fight."

By this time, I was driving our pickup truck as part of my training. Sergeant Cross flashed me that "look" again, indicating she wanted me to go "lights and siren." I didn't think this served any purpose on a small island with nothing but two-lane roads and no stoplights or major intersections. The flashing lights were brilliant blue and reminded me of the mirror balls in a dance hall. I guess it made our blazing speed of 40 mile per hour more exciting even though all the roads were designed for 25.

When we rolled up onto the portico, the Sergeant-at-Arms, Henry Jacobs, met us looking irritated and a bit impatient. Sara and a few of my guides were standing behind him grinning, which made me wonder if the prank of the year was about to unfold with me as the butt of this joke. But then my attention was drawn back to Henry waving at us and frantically trying to hurry us up.

"Finally, you're here!" he said nervously. "I need you to remove a small number of squids and jarheads who are creating a ruckus."

Sara couldn't hold it any longer. "Oh David, you're not going to believe what's going on inside. We can hardly wait to see what you'll do."

"Oh great," I thought to myself, teachers who are now acting like pranksters.

While Henry was urging Sergeant Cross to hurry it up, I was still reeling from the lights-and-siren experience and trying to imagine what lay ahead. Henry briefed us while we walked into the club.

"You gotta get those idiots outta my bar. They're all drunk and acting crazy," he said.

In her usual cold manner, she said, "Henry, calm down and tell me what you mean by, 'they're acting crazy?'"

"Well, they're gonna burn the place down if you don't stop them."

"Burn the place down?" We stopped walking as Sergeant Cross confronted the panic-stricken man. "Henry, why would they do that?"

Exasperated, he began to explain, "There's two crews from the VP squadrons and a few Marines. They decided to see who the better man was by doing the 'Dance of the Flaming Asshole' ritual. You ever hear of it?"

"Haven't heard of that one, Henry. It must be new. So what are they doing . . .really?

The cackling of my spiritual friends behind me erupted, as one of them said, "Oh this is going to be so good!"

"They came in here about an hour ago and lined up ten shots of tequila for each challenger. They shoved them down the hatch and then dropped their pants and their shorts. Their so-called judge took partially used toilet paper rolls, flattened each of them, and then stuffed one roll in between the ass cheeks of each challenger. These guys hold onto the rolls with their butt cheeks while the judge lights'm up with a cigarette lighter. The winner is the one who holds onto their flaming roll the longest without dropping it."

My perfect, blonde-headed dictator turned to me. "Sergeant Lussier, go in there and make the arrests. I'll call for backup."

I looked past her into the bar at all those half-naked, battle-hardened, drunken maniacs, and then I looked back at her and said, "I see. So you just expect me to go in there with a bunch of . . . oh let's see, battle-hardened, government-trained killers and tell them that they're under arrest. I can see that producing excellent outcomes for the new guy."

She glared at me. "Are you going to do what you've been told or do I need to demonstrate." She paused, and then added, "And before you answer, if I have to show you, you're really not going to like the outcome. Do you get my drift?"

I turned around and hesitated with my hands on the bat wing doors, trying to get a grip before walking into what I knew would be a mess. I took a deep breath, steadied myself for the inevitable, and pushed through the doors into the insane asylum.

The scene was more than I had expected. The focus of the evening's entertainment was alit as described by Henry. I wondered if this was something that only American servicemen would do in public. My Tech School instructors seemed to have passed over the subject on how to handle crazies like this. What I was now aware of, though, was how flammable human butt hair can be. The challengers were doing some sort of creative dancing trying to avoid the inevitable singed-skin consequence, while attempting to keep from dropping their flaming torch.

A tall, overly muscular male that looked like he could crush me with a swat of his hand was staring at me. This was probably because I was the only sober male in the room, and then there was that funny-looking white hat I was wearing. He began to stagger in my direction with the look of a wolf descending upon his prey. A person never knows how they're going to react to violence until they're in the moment. And my moment was certainly walking toward me half-naked. My mind began to compete with my nerves to see which would freak out first.

"You're under arrest!" I yelled in a deep voice, hoping that might make a difference. It didn't. But, all of his partners were now waiting for the second act to start. Did I mention the audience included their girlfriends? Geez, where in the hell did they come from? Again, this is a small island. I also noticed my invisible crowd had moved into the room for a ringside seat. They were still giggling waiting to see what would happen next.

Then it struck me that I shouldn't have allowed myself to become distracted by them. My new half-naked acquaintance was almost on top of me. His eyes were glowering as he took a swing at me with his massive fists.

The next thing I knew I was flying backward out of the bar through the bat-wing doors. I hit the smooth, highly polished floor and slid until I was stopped by Sergeant Cross's foot, and stared up at her. Somehow, she looked even more beautiful from my dazed perspective. Then, I felt the intense pain delivered to my body by the drunken gorilla, and knew I wasn't going to enjoy any further assaults of this kind. Had it not been for that reminder, I would have gladly forgotten about all of the drunken male egos in the bar and enjoyed this unusual view of my lovely dictator. It took only a few seconds for her to assess the situation.

"Shit, I knew I should've taken care of this myself," she said, as she pulled me up off the floor. "Since you're new, you don't know that Neanderthals require special handling. Follow me and get the plasti-cuffs ready. When they come out, you handcuff them. Backup should be here shortly. You got that, butt-head?"

As she turned around and took what looked like driving gloves out of her pocket, I was regaining my sense of balance and getting ready for the show. She slipped each one of the heavily modified gloves on as she asked, "You know what these are?"

"No," I said. All I knew was they didn't look like normal gloves.

"These are made of black leather with modified pockets across the knuckles and at the back of the hand," she said holding one of them up showing me. "These are known as 'Equalizers' in bar brawls and are similar to brass knuckles. I like these better, made'm myself," she said with an eager grin. She turned and headed into battle.

After entering the room, she approached the same god of thunder that greeted me earlier. Her "come hither" look, so typical of black widow spiders, was all she needed to lure him into the trap. When the moment arrived, she grabbed him by the shirt collar, swung him around to position him for his projected exit, and cold-cocked his drunken puckered lips. He emulated my earlier, less-than-angelic exit. The energy she generated with that one punch propelled his gargantuan body across the floor so all I had to do was apply the plasti-cuffs, secure our prisoner, roll him over to the side, and wait for my next customer.

Keeping up with her was more than just a chore. It didn't take long before she had all the party-hardy flaming male assholes outside the bar on their backs at the feet of her trusty, if despised, sidekick. Some of their butts were still smoldering from the burned body hair.

I looked over at Sergeant Cross as she walked through the opened bat wing doors, folded her trademark tools, and placed them in her pockets. Odd, she wasn't breathing hard or even sweating. She was just smiling like she had done something sneaky and beat the odds.

"Did you see that?!" Sara nearly squealed. "She cleaned house."

While I contemplated the meaning of it all, the Detachment Commander came into the club with the backup unit. Captain James Walker was a determined, no-nonsense man standing about five foot eight inches and slight of build. I never saw him without that little wedge-shaped hat and with a fat, smoldering stogy hanging out of his mouth. He always seemed to use that tobacco-stuffed tube like it was some sort of chew toy to control his nerves.

In his usual manner, he quickly approached the carnage generated by this female version of *Thor*. The stogy was bouncing around clearly implying he was either agitated, or becoming uncontrollably excited.

After doing a quick assessment, he looked at the row of unconscious detainees with Sergeant Cross standing over them like a hunter inspects her kill.

His eyes locked on hers and firmly demanded, "Did she do that?"

I wasn't sure if he was talking to me while engaged in a stare-down with Sergeant Cross. I didn't know a lot about their relationship, but I figured I'd bluff my way through it. I moved closer and said quietly, "Well sir, she did most of it, but I helped."

His intense focus slowly shifted to me, which was quickly making me think maybe the new guy should've kept his mouth shut. "You just arrived on the island in the last few days, correct?"

"Yes sir."

"And Sergeant Cross has been training you, is that correct?" The stogy bounced frantically with each question. What would happen if I took the ugly distraction out of his mouth? If I didn't do that, I was at risk for cracking up.

"Yes, sir," I said still trying desperately not to laugh while forcing my hands to remain in my pockets.

"Did she happen to mention that I want backup in here for this kind of situation, so things don't get out of control?"

"Captain Walker, we had this under control within ten minutes of reporting on scene. Everyone's fine. Henry's happy, the Sergeant-at-Arms who called this in. The other customers were obviously entertained, and, as you can tell, we put out all the flaming assholes."

Yep, that did it. He lost his stogy as he looked around the room. It finally hit him that the detainees were half-naked and some of the butts were still smoldering. He looked one more time at Sergeant Cross and then back at the new guy. He spun around and left the building, mumbling something derogatory about freakin' enlisted personnel.

"Well, Lussier, you might do okay here after all," my dictator said.

Looking at her, I couldn't resist the rejoinder, "Yeah, well I hope you're gonna clean this up. I don't deal well with naked males." She smiled briefly as Henry and his men stepped in and began dragging bodies out to the portico for pickup.

While our relationship remained professional, it was safe to assume she had decided to let me live. Regardless of the circumstances, at that moment, I knew we had finally become friends, or at least established an entente. The hazing process was over.

On my way out the door, Sara put a hand on my shoulder, "There's a lot more to this woman than you think, David."

All I knew was that I had finally gotten her off my case, or did I?

Chapter 6

"Sergeant Lussier, I'm signing you off. But, we'll still do a few more joint patrols. After that, I'll be monitoring your calls and will respond with you at times. Congratulations," Sergeant Cross said in her usual clip no-nonsense manner. But the look in her eyes suggested that she was either hiding something or her opinion of me had changed.

Her eyes would linger on me a moment too long, and they seemed almost warm or something that I just couldn't put my finger on at the time. Distancing myself in an attempt to maintain a sense of professionalism seemed to be the right thing to do. When I thought about our duties, what was there to do . . . traffic stops? There wasn't even much of that on this base given there were so few cars. Answering domestic dispute calls and dealing with the drunks around payday kept us busy at times. But the way she looked at me, it was as if she was seeing someone else—someone that she longed to see again. On the upside, she no longer wanted me dead and perhaps found me somewhat useful.

Then came my "solo" review. "Sergeant Lussier, would you step into my office?" Sergeant Gary Dodd asked. He was the lead supervisor for our crew.

As a recently minted, indestructible, and well-trained male ready to fight crime, I had no idea how little I knew about the worldly realities of my fellow creatures. Referring to other humans as creatures was meant in the most respectful way. It was, though, intended to provide a vague context for what I am about to share. It was obvious that Sergeant Cross wasn't done with me yet, and I assume that was the reason for my "review."

. "Have a seat. So, you're ready to go on patrol solo. How does that feel?" he asked.

"Not sure, yet. Just getting my feet wet," I said.

"How was your training with Sergeant Cross?"

"Very thorough. She knows what she's doing. But, there were lapses, times when something seemed to be bothering her," I said.

He paused for a moment and then continued, "You're her first trainee since she lost her fiancé. Did she tell you about him?"

"No, what happened?"

"She trained him when he first came to the base about three years ago. He was reassigned to Nam and was on perimeter patrol when he was hit."

"Was it a sniper or was the base assaulted?"

"It actually looked more like an assassination. The Cong wanted to send a message that would spread fear around the base. So, a team hit him and his partner, disemboweled them and left the bodies hanging on the fence with a part of their intestines stuffed down their throats."

I could feel Sara standing next to me as she placed her hand on my shoulder. "Did anyone tell her the details of how he was found?" I asked, trying to control my reaction to the images in my mind.

"Yep, she insisted. She didn't take it well, either. I decided to give her some time off to process it all. Our local favorite priest, Father Flanagan, helped her get through it."

"I noticed she's been looking at me differently the last few days and hasn't yelled at me recently. Do you have any idea why?"

"Not sure, but this week is the anniversary of her fiancé Brian's death. And now that I think of it . . . wait." Dodd suddenly stood up and stepped over to a filing cabinet. He started searching and found something that seemed to surprise him. "Damn, would you look at this," he said as he held up a page with a picture attached. It showed a man standing next to a patrol unit.

"Who is it?" I asked.

"It's a picture of Brian when he started on duty here. Look at him. I swear he looks like you."

I had to admit there was a resemblance, but it wasn't that close.

Sara said, "There are no accidents, David." Great, I knew she was up to something, but what?

"Sarge, she still wants to ride with me occasionally, is that all right with you?"

"Good. Increases the chance that you'll both stay out of trouble. I like the sound of that."

Soon after, as I walked down the hall of the cop shop ready to start my shift, Linda called out to me, "David."

Surprised at how she addressed me, I turned to her in disbelief. "You realize you just called me David," I said.

She stopped and looked around the shop. "Well, there's no one else here. Would you prefer that I call you Sergeant Lussier?"

"No, I'd prefer we drop the Sergeant stuff completely," I said sincerely.

She stepped closer and asked in an uncharacteristic soft tone, "Are you going on patrol already?"

"Yep, guard mount's done, I'm all checked in, and the night's young. I'm ready to hit the road."

She paused for a moment and asked, "Would you mind if I rode with you tonight? There are a few things we could cover that might keep you out of trouble."

I could tell that this was just an excuse. Something seemed to be bothering her.

"Anything wrong?" I asked.

"No. I just thought, since you haven't gone solo yet, and there are so many things that can catch a person off-guard, that further . . . oversight might help." Her voice trailed off and she looked over my shoulder, as if seeing something or someone else.

Linda now turned back to me with her eyes almost glistening with tears. It appeared she was literally asking permission.

"Sure, I'd love your company. I asked Dodd if he minded us occasionally riding together, and he said he actually preferred it."

She chuckled. "I told him I needed to do some fine tuning on you. He laughed and said to make sure I kept you in one piece."

We stood there looking at each other in silence. I was taken aback by this change from her normal cold command-and-control persona. She seemed to be warming up to me, and I was hoping it wasn't my imagination.

A quick smile flashed across her face while she wiped her eyes and said, "Good, let's get started."

Normally, she would expect me to follow her down the hallway. But today, she walked next to me, talked about her day, and smiled. She felt more like an old friend than a dictator training her subject. I began to wonder if this was an invitation to probe deeper?

I could still feel Sara silently walking with us. When Linda walked through the door, I looked back at Sara. She was smiling. I knew then that something else had changed but I didn't know what or why.

After the bar brawl at the NCO Club, I looked forward to going back on patrol with the intention of avoiding any future conflagrations of that kind. Surely there would be a place I could hide. But, then I had to ask myself, what was I really trying to avoid? Was it the behavior caused by over-inflated male egos powered by excessive testosterone? Or, did I simply want to avoid the dark, raw frailties of human differences in this life?

Even though she had signed me off to work on my own, it appeared Linda seemed to be looking for any excuse to keep us together. The first few patrols were much like the earlier ones. Then I got the feeling that she was working up to talking with me about something that troubled her, but she just couldn't quite do it. Since I clearly understood my duties, I wasn't sure how to help her open up. But then Sara decided it was time for a little guidance.

"David, look at her. Do you see the profile of an injured woman trying to keep you out of her life? Or, do you sense something else," Sara asked gently, leaning over my shoulder.

For some reason, Sara's question changed the way I looked at Sergeant Cross. She had now become Linda for me. I began to see the softer side of her energy, a part she had kept buried to insulate her heart from any further pain. It appeared that she had decided to risk opening herself once more. She had changed, and I liked the person I was with now. Linda noticed me staring and said, "What are you looking at?"

"Oh, someone that has finally accepted me as being something other than a fresh recruit to fill a slot on the patrol board back at the shop," I said with a grin.

She smiled and stole a few looks of her own while driving. "You look as if you've been transfixed by something."

Sara whispered, "Tell her you're feeling that her heart is damaged for some reason, and would she like to talk about it."

When you have this kind of spiritual support, you learn early on to follow their lead. "Yes, I am by you and what's troubling you." I paused, as she turned back to the road. "It feels like you've been hurt by something. You know, I like listening and trying to help people work through things. Is there something you want to talk about?" I asked.

Linda and I were patrolling the flight line in our luxurious dark blue government-provided ride, a 1960-something Chevy pickup. Keep in mind that this was 1972 and these air-conditioned-less motor pool workhorses were used a lot. I was now panting with relief and thanking God as the sun began disappearing beneath the horizon. Sweat was already making the fatigues I wore look wilted, but the look on Linda's face made me sweat even more.

"Why do you think that?" Linda asked, stealing yet another look at her passenger, but this one looked a bit strained.

"Oh, let's just say it's something I feel. How close am I?"

She didn't say anything at first. Instead, she pulled the patrol unit into the shadow of a hangar and stopped. The moon wasn't up, yet there was just enough light to see the ocean waves offshore moving gently toward the rocky beach in the twilight. Why was it taking her so long to come up with a response?

Sara gave me a hint. "Give her time, David. The barriers are coming down slowly."

"When I began to work with you, you reminded me of someone," she said, looking down at her hands.

"Well, I hope it was a good comparison. I wasn't sure if you hated me when we first met and wanted me dead. But, after the Dance-Off at the NCO Club, I was pretty sure you were going to let me live," I said with a smirk.

Linda looked a bit confused. "I know I've complained about your attitude and some of your odd humor. But you do still remind me so much of him. It's like he's here but in a different body."

Maybe Dodd only mentioned the obvious. Then Sara pushed me along. "Do what you think is best, David. Brian crossed over and she's still having difficulty. She needs to let him go. That's one of the reasons why you're here."

"Oh great, I haven't done something like this before," I said to myself. I could feel Sara's hand on my shoulder again suggesting I should trust her. Talk about learning as you go.

"Linda, Sergeant Dodd showed me a picture of Brian. I have to admit there is some resemblance. But, I'm not him," I said.

She looked surprised as she began to tear up, but I could tell she was going to deny her feelings. "How did you know his name?"

"Sergeant Dodd told me a little about him."

Since we were already on the flight line parked next to an old hangar, Linda began her cover-up with, "Our patrol area is restricted to the flight line. Try to remember that we never, ever leave this area for any reason unless we're directed. If you want to leave, you have to request permission from dispatch, the watch supervisor must approve it, and one of the other units must report on-site before you can leave."

"Yep, you guys don't want me wandering off and visiting the NCO Club unless I'm invited. How about the Airmen's Club? Do I need an invitation or do I just go there? And, by the way, what does that have to do with Brian?" I asked.

She continued trying to hold back the tears. "Your smart mouth is going to get you in trouble one of these days, Sergeant," she said in exasperation, while giving me a smoldering glance. The old Linda was back, shields up, but I knew I had to press ahead.

"Maybe, but can you blame me for trying to lighten things up a little. After all, Sarge, we're on an island. Where's the criminal going to go? And again, what does that have to do with Brian?"

The sun had set and it was now dark. The lighting from the dashboard barely allowed me to see her face, let alone how tightly her blonde hair was pulled back into a bun beneath her hat. Turning to face me, she gave me one of those, "I mean business looks," again. "This is a serious job," she began tersely, wiping tears from her face. "If we make a wrong decision, you, me, or others can be hurt or killed. Do you think you can get that through your thick skull?"

"I know that Linda, but keep in mind that you don't know me. Are you even interested in who I am or am I just another warm body," I said as I slid down in the seat placing my knees on the dashboard trying to relax. Her tension meter seemed to be increasing as I imagined her face turning red, and her lips tightening.

"Linda, look at me." She turned toward me, but she was beginning to unravel again. "There's a part of me that no one here knows anything about. It's a part that drives me to help people who are having the kind of pain you're experiencing. You need to let go of Brian, Linda."

"I can't let him go. He's all I have, David, and now he's gone," she said, breaking down completely. Then it occurred to me that she never had the chance to say good-bye. As that revelation occurred, I heard Sara say, "Finally, you know what to do now."

She took out a handkerchief and blotted up her tears.

"Linda, I want to try something. But, I want you to know that if this works, there's nothing to be frightened of. Just stay with me and do as I ask."

She looked at me quizzically, but said nothing. Apparently, she accepted the idea she could trust me, or at least in this moment. I turned so I could face her and placed my hands, palms up, in front of me.

"Here, rest your hands on top of mine. That's it. Now, close your eyes and relax, breathe slowly and relax. Let me have all of your tension, all of your stress, all the pain that you feel. Let everything pour through your hands into mine. Release it to someone who cares about you.

"Breathe again, slowly. Feel yourself released from all your stress and pain, from everything you just gave away. Breathe again. Now, open your heart and see Brian standing in front of you." As I began to say that, I felt a rush of wind pass through me and suddenly, I felt myself being pulled out of my body. Concerned I would lose Linda, I tightened my grip on her hands. I opened my eyes and saw her still across from me, but we were no longer in that rattle-trap pickup. We were in a void moving some place rapidly.

Someone else was with us and I turned to see Sara. She was guiding us to a distant valley that stretched out before us as we left the void through a portal. Sara helped us settle onto the grassy knoll that provided a beautiful view of the surrounding forest.

"Linda, I'm one of David's friends. You can call me Sara."

Linda looked surprised. She glanced around in disbelief and then checked herself and touched me. Thinking everything okay, she quickly asked, "How did we get here. Where are we?"

"We're in a place, Linda, where you can heal yourself. David helped bring you here."

Linda looked surprised, perhaps not knowing what to think. "What do you mean: he helped bring me here?" Linda asked.

"It's unimportant. Someone is here to see you," Sara said, as she turned so Linda could see someone walking toward her.

As the figure came closer, she realized who it was. She excitedly yelled, "Brian . . . but I thought you died." She ran into his arms and they held each other. I could tell the love they had for each other in life was still very strong.

"Oh honey, my body died, but my spirit lives on. I've been told you needed to see me."

Sara wrapped her arm in mine and pulled me away. "Let's give them some privacy. He doesn't have long and they really need to talk."

We walked and talked about different things. But, Linda eventually caught up with us. "Thank you, Sara. I didn't know any of this was possible," Linda said.

"Oh, dear, this and much more. And, you have David to thank for this one. He's been in training for all sorts of things with us. But, he's getting good at helping others. Don't you agree?"

Linda looked at me, and this time she allowed me to see her without reservation. Looking into her eyes allowed me to experience an entirely different person than who I met the day I arrived on the island.

"You are a complete surprise to me, David," Linda said in a soft voice that melted me.

"It's time we went back," Sara told us. "David will explain all of this later if you have any questions."

Linda hugged me and I closed my eyes as I felt her pressed against me. I opened my eyes and found myself sitting in the truck across from a new person. She was smiling, and without a word, she pulled me into her, kissed me on the cheek, and said, "Thank you. Being with Brian seemed so real. I didn't know a person could do that."

"I've been doing things like that all of my life, Linda."

"So this is what you wanted to talk to me about?"

"Well, I was hoping you'd take the time to know me, as a person, not David the cop."

"This was quite a surprise. Is this something we can do again?"

"Yep, but it depends on the purpose. This gift isn't a toy. I use it to learn and to help others, nothing else."

"I hope we do this again. It felt like this would be a way to deal with a lot of unfinished business for me," Linda said.

"It has been for me. So, does this mean I passed training or is there something more I need to learn," I said with a smirk.

"Oh dear David, you have a lot more to learn and I do, too. Maybe we can teach each other. Would you like that?"

Yep, I knew she wanted me to live, and she definitely trusted me now. I wasn't sure where our relationship was going as I looked at how she was still holding my hands. But, I knew I didn't want this entendre to end any time soon.

Chapter 7

The staff dwindled when reassignment orders arrived. Being cycled back to the states on certain overseas assignments was part of the deal. And being short-staffed meant Linda and I were assigned different patrols to fill in until replacements arrived. The unit I was driving seemed empty without her. When everyone on base is behaving themselves, solo patrols become boring real fast. A look at my watch gave me an excuse to take a break. I had hoped Linda could join me, but obviously the fates had other ideas.

The Coffee House was usually busy with folks who dropped in from the 1605th Air Base Wing office building across the way. All of the core command offices were located there including the Staff Judge Advocates group.

I bought my lunch and sat down at a table to relax.

"Are you Sergeant Lussier?" I heard a woman ask.

I looked up and saw a tall, well-dressed woman in heels holding a cup of coffee and smiling. I couldn't help but notice how beautiful she was. "Yes, I am and you are?"

"I'm Julia Madison. My husband is Major Madison. He runs the JAG office. May I sit down?"

Beautiful women never asked to sit down to lunch with me, so I could only assume there was some other purpose for her request, but Sara was silent on the matter. I thought I'd let this play out anyway.

"Sure, have a seat," I said, while mindlessly holding my sandwich in midair as if I had forgotten what to do with it.

"I hope you don't mind," she said as she paused to sip her coffee. "I was hoping you were Sergeant Lussier."

"Why's that?" I asked.

"I heard a rumor that we had a cop on base that has vivid dreams or visions, and I wanted to speak with him. Do you have time to talk?"

"Yes, but I'll have to get back on patrol soon."

Julia smiled and said, "I understand. You'll need to eat while we talk." I nodded my head and took a bite of my sandwich. "I have a few friends who have unusually vivid dreams, and I heard you might have something similar."

I thought about how to answer her because I didn't understand her interests. "And why would you ask me that, Julia?"

"Oh, my housekeeper heard about you from one of her neighbors. You responded to a domestic dispute call across the street a few weeks ago, and she overheard you talking to the couple having trouble. You mentioned something about your dreams to them which seemed to help them calm down. Is that right?"

I had forgotten about the incident. The couple hadn't been on the island long when their troubles started. Life on an island isn't for everyone. At the time, it occurred to me that one of my experiences might help them deal with their anger. "Uh, yeah, I guess I did."

"Would you mind sharing the dream with me and why you thought it might help them?"

I wondered whether I should confide in someone I didn't know. I felt Sara's reassuring hand on my shoulder and nodded my head.

"Actually it was a dream within a dream within a dream. That's what I call these things when they happen," I said.

"Really, I didn't know a person could have multiple dreams like that," Julia said, as her eyes narrowed and she stared back at me.

"Yeah, it was a first for me. I was sleeping one night and dreamed that I was coming home from work exhausted. I walked into a house that I thought was my home and a woman, perhaps my wife, began complaining about her day without considering how mine went. I tried having dinner with her, but her complaints were endless.

"Feeling even more drained, I struggled to go upstairs and fell into bed. She followed me and continued her complaints as I drifted off. Suddenly, I felt myself pulled from my body and placed in a thick forest next to a stream. The animals around me were all in need of care, so I did what I could for them.

"As the sun set, again, I felt exhausted and laid down in the soft grass next to the slow moving stream. The sound of the water was so relaxing. A few minutes passed, and I felt myself drift into sleep. And, as before, I was pulled quickly from my body.

"This time I found myself standing in front of an ancient temple of some kind that had a number of steps leading to what looked like the main entrance. There was a line of people slowly making their way up those steps.

"I thought about joining the line as it moved upward and into the temple, when someone motioned for me toward her, and said, 'Come, you need to be here with me.'

"I joined the young lady but I had no idea why. Once we entered the temple, I understood. As we moved inside, everyone there knew why this was necessary. Each person who entered the temple merged with all of the others that had come before them. We had become one and that was the lesson."

"I'd like to hear more about your dreams. Do you mind?" she asked, leaning forward in her chair. Before I answered her, I recalled hearing something about her husband that caused me some concern. While he was a lawyer who took care of issues for the Wing Commander, there was a rumor that he had something to do with the intelligence community. Linda had mentioned that she heard he had partners working on the island, but no one knew why they would have an interest in a small, low-activity island.

Julia, on the other hand, was definitely her own person. I had heard her social circle included some of the most important people on the island. And, since Sara wasn't giving me any hints, I decided there wasn't anything to be concerned about. Perhaps Julia just had an interest in the paranormal.

"So, David, why do you suppose this helped my neighbors?" she asked.

"Well, people can interpret dreams or visions differently, but in the dream my wife and I went from her complaining and me not caring about her trying day, to realizing that there was a higher reason for us being together, and if we climbed out of our small world, there was a greater world waiting for us."

Julia just blinked her eyes. "Wow. I would've never seen that much in it."

Given her wholehearted response, I decided to share something that happened when I was three years old. It was my first vivid dream that I could remember. "Would you like to hear about my first experience with all of this? It happened when I was three."

"Of course, do you have time?" she asked.

I looked at my watch. "Yep, I think I can squeeze it in," I said, realizing that the rest of my lunch was coming with me.

"My parents decided to visit my uncle in California one summer. On our way, my father decided to stop for the night at a small motel in the desert. He could only afford one room, so he and mom got the bed while us kids picked a spot on the floor.

"I remember falling asleep quickly. The day had been hot and tiresome, putting up with my siblings complaining about the heat and the dusty roads. Then, I thought I heard a deep, but soft roaring sound outside. I got up and looked out the window. Swirling around behind the motel was something that looked like a small tornado.

"I heard a soft voice next to me say, 'What do you see, David?'

'Something big twirling in circles,' I said.

'Are you frightened of what you see?' she asked.

"I turned to her and said, 'No, I'm not frightened.' I felt some energy coming from her that I didn't want to lose.

"She smiled and her warmth enshrouded my small body. She put her arm around me and said, 'Good, it's time for us to sleep.'

"She curled up on the floor with me. I thought I had found a new friend that was staying with us. When I awoke in the morning, she wasn't there. When I explained what had happened to my parents, they just wrote it off as my overly active imagination."

"How did your parents handle your visions?" Julia asked.

"That was my first detailed dream. After I had my third one, I realized that I shouldn't share them with my parents, especially after they said that if they didn't stop, I'd be lured into the bowels of Hades."

Julia listened intently and asked some clarifying questions. When it was time for me to go, she asked if we could meet occasionally to talk more about these experiences.

We left the Coffee Shop together and agreed to meet here again. I watched her walk back toward the main office building still wondering why this had happened. As I turned to make my way back to my unit, I almost walked through Sara.

"Whoa, you should tell me you're here."

"Why? You're only going to walk through me, not into me," she said smiling.

I chuckled. "So, what do you think of Julia?

"There's something shrouding her and preventing me from understanding why she's interested in you and your dreams. But, I think it's safe to say this needed to happen for some reason."

"Geez, I never thought I'd hear anyone on your side say you didn't know something that an embodied person was doing or what their intention was."

"Well, when something's suppose to happen, we're not to interfere. Has anyone spoken with you about critical decision points or a triggering event?" she asked.

"No, not yet."

"Critical decision points are just that. The choice you make can trigger a series of events that can, and oftentimes do, affect you and a large number of people. It can change the direction of their life. That's what this feels like it's leading to, David."

"It sounds like I need to be careful, then. Would that be a fair assessment?"

"Perhaps, but let's see where it goes."

Julia's interests in my "events," as I called them seemed to increase each time we met for lunch which happened a couple times a week. Occasionally, we would run into each other at the NCO Club after hours and talk. Eventually, her talks expanded into the same spirituality issues that I had been working on for years. I felt conflicted because I couldn't figure out why a woman like her would take a deep interest in such explorations. The more time I spent with Julia, the more I could sense what Sara had said earlier was true. I knew that as with Linda there was a connection between Julia and me, but I didn't understand it.

The deepening connection with my new friend continued with each meeting. It wasn't some sort of desire or attraction. It was something different that even today, as I think back about her, I still cannot explain even though I have tried to forget her.

At the time, I interpreted it as me being pushed to protect her as if she were in grave danger. Periodically, I would have brief dream-like flashes of her being attacked, yet I could never see enough detail to know what to do.

One of these events occurred after a swing shift. My day had been complicated and rather draining. But with Linda's help, I was able to get through it. The bed in my room never looked so good as I fell into it. I was out in more ways than one that night. My body was in deep sleep, but then my consciousness was pulled, almost yanked out of my body by some Spirit in a hurry.

Before I knew it, I was standing in Julia's backyard. I saw someone break into her home through the patio door. He was dressed in black and moved in a way that made me think he wasn't your average midnight thief. As he made his way through the house, he kept searching for something. He moved into a small office and began searching through a file cabinet. While doing this, his jacket opened when he leaned over to pick something up, and I noticed he had a large caliber hand gun strapped to his waist.

I moved up to her bedroom thinking that perhaps I could find a way to wake her. I saw my friend and her husband asleep. Neither of them slept with a sheet over their bodies which allowed me to see more than I wanted, especially since neither of them wore pajamas. Why I didn't hesitate to look more closely at a tattoo Julia had on the outer thigh of her right leg is beyond me, but I did. Whoever had pulled me into this adventure still didn't want to make themselves known, but they were helpful. Somehow, they cast just enough cosmic light on Julia's thigh that allowed me to see a rather ornate image.

The background of the tattoo was dark. A bright, silver colored eye appeared in the center. Large wings were attached and they were surrounded by stars. I couldn't imagine what the artist used to make the silver color so vivid on skin, but it worked in this light.

The cosmic illumination disappeared and I continued looking for a way to wake them up. Sara almost laughed as she said, "Concentrate, David. It's not that hard to tip something over if you just focus."

Guess I focused too much because everything on the dresser fell onto the floor. They were definitely up now. As they were figuring out how that happened, they heard noises from downstairs. Both of them quickly put on robes and her husband went to investigate. Julia made a short stop to retrieve something from her dresser drawer—a gun.

When I saw that, I knew they didn't need my help any longer. I turned looking for my mysterious spiritual companion, but I only saw Sara. I decided to change locations and took Sara with me.

"Okay, what was that all about?" I asked.

"You needed information and you got it. The cosmic light shown on her tattoo means it has greater esoteric significance. She was probably an adept in another lifetime."

I thought about this insight. "Yeah, but I felt like Julia needed to be protected for some reason."

"She does, David. This time it was the guy trying to steal stuff from their home. The next time it could be worse."

"That guy stealing stuff wasn't a normal thief. He was looking for something specific. What I'd like to know is who jerked me out of my body like there was a fire someplace. Was that you?"

"No," Sara said.

"It was me," I heard a male voice say from behind me. The look on Sara's face showed shock which I had not seen before. I knew he wasn't part of my spirit clan.

I turned and saw only a darkened area behind me. "Who are you?" I asked.

Sara and I had moved ourselves to a small alley not far from Julia's home. The light in this area was better, and I saw a translucent image of an old man.

"I'm new at this," the old man said.

"New at what?" I asked.

"Everything," he said, obviously embarrassed. "When I was alive, I was known as Jim Bassett. Julia's my granddaughter. She called me Opa Jim."

"You and Julia were close?"

"Yes, but she's doing things now that I don't approve of. I heard about you, and thought maybe you could help me."

"How did you hear about me?" I asked and turned to Sara to see if she was part of this setup, but she just shrugged her shoulders pretending innocence.

He continued, "They gossip about people on this side too."

I shook my head. "What are they saying?"

"That you've got a big heart and that you could help her."

"So, what do you want me to do?" I asked.

"You already saved her from being hurt by that nut. He wasn't a thief. He was trying to find something her husband was working on and take it."

"Can you tell me what he was working on?" I asked.

"All I know is that it was important and it was classified."

"Is there something else you wanted my help with?"

"Just do what you can to make sure no one hurts her."

"Just curious, but do you know the meaning of the tattoo on Julia's thigh? It's very unusual," I said.

"That's part of why I'm hoping you'll continue being her friend. When the time comes, she'll tell you what it means." And with that, he disappeared.

Not knowing what to do next, I turned to Sara and said, "Can I go back now and get some sleep?"

Sara smiled and disappeared herself.

The next morning I woke up exhausted. It was my day off, but I had things to do. Then Julia called and wanted to meet for lunch for some reason. She was waiting for me at the Coffee Shop.

"How many times have we had lunch together this week," I asked, as I sat down across from her. She looked serious today as if something was troubling her.

"Oh, I think three. Why do you ask? Are people talking?" Julia said, as she sipped her coffee.

"Yes, but not from here."

She looked at me quizzically. "You have something to share, David?"

"Yep," I said and proceeded to give her the highlights of what happened the night before. She remained silent and highly focused until the end.

"Since you were in my bedroom, did you see something that will convince me that you were actually there," she said with a note of seriousness in her voice.

"You have one of the most intriguing tattoo's I have ever seen on the outer thigh of your right leg. And you have a gun stashed in the dresser drawer near your side of the bed. What else would you like to know?"

She looked at me both delighted but somewhat miffed by my intrusion.

"Look, Julia, I'm sorry. Obviously I violated your privacy. But, your grandfather was insistent that I help him protect you. He said the guy that broke into your home wasn't a thief, but he was looking for something that was classified. He just didn't want you to be hurt."

"My grandfather? You met my grandfather?"

"Yeah, Jim Bassett. He said you called him 'Opa Jim.'"

Julia began fighting back tears. "How was he?"

"He's fine. In fact, he's learning how to be your protector. I guess you two were pretty close."

"Opa Jim was a special man, David. He worked all of his life protecting our country."

"Yeah, I kinda got the hint he did something like that."

"He did more than just military law enforcement. But, let's get back to your dream or vision. Did anything else happen?" she asked.

"Nope, he thanked me for helping him out and left."

"Okay, good, well I need to go myself. I hope you don't mind," she said.

"No, I understand. Stay safe," I said, as she stood up and left hurriedly.

After the meeting with Julia, I felt a heaviness drain my body of its energy to such a degree that I had to return to the barracks and lay down. I never made it. A small park on the way had some trees that looked inviting, almost saying, "Come here, little boy. Sit with us for a while," which I did and it was under one of those trees I closed my eyes and instantly drifted away.

I could feel the afternoon ocean breeze gently caress my body relaxing me even further. As I felt myself fall deep within, I knew this was going to be a different journey. This time, I felt two sets of hands pull me from my body and carry me into the sky above the base.

We flew several hundred feet up, which allowed me to see the rolling terrain of the island's green countryside. The mountains in the distance bordered the base in a way that made what I was seeing appear like a perfectly framed picture.

As we soared above small villages, I felt us being pulled toward one of the cliffs near the port city of Pria. My unseen companions stopped and kept me suspended high above the docks. "Look carefully at the cliff's edge. Do you see someone?" one of the two guides asked. It sounded like Opa Jim, but I couldn't tell.

"Yes, I see a man struggling with a woman," I responded, wanting to move closer to see if I could stop the violence.

"You must stay here. Just watch," the same voice said.

While being held motionless, I saw the man hit the woman hard with his fist and she doubled over. Then, he picked her up and threw her over the cliff's edge. I watched in panicked horror as she fell to the rocky seashore below. The only movement I saw then was her body being pushed back and forth by incoming waves across the volcanic rock of the shoreline.

"Hey, David, you should try sleeping in a bed," a voice said as I found myself back in my body and sitting up slowly.

I looked up and saw Ed Smith, one of the other members of the Security Police Detachment, kneeling next to me. "Ed, didn't expect to see you. What time is it? I asked rubbing my back.

"Who cares Dave, it's dark. Go back to the barracks and try your bed. You've got training tomorrow," he said.

Chapter 8

Julia seemed to be busier in the coming weeks, since she always had a reason to cancel our lunch meetings. I wasn't sure if what I shared about my late-night "visit" was too much for her to handle, or perhaps she felt I had violated her trust. Either way, I felt something wasn't right at home. I chose not to press her any further. If she wanted help, she knew how to reach me.

For some reason, Sergeant Dodd decided to take a risk and assign the off-base patrol to me. There was always a Portuguese interpreter on these patrols because you never knew when you'd have to deal with a civilian.

I became close with one of the interpreters, Braz Mendoza, over the next month. He felt more like a father to me and I think he saw me as the son he never had. Braz often invited me home for dinner with his family, and it didn't take long for me to become a part of this clan. Sophia, his wife, immediately took me under her wing.

They were a great match, which was reflected in their auras. Braz was stocky, of medium height with short dark hair, and always with a smile on his face. Sophia, on the other hand, was a short woman but attractive with a womanly quality about her. Was I looking for the motherly love that I had craved most of my life? Or, was there something more about her spirit, perhaps we had known each other in a prior life? What intrigued me most, though, was how her aura would change or intermingle with Braz's when she was around the love of her life.

She would fuss over both Braz and me every time I was with them. And tonight, she insisted we enjoy the peacefulness of the sunset from the rough-stone patio of their home. It was truly gorgeous, a perfect evening with a sea breeze that wafted through the shaded retreat. It wasn't long before Sophia brought us into the dining room for the sumptuous meal she had prepared. It was a lively get-together with Sophia prodding her two daughters to share their day with us.

Her whole family was such an extension of her heart, and they had befriended me as if we had been together for a long time. I never felt so loved as I did when I was with them. Spending the evening with Braz and Sophia's family helped me to feel connected to something that had been missing in my life.

The next day, Braz and I were on patrol driving around the Pria Harbor late in the afternoon. Something began to trouble me the closer we came to the docks, but what? There was almost no traffic. The sky was a perfect blue canopy, and the sea breeze was beginning to cool off another hot day. I tried to push away the growing feeling, perhaps a warning, of an approaching darkness. Then Braz suddenly shouted while pointing out the window, "Look, they fight near the cliff!"

I stopped the patrol car and followed Braz's point-out. That's when I saw what looked like a man and a woman struggling near the cliff's edge that overlooked a rocky estuary at the edge of the harbor. All of a sudden the earlier vision I had of this encounter came back to me. I knew what was about to happen as I picked up the mic to call for backup.

The ledge was about 100 feet above the rolling surf. My attention was briefly drawn to the shore where waves rolled across jagged volcanic rock. I turned on the emergency lights and siren, as we made our way through Pria to the small road that went up the side of the cliff. A persistent sense of urgency continued to push at me as I sped up, trying to reach them and change the outcome of this altercation. But I was too far away to reach them in time, even if I didn't want to admit it.

As we left Pria behind and started up the cliff road, I watched the two of them continue to fight, which created an ugly sick feeling deep within me. I finally had to accept who the woman was and that I had failed to do what I had promised her spirit protector, Opa Jim. Then I wondered what could I have done to stop this? Perhaps something fateful was happening—a critical decision that Sara spoke of earlier? We were almost there when I saw the male aggressor pick Julia up and throw her off the cliff. He then jumped into his car and sped away. The pain I began to feel was the most intense I had ever experienced. Could a hunting knife thrust forcibly into my abdomen feel as bad?

I was breathing heavily, nearly clutching my stomach as we arrived; Braz looked at me and asked, "David, are you sick?"

"I don't . . . no, it's something else. I'll be okay. I'll see what happened to her. Will you call it in?"

Braz updated the dispatcher and learned that the Watch Supervisor and Detachment Commander, along with other units, were almost to Pria. Braz gave them a description of the murderer's vehicle and where it was headed. They would see him because there was only two ways up and down this cliff, and we had taken one of them.

I looked over the edge and saw the body sprawled on the rocky shore below. We jumped back into our unit and sped back down to the harbor. Braz commandeered a boat to get us to the rocky beach where Julia's body was being tossed relentlessly by the waves across the sharp volcanic rock. As we approached, I saw streaks of blood had appeared around her as the surf caused parts of her body to be shredded on the sharp volcanic rock.

When I finally reached her, I turned her body over and gasped in agony. In life, Julia was my intelligent, very articulate, and beautiful friend who shared an interest in spiritual matters and vivid dreams. I checked her carotid artery for a pulse. Having found none, I was left to live with this image of her lying before me, which I wanted to block from my mind forever and that's when time stood still.

I don't remember Braz helping me back into the boat and waiting for a special evidence forensic and recovery team. In fact, the next thing I remember was sitting in a darkened office back at the cop shop. The Watch Supervisor, Sergeant Dodd, came in to check on me.

Being from Oklahoma and having younger siblings in his family, Sergeant Dodd always felt like the youngsters that the Air Force sent to Lajes needed more parenting than supervising. He surprised me this time when he asked, "Sergeant Lussier, are you back with us yet?"

Curious, but somewhat dazed, I asked, "Why do you ask?"

"You, son, have been unresponsive since I picked you up at the pier. You know, David, people talk on a small island. Rumors begin to circulate especially about anything that's unusual. So, when I saw you on the pier looking as if you had tranced out, I hurried you into my car and got you out of there before any OSI agent or medical team members noticed."

"Sorry, I had a lot to process back there. I knew her, Sarge," I said, leaning forward and looking at the floor, hoping the weight that pressed hard against me would dissipate.

"Yeah, I figured as much, given the rumor that's been going around. Your lunch rendezvous with her had been noticed."

"I just don't understand why anyone would want to kill her. I saw this before it happened in a . . . dream, and yet I still couldn't stop it. I don't understand why I would get a heads-up and a request to protect her, if I wasn't going to be able to do anything."

"David, I don't know about your dreams and the stuff that Linda told me that you're able to do," Sergeant Dodd said and then paused. "But it might've been more about you than her."

This stopped me, and I looked up at Dodd. Was he right?

"Another thing, David, I haven't known you all that long, but it seems to me that you're always there for everyone else, but when you need someone, where are they?"

"It's always been this way, Sarge."

"Would you talk to someone if they offered?"

No one had ever asked me that question, but for some reason, Linda came to mind. Since she was on leave, I sadly put this possibility aside and said, "Maybe."

"Okay then, let me get them."

I couldn't image who he had in mind, or who would be open to talk about my relationship to Julia. My curiosity grew as I watched Sergeant Dodd leave the room. When he came back, my heart leaped when I saw Linda walk in behind him. The weight that had been trying to crush me immediately vanished.

She strode up to me and hugged me tightly. She whispered in my ear, "Wait til we're alone. Dodd doesn't need to see either one of us break down."

I nodded my head, still in a daze.

"Let's go for a ride and talk," Linda said. We left Dodd's office and quickly walked out of the old wooden clapboard-sided building that housed the Security Police Detachment. We got into her recycled island car, which was actually an ancient off-white Volkswagen bug accented with salt-air rust. Having been on the island for at least a decade, the car had developed a reputation for reliability and its unique appearance. Previous owners, and now Linda, had provided the care needed to prevent the ocean salt water spray from rusting the car into oblivion.

We started down the road and made our way off base before she asked her first question.

"So David, crime scenes involving DBs don't seem to set well with you."

The image of Julia's body on the beach began swirling through my mind again and drained me. "Wouldn't any normal person be affected like that when they discover they knew the person they just rolled over?" I said, looking out the window while the sense of utter numbness continued to dominate me.

Linda continued, "David . . . look at me," she said firmly, trying to bring my attention back to her. I turned to her. "Sergeant Dodd mentioned that you knew the victim."

"Julia Madison. I'm surprised you didn't know."

"I heard the rumors, about you two, but I wanted to make sure. Was there anything more to your relationship with her than your lunch meetings?"

"No, Linda. She just had an interest in out-of-body experiences, lucid dreams, things like that."

"How did she know about you?" she asked, then paused apparently thinking about something. "Wait a minute, Major Madison, the JAG lawyer. We responded to a domestic dispute on their block a couple of months ago."

"Yep, her maid heard the neighbors talking about what I told them. And that lead her to find me."

Linda was quiet, thinking about something, and then said in a serious tone, "David, I think her husband plays more than one role on this base, and she may have been involved somehow."

Sara jumped in and offered, "David, tell her about the OBE you had when you saw the break-in at her house."

I told Linda about what had happened. Again, she was quiet and then said, "I can't prove this, but I'm betting Julia was in the intelligence game, too." She paused, "We need to be careful, David."

"We? Why is it now we?" I asked in alarm. "You're not involved in any of this, and I'd like to keep it that way."

Linda pulled the VW to the side of the road where we had a beautiful view of the waves slowly rolling onto the shore as the sun set in the distance. Linda turned toward me and reached for my hands, holding both in hers. "David, I know you're not Brian. But, I just don't want anything to happen to you. What you've done for me is something that no one else has been able to do. I just don't want to lose you, which could be avoided if we worked together."

No one had ever said anything that endearing to me. It felt as if a hidden hole in my heart was finally being filled with someone who cared for me.

"David, I know you were just trying to help Julia as with everyone else that you've met on this island including me. But there's a lot more to Brian's death than you know. In fact, when I came back to the base, I wanted to see you and explain that."

I smiled. "Well, guess what. There's a lot more to Julia's death, too."

Again, Julia's image and all the conversations we had about spiritual practices, dreams, and divination came back to me. I just couldn't believe that she was murdered that way, simply tossed off a cliff as if she was today's garbage. What kind of person does that? I gazed out the window at the sunset and said softly, "I knew her well, Linda, and I thought she was becoming a friend, someone who understood what I've lived with all of my life."

"David, again I need to ask about your relationship with her. The rumors make it sound like you two were doing a lot more than just talking."

"Linda, when I spend time with someone who seems to have common interests, especially in the area of energy sensitivity, it's likely a strong bond will form. But that's all."

"Well, you know that's not normal. Most men would pursue something more," she said.

I turned back to face her not believing what I just heard. "You've been riding with me and seeing how I deal with people. How can you say that I would essentially deceive a woman just so I could what, get into her pants?"

"So, you're not like other males?" she asked with a smirk.

I looked at her and said, "Get rid of the smile, Linda. Lumping me into the Neanderthal cage is personally offensive," I said firmly. "Look, I'm just trying to deal with losing a new friend. Someone I could talk with about my visions and not get a reaction out of her like I was some kind of nut or evil person."

Given the extreme conflict in which I grew up, I placed significant emphasis on the quality of the relationship two people can have instead of the manipulation I had seen others use.   "Linda, I want you to understand something that's at the core of my being. I respond first to a person's desire to be open, and their willingness to speak candidly. If that person happened to be in the throes of conflict and was open to my help, I'd gladly offer whatever I could, even if it's nothing more than just being a good listener."

Linda thought for a moment before responding, "Well, in your case, right now, it looks like the shoe's on the other foot. You give help, but you don't seem to be accepting it very well," she added.

Feeling myself being drawn inward, I decided to stop shielding my past from her as I had done with everyone in my life. Besides, she had already experienced a part of what can be done when a person travels outside the body. Most of the time, people had either made fun of my history or thought I was crazy. But, there was something growing between us, something I could trust, something akin to the sense I had with Braz and his family.

"Maybe I should tell you a little more about myself, and then you can decide whether or not I'm telling you the truth."

Linda focused on me as I was preparing to confess something that was perhaps profound or that I had committed a major crime. "Okay, let's hear it."

"I grew up in a household that converted from Quaker to Methodist. I got a lot of beatings from an abusive father, and there were times he almost killed or blinded me. I just about killed him once when he attacked me while I was sleeping, but my mother intervened. My parents refused to allow me to have friendships with girls until I left home. And let's top it off with the fact that I haven't been on a date in my life, and yet I was thinking about asking you out. But, I was concerned if you agreed that you'd be doing it because of Brian and not me."

Linda looked at me oddly conflicted as she nervously shifted in her seat. She knew up to this point that I had never lied or exaggerated about anything. "So, what are you, 18?" she asked with a snicker. "And you're telling me you're a virgin, right?"

"Yes," I said, not believing someone, least of all a woman, would ever ask me such a personal question. "Let's not forget that I grew up in a reformed Quaker home. Add to that, I had two uncles that were circuit-riding Methodist preachers. Because I was such a problem child, according to my parents, one of the preachers became my counselor. So no, I was never allowed to date and I just got my driver's license a year before I enlisted in the Air Force. Anything else you wanna know?"

"Wow, I can hardly believe what I'm hearing. I take it that those are the *Cliff Notes*. You don't seem like a bad boy. What the hell did you do that required counseling?"

"It wasn't normal teenager stuff, Linda," I said.

"Hey buddy, I doubt seriously you can scare me. I've seen more of the human underbelly than most women my age. And, after working with you for the last few months, not to mention what you and Sara did for me, why don't you give me a shot?"

I thought about it. I kept remembering how my mother responded the first few times I went to her thinking she would help me understand my visions. But instead, I came close to being locked up in an institution for people who talk with spirits and see things that are not there. Besides, what I was about to say wasn't any stranger than what Linda had experienced with me so far.

"Okay, I'll take a chance, but I need your word that this stays between us. Do you agree?" She nodded perhaps anticipating something enticing.

"There's not much more to say than much of the time what I see is in the past. But, there are times that I see things that provide a window to future events. It's similar to what we did so you could say goodbye to Brian. And, there are times I see myself leaving my body when I should be sleeping. It's a way of de-stressing, I guess."

She looked at me like I let her down. "That's it? That's all you got to say?"

"Well, there are some examples I could give you, but I don't see the point. Let's just say that when I dream and have those experiences, it opens a part of me that others have closed off, which helps with my relationships."

"What do you mean by that?"

"People generally find it easy to open up to me when we talk about my paranormal experiences like what I did with Julia's neighbors. And when they do, some feel comfortable, a kind of strong connection forms because they have had them too without recalling the experiences. For me, I know it's happening when I feel something being drawn from my chest that's like pulling a balloon and stretching it toward them. In other words, I feel a kind of pulling, so to speak. I don't know how to explain it any better than that."

Linda thought for a moment and asked, "So, how does this relate to Julia?"

"I was on patrol one day and stopped for lunch at the Coffee House. She asked to share my table. Then, she started talking about things in general and eventually she mentioned she heard I had visions. As we talked, I could feel something that was drawing me to her. But, it wasn't until I had a vision involving her grandfather that it began to make sense. He had asked that I look after her, and then the vision occurred where I saw a man and a woman fighting on the cliff just before he threw her over the side."

"Really, that's interesting." Linda said, her eyes widening.

"Yep, after that Julia and I met several times and talked in more detail about my visions. She also talked about hers, which I found interesting. Meeting someone who has had similar experiences is rare. But, these past couple of weeks, she kept coming up with reasons why we couldn't meet."

I waited for a response, but Linda seemed to be thinking. So, I continued, "When we first started the lunch time discussions, I realized that she also shared an interest in unusual spiritual-based human events which goes well beyond her own visions. In fact, the last conversation we had she was telling me about a project that a branch of the military had started a few years ago involving remote viewing."

It finally occurred to Linda why this was too much of a coincidence. "David, she has to have had something to do with the intel community."

"I heard rumors about her husband, not her," I said.

"David, she's got to be involved somehow. Sergeant Dodd wanted us to get away from the shop before the OSI investigator arrived, and I think it's even more important now that I know more of your background and what happened between you two," Linda said.

"Why?" I asked.

"Dodd wanted to give you some time to calm down and prep for the interview," she said and then continued. "Do you know what the OSI does with this kind of case?"

"Not really. All they said in school was that they're like the FBI back in the states," I said.

"Okay, so when a crime occurs that would normally be classified as a felony in civilian life, the OSI takes over the criminal investigation. All we do is provide support for them. But, in this case, we need to be ready because they also deal with espionage and more sophisticated crimes. Julia could have also been screening you for something."

I nodded my head. This seemed to make sense.

"I also found out from Dodd that the OSI considers you a 'Person of Interest,' even if it's not related to this case. So, your interview might be far-ranging."

"Do you know anything about this OSI guy?" I asked.

"I don't know who he is, but I know he's not their normal crime investigator. He's from the Counter Intelligence Group based at Langley. So, I'm guessing this might get messy."

"I didn't know that," I said wondering what would happen next. "Linda, what does it mean to be a person of interest to the group you mentioned?"

"Man, you are a total virgin. Okay, have you ever been attacked by a bully at school?"

"Yeah, a lot, why?"

"Take all of those experiences and multiply them by 10, and you might be close to the pounding you may take by this investigator. It all depends on their mood, how much pressure they're under to solve a case, and how valuable they think you might be to them. So, as an example, if Julia and her husband are both in the intelligence community, which is entirely likely, recruiting might be one her roles. If so, then when she was talking with you about your sensitivity, she might have been screening you for something, like a project, or a special team. Keep in mind, if they want you, you could be ordered transferred into their group.

"So, let's say she's screening you. It's likely she started a file and talked with her upline about this new kid she found that might be trainable for something we don't know anything about. If she did, then her upline may have shared the file and their interest with the OSI, because if nothing else, they're seriously interested in finding who took out one of their own."

The more Linda talked, the more I kept seeing some ugly currents of energy coming my way, and the more intense my negative feelings became. "I got it, Linda. They might want me to give them leads to the killer or to 'scope out' other targets which would make their job easier. What if I refuse to cooperate?"

"Remember my comment about ordering your transfer to their group?"

"Yeah, I got it. I'm torn because I want to find out who killed her, but at the same time I'm seeing a path into the future that's extremely dark if I allow them to use me," I said worried that a door might have been opened that could not be closed, especially since Sara wasn't saying anything.

"Well, that's why we left the base. Sergeant Dodd has a campsite on the opposite side of the island. The beach area is remote and there are no landlines there. So, even if Sergeant Dodd is ordered to produce you, he could say that he gave you leave to gather yourself and doesn't know where you are. We'll head back once you make up your mind. The only caveat is that you've got a week to get it done."

Damn, I thought, *only a week?* "Are you staying with me?"

She chuckled softly then said, "Hey genius, how do you think you'll get back? There's no phone out there, remember? Besides, since you're the complete virgin, you'll need me to survive in the wilderness."

"Ha, ha . . . you're so funny. I can survive on my own just fine. All I need is a tent and some tools. But you're right, I'll need a ride back."

She smiled.

Chapter 9

There were few options on how to deal with this OSI Investigator. Days later when we approached the Main Gate to enter the base, one of my fellow super-troops waved us to a secured inspection area. The gate supervisor called the dispatcher to report our arrival and then came out to speak with us.

"You two finally decided to come back from vacation?" Sergeant Ford said sarcastically. Jerry Ford was a good guy, but he had issues like most former Viet Nam NCOs I had met who usually carried around a ton of emotional baggage. In fact, the military sent some of the active-duty Viet Nam vets to Lajes Field, Azores to recover. Jerry seemed further along in that regard than many of the others whom I had dealt with during domestic disturbance or public intoxication calls, but he could still be challenging.

Linda was pretty blunt when dealing with burnouts like Ford. "Sergeant, your vacation crack sucks, and if you don't have a good reason for detaining us, we'll be on my way. Both of us have the watch tonight."

Jerry placed his large hands on the open window of her door, leaned down with one of those "I'm gonna dominate you, baby" stances, and slowly spit out, "You two vacationers will remain here until you're told otherwise. And you don't have duty until the old man releases you."

Linda kicked the door open with enough force to put Ford flat on his ass. He recovered quickly, jumping up to engage this female resister. She launched into him as soon as she was out of the VW bug. If this confrontation wasn't so volatile, I would have laughed seeing a short blonde dressed in a T-shirt, shorts, and sandals screaming at the chin of a rather tall muscular male idiot.

"We haven't done anything wrong. Where's Sergeant Dodd? He told us to leave the base for a few days," she yelled.

"Back off, Wonder Woman. Do that again, and I'll have you in bracelets before you can slap on those cheap, pellet-loaded gloves you carry," Ford retaliated.

"I don't need any help turning the lights off on a dork like you. Either tell me what's going on, or I'm leaving right now."

Ford waved some of his guys over. Linda added sarcastically, "You need help to deal with a woman?"

Airmen Todd Hunter and his partner, Timmy Flowers, were within hearing range of the brewing fight between these two. I learned early in this job that every enforcement group has their own gorilla. Timmy was ours, which always seemed odd to me. While he was a tall guy with huge muscles, He was also one of the most mild-mannered, soft-spoken cops I knew, and besides he liked Linda.

"What do you want Sergeant," Hunter asked as he and Flowers approached ground zero.

"Make sure these two vacationers don't go anywhere until the old man gets down here. Her highness here thinks she runs the place."

Timmy was obviously happy about keeping Linda company, "Oh, hi Sergeant Cross. What's up?"

Ford rolled his eyes. "Look Airmen Flowers, you idiot, you're keeping these two under detention until you're ordered otherwise. Don't treat them as friendlies. Do you read me?"

Both men quickly answered in unison, "Yes sir." Ford now turned and walked back to his guardhouse.

The old man, known as Master Sergeant Craig Towers, arrived a few minutes later. Craig was highly experienced, hardened but fair, and had been in the security police system his entire career. He waved Linda and me over. "Welcome back to my world . . . which ain't such a nice place right now," he said with a bit of exasperation.

Linda asked him, "What's going on?"

"After you left a few days ago, it took about twelve hours for the notifications of the murder to make the circuit. You were right about the couple, but there was a lot more to them than any of us knew." He exited his vehicle and leaned up against the door as he continued, "The major and his wife were certainly intelligence operatives, but they were very competitive in doing their jobs and it was starting to cause friction."

"Really, what were they doing besides snooping around?" Linda asked with mild astonishment.

"It seems their primary role was to collect intelligence data on various classified subjects. But, Julia was apparently much better at it than her husband," Towers added.

"And what could that sweet, innocent little girl be uncovering on a base with only us and our Portuguese allies?" Linda asked.

"Yeah, that's what I thought, until I sat in a briefing between the OSI Investigator and the Base Commander. Apparently Julia was particularly good at recruiting among other things. And, like I said, her husband wasn't getting the same high evals and so they were thinking about reassigning them to different bases. He thought it was at her request as the end of their relationship, supported by his belief that she was messing around. So, with all of that and with him thinking she was stealing his thunder, it pushed him over the edge, like he could get away with murdering his wife on an island."

"I knew there was something more to her than her cuteness. And it doesn't surprise me that bastard would do something this stupid," Linda said.

"So, if this has nothing to do with me, can I go to the barracks now?" I asked wanting to take a break before going on patrol.

Craig shook his head. "Oh no you don't. You're going back to the cop shop with me. Someone there wants to speak with you about your relationship with the Major's wife."

I shook my head in exasperation. "Sarge, the only relationship I had with her was a shared interest in the paranormal. I mean, we only met in public places and talked . . . nothing more."

"Hey, dumbnut, are you slow or deaf? Didn't you just hear me say she was a recruiter? Which means she was on the lookout for people who might be gifted, you know, like who see things that aren't there," Linda said.

"Wow. I never suspected that."

"Yeah, well that's what made her good and it got her killed," Towers said impatiently.

This took me aback, realizing I may have inadvertently contributed to her death.

Linda saw my stunned look and added, "Sergeant Lussier is ignorant about people like Major Madison and his wife. I don't think it's a good idea to put him in a room by himself with anyone connected to those two."

"Understood, Sergeant Cross. But, this investigator has some serious creds, and while he showed up claiming to be investigating Madison's death, it became obvious he's really here to talk with our new boy."

"So what are we going to do? We can't just throw David to the wolves. He hasn't had any experience in dealing with this kind of person. Besides, can you see Sergeant Lussier working for someone like that? He has a hard time dealing with a dead body as we all recently found out," Linda said.

"Yeah, I know. But you also know that if this guy pulls the right strings, there's nothing we can do."

"Maybe you can't or won't, but I sure the hell can. Since you don't need me for this, can I go?" Linda asked.

Towers waved her on and she turned to me and said, "I'm not abandoning you, David. I'll do what I can. Be careful what you say." She hugged me, which got more than a few looks of astonishment from those present.

Master Sergeant Towers delivered me to the Security Police Headquarters building parking lot. My supervisor, Technical Sergeant Gary Dodd, escorted me into the building. Though he was my supervisor, Dodd had become more like a big brother or another father-figure like Braz. He went to extra lengths trying to keep me out of trouble. But in this case, it was apparent he had no other choice but to escort me into the bowels of the Security Police building.

"David, you be careful with this guy," he said as we walked along. "You've never dealt with anyone like this, and I still don't know why he wants to speak with you."

We stopped in front of an open door to a private room with no windows. No enlisted personnel enters this kind of room unless they were being interrogated or the discussion needed to be secure. Dodd held the door open and whispered as I walked in, "Don't say too much."

Sitting in an old wooden chair behind a drab looking table was a short man in a dark suit. Obviously, he had been waiting for us. I immediately noticed a faint dark shadow hovering behind him, and my internal alarm bells started going off. Yup, this was not going to be a lot of fun.

The visitor, or perhaps my inquisitor, stood up and smiled at us. My skin began to crawl as if millions of ants decided to bivouac there.

"Sergeant Dodd, is this the young man you've been telling me about?" asked the inquisitor.

Superior ranking officers and noncoms never held a door open for us "pee-ons," and they never talked like this in front of us. I had all sorts of yellow flags flapping along with the inner alarms now. "Yes, Agent Bullard. This is Sergeant Lussier," Dodd responded.

As I sat in one of the two remaining chairs, I had no doubt that this mini wannabe secret agent was my adversary. But, my sense was that Bullard was far worse than that. I couldn't put my finger on just how much worse, but it was obvious the dark spirit behind him was here to compromise me. But then an unrelated thought crossed my mind. Why do I keep running into short officers since I arrived at Lajes Field? I was hoping he wasn't like the Captain Walker, the Commander of the Security Police Division. Ego and self-esteem issues can be difficult to get beyond in most cases.

Besides the dark suit, Bullard also had a Marine buzz cut, with standard-issue secret agent black-plastic framed glasses, and a smile that would make a used car salesman jealous. But it was his eyes that drew my attention. They had a dark, shiny coal-like quality that reminded me of staring into a bottomless pit; what was down there is what really concerned me. Something lived there, if that was the word, which was at the core of the man I was seeing.

He extended his hand to shake mine and said, "Good to meet you, Sergeant Lussier. I'm Steven Bullard."

As we shook hands, the ants vanished in utter panic as an intense chill traveled up my arm like a wave of fast moving Arctic water. It was obvious that I couldn't trust most of what was about to happen, let alone anything that might come out of his mouth. The challenge was how to respond to him in a way that would avoid an undesirable outcome. I had heard rumors of how certain military personnel would disappear from duty assignments for various unsavory reasons, and I didn't want to be one of them.

He flashed his ID card to verify that he was an investigator for the Office of Special Investigation (OSI), the Air Force equivalent to the FBI. "Says here you're a captain. How long have you been with the OSI?" I asked as my attention moved back to him. The eyes are said to be the portal to the soul. In Bullard's case, his eyes were the secret passageway to his other world. This was where that tag-along dark spirit lived, and this was the pathway it used to enter and exit physical reality at will.

Something unseen to anyone present opened in front of me. I was drawn deep within this dark spiritual energy, touring a realm that defined the real entity here, not this person standing before me. The tour was like being on a rollercoaster ride through Lucifer's valley of evil, a place completely devoid of light that possessed an abundance of tortured souls pleading for mercy while screaming for vengeance.

Bullard's facial expression changed as he realized I had just exposed his secret self. He withdrew his hand and backed away to sit down in his chair. He scrutinized me carefully. "Did you enjoy the tour, Sergeant Lussier?" He paused and waited for an answer. When he didn't get one, he continued, "I hear you're not much for military protocol."

I offered Sergeant Dodd my chair hoping he would finally sit down. "What tour? Did you go on a tour before you came back to the base?" Dodd asked me as he sat down.

"No sir, that's not the kind of tour Bullard's talking about." I turned to him and responded to his question, "Not true Captain. I believe in protocol as long as everyone is on the same page and the participants are fair with each other. What's more important to me, though, is the issue of respect and honesty." I paused for a moment for effect and then continued.

"Take Sergeant Dodd for instance. He's honest with me all the time. He also respects me so I have no problem with covering his six and properly addressing him. If someone behaves contrary to that, then I see no reason to extend to that person the respect upon which military protocol is based. Don't you agree?" I asked as I continued to lock eyes with him, refusing to let go. Obviously, the battle had begun.

Sergeant Dodd became observably nervous as he shifted in his chair and moved his attention between what looked like near-future combatants. Still looking at me, Bullard asked in a firm tone, "Sergeant Dodd, do you allow all of your charges to speak like this with officers?"

"Sir, I don't think rank has its privileges in an interrogation. I would prefer that everybody speak their mind."

"That's a rather liberal attitude, Sergeant. Must be the island life here. Brains get soggy," he snickered. Bullard looked back at me. The dangerously powerful spirit that had been behind him now fully inhabited this sterile secret agent. "Well, then David . . . perhaps we should get to know each other on a more personal basis. Sergeant Dodd, why don't you take a walk?" he spit out, then glared at him and continued, "Right now."

Dodd wasn't offended or didn't show it. He stood up, gave me a look, and walked out.

Alone, I couldn't resist, "So, do you prefer Steven or Steve?"

"Does it matter, really?" he asked, then added in a serious tone. "Do you know why I'm here specifically to speak to you?"

"You know, Steve. This is one of the fundamental differences between us. You want to talk *to* me as compared to talking *with* me, which I would prefer," I said with a smile.

"What are you talking about?" he asked more intensely.

"That you're here because of something Julia Madison said to her guys about me. Odds are, everyone misinterpreted whatever she said or wrote. And so you're here to either figure it out or tell me I just won the lottery and am about to be reassigned to some exotic place for a truly exciting experience that I'll just love . . . provided I live through it. How close am I, Steve?"

He sat back in his chair and folded his arms. His eyes narrowed, apparently calculating his next move. "So, you're telling me, Madison was wrong? In fact, that she simply misinterpreted you and your discussions. Is that right?"

"Well," I said, as I leaned over and propped my elbows on the table. "It's hard to say that without having reviewed what she submitted. But, I already know what you do for the OSI and why you're really here." This got his attention. He pushed his chair back, walked around the table, stood next to me, and leaned over trying to physically intimidate me.

What he didn't know was that having grown up in a challenging household, he couldn't bully me. "Oh, and Steve, let me share something with you since we're being so candid with each other. You can't physically force your power on me. Believe me, it ain't gonna work, buddy. You might as well relax and save your energy. It's likely we're going to be here a while. If you burn yourself out early, you'll miss some of the fun."

He leaned back and walked around to his chair and softly chuckled to himself. "You think you're so smart. If you can read my body language, then let's try something a bit more challenging. Tell me what I'm thinking," Steve said flippantly.

Again, I couldn't resist laughing, but then Sara spoke to me. "*David, be careful. He's linked to a powerful evil. He actually murdered someone just last week in a wooded area near the Frederick, Maryland Municipal Airport and buried the body in the woods on the west side. If he pushes too hard, tell him you know who Professor Timothy Mallard is and you know why he murdered him."*

The smile abated and I said, "Steve, all you know about me is what you've read in my personnel file and the reports that Julia sent. If I were you, I'd be careful about any conclusions you might make."

"Well, I hear from others as well that you have an unusual ability to see things and read people."

"Again, Steve, I can't comment on something she wrote or hearsay for that matter. A person can write or say anything based on what they think they understand. The question is how accurate is their interpretation?"

"Look Sergeant, we could continue this dance all day, but I don't have time for it. I'm ordering you to answer my questions."

"No, Steve, what you're ordering me to do is provide answers that you can twist around, to enlist me and put me in a position of providing you information that will allow you to harm others, control situations that you have no right to, and to deceive everyone. Oh, and just so we have complete disclosure, I know Julia reported to you, not her boss, and your upline doesn't know you're here. One question would be why she would do that and the other would be why are you working so hard to expand your ... 'reach'? How close am I?"

That used car salesman smile reappeared. He thought he had just tricked me into revealing what he needed to know. "Well, smart ass, I can tell you she was right. You're pretty good. I can't wait to get you back to Langley and have you tested. You should feel right at home there," he said, as he relaxed momentarily.

"You say that, Steve, as if you were certain I would accept a reassignment taking me away from this island resort and all my friends."

Another smile of confidence appeared as he settled further back into his chair. "You're not being offered a choice. I'll have your orders cut shortly and take you back with me. Besides, like I said, you'll like Langley. Wait until you see all the other talented colleagues there," he said, as if he were offering me leather seat covers for free.

"Nope, I'm not going there," I said, sitting back upright in my chair.

"Maybe I haven't been clear, Sergeant," he said with emphasis. "You will be reassigned to my unit at Langley and, because you are now considered to be an invaluable military asset, your very existence will be classified. And, as an extra benefit, I will assign one of my . . . agents to ensure your safe transit."

I leaned forward and said with noticeable force, "What you mean is that you are going to force me to do what you want, when you want, and to whom you want. What you're forgetting is what I told you earlier. I will not work for you regardless of any order you may issue."

Bullard was now oozing overconfidence with a bit of sadistic dictator mixed in as he said, "Oh, you will do as you're told. You, my young idealist, forget the business I'm in. I know oh so much about you, the things you like and dislike, including your horrid family history, and the things you've done. In fact, my little birdie's tell me you've got a thing for . . . oh, what's the name of that bitch . . . ah, yeah, it's coming to me . . . Sergeant Linda Cross."

I could feel the intensity of the spirit pushing him grow as he leaned across the table attempting to physically threaten me again.

"There you go again, Steve. I'm not sure what's bigger. Your grotesquely overinflated ego or your well-established narcissistic self-image fueled by that bizarre creature that resides within you."

I stood up and stretched my arms and said, "Let's keep something in mind, my evil friend. I will never work for you or anyone remotely like you. I will never confirm to you what I can or cannot do with any God-given talent I might or might not have. And, if I did have that talent, you'll never know just how far I'll explore creative solutions to protect those who are special to me. In other words, Steve, make your decisions wisely. You don't know what I'm capable of."

"Are you threatening me?" he asked in disbelief.

"There you go again, Steve. If you knew as much about me as you say, you wouldn't have to ask that question. But, I'm a nice guy so I'll let you in on a secret. I have never threatened anyone in my life. I learned early that threats mean nothing. On the other hand, actions speak volumes. No Steve, I'm not threatening you. I am promising you that if you harm anyone thinking that you can force my hand, I will bring things back into balance and I guarantee that it will not be a pleasant experience for you."

I stood up as I finished explaining my decision and walked to the door. "Oh, there's a couple of things you should know. Your evil core showed itself to me when I sat down and oddly enough, it didn't frighten me. Gee, I wonder why. And, you really don't want me working for you when I know where you buried Professor Mallard's body in the woods back in Frederick, Maryland and why you murdered him," I said to him calmly. The look on his face was a priceless. He seemed caught between the shock that someone could prove he murdered another human being and that he had hit the jack pot after all, even if he couldn't spend the money.

"Steve, I think we're done here. And you know something? I can tell by the look on your face and the thoughts that are currently running through your puny mind that you know what I'm talking about. By the way, you should clean up the language you use when talking to yourself. It makes you look rather juvenile." With that, I opened the door and began walking down the hall. I saw Dodd and Linda coming toward me from the other end.

"I guess we'll see how this turns out, won't we Sergeant Lussier?" Agent Bullard shouted as he stood at the door to the interrogation room and watched me walk away. I held my hand up behind my back and flipped him off.

Chapter 10

Sergeant Dodd escorted Linda and me out of the building. As we were walking into the parking lot, Linda's face lit up when she saw who was coming toward us.

"Good day," Father Mike said with a huge smile. Linda had introduced us while we were on patrol several months ago. He wasn't the typical Catholic Priest that I knew growing up. Father Mike Flanagan was tall, in great shape with thick, dark, wavy hair. For a man in his mid-forties, he looked fit. He and Linda had invited me to attend services, but they could tell there was some reluctance on my part. At one point Father Mike said if I ever needed his support, he would always be there for me. Maybe he sensed that day would be sooner than later.

Father Mike seemed happy to see us as he approached with an obviously important career officer, as denoted by the lines of campaign ribbons pinned to his uniform. For me, what first caught my attention were the miniature eagles on his collar that signified he was a full bird Colonel.

Father Mike continued, "I want you to meet Colonel Richard Smith. He's visiting from the 21st Air Force at McGuire Air Force Base. We're old friends, and he decided to take me up on an offer to play at our lovely golf course here."

"Hello, it's a pleasure to meet you both," Colonel Smith said with a gracious smile as he returned our salutes.

"Well, I hope you enjoy your stay," Linda said, then smiled knowingly. "So, I gather Father Mike also enlisted you in more than a round of golf?"

Father Mike shook his head. "Not the case, Sergeant Cross. Rick just happened to overhear our phone conversation and offered his assistance," he said with feigned surprise.

Colonel Smith laughed. "Sure, that's it, Father." Smith now looked back at us and said, "I'd do anything for this man as long as it didn't get me into trouble." He paused, and in a more officious tone and said, "So, you have an OSI agent going after you about something that's beyond the scope of his murder investigation, is that right?"

"Yes sir," I said. "He's trying to recruit me to work on some kind of psychic program at Langley he apparently is putting together, or maybe just testing at this point."

Richard nodded his head. "Yeah, I got wind of something like that going down."

"Well, I have no desire to become involved in anything that remotely looks like cloak-and-dagger behavior, or that requires deception to succeed. I am more than willing to help people, but what he seems to be suggesting would do more harm than good." I paused. "Besides, my friends and family are here. I'd rather be left alone."

The comment about friends and family got Linda's attention. She was looking at me with a bit of shock, perhaps wondering what I meant by that.

I glanced at her but she gave me one of those "we'll talk about this later" looks.

Father Mike picked up on this exchange. "Families come in all shapes and sizes."

Richard looked back and forth between us, then continued. "This Captain Bullard is no stranger to my colleagues at the 21st Air Force Command Headquarters and we'll leave it at that. I can understand why you would prefer to continue working in something you find more rewarding than 'cloak and dagger.' Since it's outside the scope of your 'known' qualifications, I can use that to pull some strings and keep you here. It won't matter how far up the chain of command Bullard goes, he won't be able to change this one. So forget anything the agent told you."

While this was a great relief, I could sense a dark cloud still hanging over me like this wasn't over yet. "Thank you, sir. I appreciate you doing that."

"Yes, Richard," Father Mike said. "Your help will be greatly appreciated. And if I may add, I think it's God's will in this case."

"Yeah, that's what you always say when you beat me at golf," Richard laughed, patting the priest on the back.

This broke a little of the tension. Father Mike now turned to Sergeant Dodd, who had stepped back and deferred to the Colonel. "Sergeant, I have something I would like to speak with you and Colonel Smith about. Let's go over to the church." Once there, he turned to us. "While we're talking in my offices, why don't the two of you wait here in the sanctuary?"

After they left, Linda looked at me as if I should already know what she was thinking,

"What? Why are you looking at me like that? I asked.

"I didn't know you had any family here," she said.

"Well, Sergeant Dodd feels more like a big brother, and Braz an uncle who has brought me into his family. And then there's you," I said, wondering how she would respond.

"Me? What about me? How are we family?" she asked in surprise.

"Well, the way you stood by me when I was about to railroaded by Bullard speaks volumes."

We sat in a pew in the back of the church or what was called the nave. The balcony hung low over these pews casting a shadow over us.

She finally said, "I do feel close to you, David. I've thought about how similar you are to Brian. It's almost like being given a second chance to find something that's been missing in my life," she said and then turned and looked intently at me. I could feel her venturing a bit further and perhaps exploring our attachment to each other, which she hadn't done before.

While I opened myself to her, I also noticed sunlight streaming through the church's tall stained glass windows and making them feel alive. The scenes they depicted held as much mystery and spiritual energy as any I had ever seen. This always seems to happen to help those of us, who truly understand the illusion of physical reality, to remind others of the true source of our lives. And, when this unique presence is felt, those who can respond usually have a profound experience. Linda was beginning to open herself to this grander vista, and I could feel it in an unexpected way. She seemed to be trying to join, if not merge, in some way with me as the spiritual energy of this holy place affected both of us.

Then my attention was drawn to the altar which was unusual in that it was very ornate and the focal point of the church. Handcrafted, the altar was unlike those in the churches I'd been to in the U.S. Some unseen entity allowed me to see how decades ago spiritually sensitive Portuguese Catholics presented all of this to the priest of the day.

Oil paintings of Saint Mary, the baby Jesus, and a few other saints of the Christian faith came alive in the windows and at various worship stations. The wood surrounding them was richly textured and well-carved. All of these spirit-filled artisans understood what lived here, and they gave of themselves so that others might have a chance to perceive as much.

Linda was holding my hands, and I could feel our auras mingle to familiarize us before delving further. Our hearts opened to each other as incredible energy enshrouded us. Then, a cloud must have parted, because the sun shined even brighter through the stained glass windows. I felt us spiritually bonding and knew that we had become linked together perhaps forever. As we gazed at each other now, I saw the undulating radiance of merged souls.

Our moment ended and Linda asked softly, "Do you know what just happened?"

"Huh, sorry," I said as I came back to her. "I should have mentioned that churches were what the embodied spirits created to convey their understanding that this life is just an illusion. These were places that represented momentary gateways for others to experience what was real."

Linda nodded her head.

After taking a moment to collect myself, I asked, "Did you want to talk about something?"

Linda took a moment to answer and then said, "Being with you is something that I'm not sure I can explain to anyone. I've never experienced anything like this moment, including with Brian. Whatever we just experienced was . . .

special. But, right now I really want to know is what the OSI agent told you."

"Nothing much, he was testing me and my psychic reach. It seems my so-called friend, Julia, had been filing reports on her impressions of my ability. I really don't think Julia's murder was why Bullard showed up here," I said.

"So you think he came here to finish what she started?" Linda asked.

"Well, he said he had a group of people working for him back at Langley. He didn't say it, but it was implied they were psychics. I'm not sure what he uses them for, or plans to, but he's serious about fattening his tribe. My sense is that no one upline from him knows exactly what he's really doing."

Suddenly I could feel myself drifting quickly out of my body, again as if someone was pulling at me with a sense of urgency. I've had that feeling before when Sara wanted me to go "elsewhere" with her for some reason.

"Come with me, David. Someone wants to meet you," Sara said, as she led me toward the altar. We hovered near the oil painting of St. Mary and the baby Jesus; the imagery now became liquid as if it were a simple wave being moved aside by a large pair of hands. We slowly moved into another room filled with brightly decorated colors, old paintings, and dark wood before coming to rest near two small chairs that sat across from what looked like an old wing-back chair. I felt

Sara's hands release me as another tall figure entered the room dressed in a blue robe.

As this figure came closer to me, I could see that she had long, smooth, flowing brown hair. The purity of her skin was incredible, and her eyes were eagle-gold penetrating me easily. She was obviously more highly evolved than Sara. The woman smiled gently and asked, "Do you like where you are?" she asked with a lilting voice.

"Yes, I do, it's . . . very relaxing to be here, wherever this is."

"This is where you were, but in a different dimension," she said in her almost melodic voice. "Do you know why you're here?"

"No, but I wouldn't mind staying for a while," I said half-joking.

"Sara is right; you do have an unusual wit about you," she said with a gentle smile.

"Thanks, I take it this isn't a social call?"

She moved to the opposing chair and sat gracefully. "No, I wish it were. Something tells me we might have some fun though. It depends on you."

"So, if I may ask, who are you and why did Sara bring me here?"

She seemed to look inward for a moment perhaps thinking how to respond. But then, she zeroed in on my eyes and I could feel her connect with me in a very intense way.

"David, I asked Sara to bring you here because the Council wanted to ensure that you are aware of certain things, and also to express how delighted we are with your progress. You are one of several that have a unique ability that is quickly becoming important to us." She paused to let this sink in. "As you've discovered, the OSI Agent, Stephen Bullard, isn't what he appears to be," she said in a serious tone.

"I did get a bit of a warning from Sara. So, what am I really up against?" I asked.

"We have given you foretelling visions of Maridon. What we have not shared are his specific methods. This is something you need to learn about and understand. Steven is one example of that, and you immediately saw the darkness that controls him. This is what happens to young souls who chose to make a deal with such a dark spirit.

"Maridon has never been embodied and yet he thrives on those who have. He's even gone so far as to challenge us light beings by enslaving what he calls living vessels to do his bidding. The difference is that his creatures no longer have free will, and they are completely devoid of any sense of love. They live in complete fear of him."

"So, was the spirit I saw in the room Maridon?" I asked.

"No, it was one that belongs to him. You'll know when Maridon's present and in control. Just keep in mind that it will be easier to defeat Steven if Maridon is not present, since this man's body is still subject to physical law."

"Yes, but I won't have anything more to do with tasks that involve violence. I really dislike the entire concept," I said.

She leaned forward trying to emphasize the importance of her next point. "We understand, David, but hear me when I say it doesn't matter what your preferences are. He will continue to pursue you until he's either killed your body or taken your soul just as he has done with Stephen," she said in utter seriousness.

"But why am I a threat to him?" I asked in desperation. "How in the world did I become the focus of such a spiritual maniac?"

"Powerful souls like you and others will always be a threat to Maridon because as a group, you will be able to defeat him. And that's what we had been hoping. The more you learn, the closer you come to being ready for the fateful day that's coming. But, as he has managed to foresee this eventuality, he has put in place his own plan to defeat us. So, please be careful and remember that whatever you do, there will always be consequences," she said as her hands gently held mine to comfort me.

That look of hers demanded answers to a few more questions. "What are you saying? Is something bad going to happen? Why? And by the way, who are you?" I asked firmly as I pulled back from her.

"Just call me Mary. You might say I'm related to your Spirit Guide Sara. As for your other questions, David, life is composed of both good and bad experiences. It's how we learn. And learning is all you are here to do. So, just remember that when you push through something that seems bad, there are good things that will follow. You just have to be patient."

And with that, she stood while still holding both of my hands. I stood with her. She hugged me tightly and said, "No matter what comes, David, you are beloved by so many—far more than you can imagine."

She pulled back, walked away, and dissolved into the light.

"David . . . David, are you all right? Do you hear me, David?" Linda yelled not knowing what had happened to me.

I blinked my eyes trying to refocus and made sure I was back in the church proper. "Yeah, I'm okay." I leaned back in the pew and took a deep breath, then slowly let it all out.

"I thought you were having a stroke or something. Your eyes got big, and then you just fuzzed up on me, and wouldn't or couldn't answer my questions. What happened?" she asked in near panic.

"Linda, I just had what's called a spontaneous out-of body-experience."

"You mean, like when you took me to visit Brian?"

"Yes, but that was initiated by me, and then sometimes I just get pulled out of my body by my Spirit Guides."

"Yes, you explained that to me before, but this was rather alarming."

"Sometimes these spontaneous experiences are just for fun and other times, they are to forewarn of something that's about to happen." I told her about my meeting with Steven Bullard, the warning I received while in the interrogation room, and how someone else, Mary, gave me further insight.

When I was finished updating Linda, the look on her face was hard to interpret. "So, do you just wanna run away screaming from the crazy guy, or do you wanna hang around for more?" I asked, curious to see what she would say.

She looked away obviously thinking about it. Then she turned back to look at me and said, "I don't think you're crazy, David. As you know, Brian had similar experiences. Some of his frightened him a lot, especially the dreams he had of being murdered."

She placed both of her arms around me and pulled me into her, resting her head on my shoulder and said softly,

"I want you in my life, David. Please don't go anywhere without me."

She began to cry as I held her. "Linda, I won't, and I won't let anything happen to you either. Will you trust me when I say that?"

I heard a door open, and then a voice. "Oh my dear, no hugging in the church," Father Mike said jokingly. "I knew there was something special about you two when I first met David. Seeing you two together now makes an old priest's heart feel good."

Father Mike sat next to us and continued, "David, you have nothing to worry about. Sergeant Dodd explained to Richard how you are better suited in aviation, and your desire to pursue a career in air traffic control. When the time is right, Richard will work with Dodd to make that happen. And, my dear," he said as he looked at Linda, "if you're still attached to this young man at that time, you'll have the option of going with him. How does that sound?"

I was gently wiping the tears from Linda's eyes when she said, "You seem to have married us off already, Father. I don't know him that well yet."

"Hey, wait a minute, you just said . . ." I began, before she used a finger on my lips.

"I know what I said. And you don't have to share everything," she gently said.

"Never forget," Father Mike continued, "you are loved by so many here, far more than you can know or see."

That caught my attention. Mary said something similar when warning me about Bullard and Maridon. I began to wonder if Father Mike was in contact with celestial beings, too. If so, we had a lot more in common besides our appreciation of Linda.

Chapter 11

Part of my agreement with Sergeant Dodd before leaving the island was to first complete SWAT certification training which I did in 1972. Violence was not my first option in disputes, but given the small size of the island, what could go wrong? What I didn't know was that things were about to change.

Lajes had experienced an unusual increase in on-base crime, which was causing Sergeant Dodd to reconsider our agreement. The kind of criminal activity was what I would have expected at a larger base. This included transporting small amounts of well-hidden drugs and high-value contraband onboard military aircraft. We were all perplexed by how someone could organize a group of enlisted personnel on different bases to deal with such illegal cargo.

Then one night we had a perilous traffic stop.

"Can you clearly see the target vehicle?" Linda asked, as I concentrated looking through the old surplus World War II binoculars.

"I think so. Wish we had a full moon tonight. It's hard to see much more than shadows in this light," I said.

Linda commented, "Well, if it's going down, we should be seeing something soon."

We were tracking a vehicle owned by a Navy enlisted man whom the OSI thought was involved in a smuggling ring. It wasn't long before I spotted some guys getting into the car with a couple of women. "I've got a small crowd driving off in the car, but they don't seem to be carrying anything."

"Tail them and see where they go," Linda added.

We followed discreetly reporting the activity to Sergeant Dodd, the Watch Supervisor, who was with the Lajes-based OSI Investigator on duty. Agent Bullard had left Lajes the day after our interview. As we followed, it became apparent that the driver was under the influence or being distracted by his companions. The car maneuvered down the road nearly hitting oncoming traffic and then he ran a stop sign. We reported this violation to Sergeant Dodd who gave us permission to conduct a traffic stop.

After pulling the vehicle over in a safe spot, Linda approached the driver's side. I observed from the right rear of the vehicle. "Good evening, I'm Sergeant Cross. Do you know why you were stopped?"

The driver's speech was slurred. "Naw, and I don't give a fuck," he spit out.

Linda shook her head but let this pass. "I'm stopping you because you're having trouble keeping your car on the road, and you ran the stop sign at the last intersection. Step out of the vehicle and go back to where my partner is standing."

As the driver got out, we recognized him as an off-duty security policeman. "Come on Sarge, why are ya be'n such an asshole?" he asked with distain. Linda grabbed his arm and put him in a rather painful come-along hold as she moved him back to where I was standing. She then tried to conduct a field sobriety test, but he resisted her.

"What the hell are you doing with my friend?" a deep voice rang out. The shocking chill of that voice was palpable. The dimly lit area prevented me from seeing the rather tall, foreboding shadow exit the passenger side of the car.

"Hey . . . I'm speaking to you. What are you doing to him?" the voice yelled aggressively. As he slowly approached, I saw that he would tower over me if I allowed him to come much closer. It was then I became acutely aware of his muscular dominance.

I had only one chance of surviving my imminent destruction, and nervously grabbed the butt of my service revolver. Linda immediately reacted to the threat. In only seconds she firmly grabbed the inner thigh of her detainee's left leg below the crotch that shot a sharp, debilitating pain into him as he collapsed screaming. Somehow, she managed to cuff him on the way down.

She was now standing next to me with a determined look and focused on the approaching threat. She called out, "You must be a fan of, 'stupid is as stupid does.' Would you like to join your friend?" Linda said with authority, almost a growl and one that I had not heard before.

The guy stopped as if he were locking horns with the short woman in front of him. I had my gun out, holding it behind my right leg so he couldn't see it. I'd seen Linda take down guys his size before, but there was something different about him. Above all, he wasn't under the influence of anything other than his own ego and a flood of testosterone.

The only thing these two weren't doing was walking around each other in a circle like sumo wrestlers. She said with a disdainful smirk, "I'll be nice and give your oversized ass one last chance to get back in the car."

Her unknown, stare-down partner sneered, "Really, Sergeant Cross. I heard you're so full of yourself that you might benefit from a real man teaching you a lesson."

I thought to myself, *Oh, I wish he hadn't said that.*

Linda wasted no time in countering him, "How does an animal like you even know my name?"

He seemed ready to launch an attack as his evil aura began to overtake me. While I was used to the physical manifestation of danger, the dark bubbling energy that crawled up my legs and into my torso was never as obvious as it was now, and this time it was intense. I've learned to pay attention to this kind of alert because every time it occurred, there was a nonhuman quality to whoever was present.

"Sir," I said. "look over here." I could feel his anger flowing out of him toward Linda like a merciless river flows from a broken dam; I knew then it came from some demonic entity attached to him. Its intention wasn't just to defeat Linda; it was to destroy her. I now felt the intensity of that destructiveness slam into me as he switched his focus. Now, I realized who had sent him and why he was here.

He had moved into the dim illumination of the street lights around us. I could see his facial expression clearly and saw that it had acquired a kind of darkness that I had never seen in a human. I warned him, "Do you see the weapon I have in my hand? It's aimed at your heart." This was the one card I had to play, and I knew that if it worked he and his demonic friend would know that I would at least take the body down if I couldn't do anything else. "And, if you noticed, my weapon is calmly positioned to take the shot."

"You won't shoot me. I'm unarmed," he said in the now familiar evil-like resonating voice. Every time he spoke, my demonic alarm system would increase in volume.

"I may not kill you, but if I kneecap you, you'll go down and limp for the rest of your miserable life. So stop threatening my partner."

"I just asked what the hell she's doing with my friend." Again the alarm was blaring in my head.

"She's given you a lawful order. Return to the car, now. Your presence here constitutes a threat. Back off or I'll take you down."

Linda now spoke up. "You're under arrest for interfering with a police investigation. Drop to the ground and spread your arms and legs . . . NOW," she demanded.

He turned to attack Linda when I heard a shotgun round being chambered, and a familiar voice yelled out from behind us. "Do as Sergeant Cross has ordered, or you'll see that oversized chest of yours disappear."

Sergeant Dodd had pulled up with his lights off and was watching from a distance. When he saw things going south, he quietly approached with shotgun in hand and his OSI Investigator in tow.

The dark monster masquerading as a human did as he was told. Linda cuffed him and another backup unit arrived. The female occupants of the car were released. Both suspects were transported back to booking and put in a holding cell.

"Would you two step in here for a moment," Sergeant Dodd asked as Linda and I were leaving at the end of our shift. "Have a seat. You met Agent Chad Meadows from OSI earlier." We nodded our heads and sat down. "As you know, they've been conducting an investigation into the smuggling on the base. He has an update that you two need to hear. It appears that you've met one of the major operators of this smuggling ring tonight as a result of your traffic stop."

"The collar was a nice break for us in a way, but it might be bad for you two," Meadows said as he opened his file. He was of medium height with a strong built and someone who could handle himself.

Linda said, "The big guy with the attitude problem?" Linda smirked.

Chad looked up at Linda and said, "Yes. It was good for the smuggling investigation because the man you arrested happens to be a soldier in more than one way. Umm ... I should be more specific. He's a former Army Intelligence Operative, but we're pretty sure he's also an enforcer for the group that's coordinating the smuggling activity here and elsewhere. It seems that he's either recruited your off-duty cop, the drunk driver, or is in the process of doing so. That would give his crew access to information related to our stakeouts, or he could use him to interfere with our investigation.

"Not sure why he confronted you two over a potential DUI, though. That doesn't make any sense. Maybe he thought he could pick up a couple more recruits." Meadows paused, thinking this over. "Could be you, being a woman, threw him a curve he couldn't get past. It was a good thing we were there because you two had no idea who you were dealing with."

Linda sat back in her chair to consider what she had just heard.

My evil monitor was peaking off the scale. "Great, so what does that mean for us?" I asked.

"Well, he's going to do either one of two things. One possibility is that after his release from custody, he might test you again to see if he needs to move to his second option," Chad explained.

"And what would that be?" I asked.

"He's the kinda guy that doesn't like to be . . . how should I say this . . . manhandled by a woman, or anyone he considers to be a lesser human being," Chad said.

I pushed further. "If he's former Army, why is he being allowed to do this crap? And why would he be released from custody?" I asked not believing what I just heard.

Chad leaned forward in his chair and continued, "You don't need to understand the why in this man's case. What you need to understand is the threat he poses. Option two is that he may decide to use one or both of you as an example to test whomever he recruits here. But, I'll tell you this, the government is willing to give him a little leeway, shall we say, hoping he'll lead us to bigger fish. The group we think he's tied to is big and complex. That's all you need to know. In the interim, be careful both on and off-duty."

Linda had been listening intently to the conversation. "So we'll be selectively enforcing the law when it comes to him. What's his name?" she asked.

Chad looked at her for a moment before answering. "Dominic Rigusso." He paused, then continued as if thinking aloud. "This still doesn't make any sense. Someone like him doesn't make this kind of mistake. There's more to this that I don't understand."

Both Linda and Dodd looked at me, knowing what the missing element was, but didn't say anything.

Chad now turned to Sergeant Dodd. "They need to be really careful, Sergeant."

"Okay, I'll talk with the old man to see what he wants to do," Dodd said.

"I think we should continue with what we've been doing," said Linda. "I don't see Dan as being that smart to begin with, so if your target is doing something out of character, then why not draw him out further?"

Chad asked, "Dan?"

Dodd responded, "Dan Chambers is the kid they arrested for DUI. He's been assigned here for less than three months."

"Well, Dom is definitely recruiting local soldiers, a crew that does what they're told with no mind of their own. But, whatever you do, be careful and check with me before any takedowns. I don't want this investigation jeopardized," Chad said.

In the weeks that followed, the unusual uptick in criminal activity continued. Our division commander decided that we should maintain the status quo. One day Linda and I were on the evening watch assigned to different areas of the base. The shift was slow until about midnight.

"All units, silent alarm at the base gun club. Eagle-5 en route; all units respond and report ETA," dispatch said.

We were short-staffed leaving us with two on-base units, a flight line unit, and the off-base patrol. "Lima-2 ETA two minutes," Linda responded.

"Lima-3, on scene," I reported. I was a few blocks away when the call was received. "I don't see any vehicles in the vicinity," I reported.

"Lima-3, Eagle-5, observe but do not approach. I'll be there shortly," Sergeant Dodd ordered.

As Eagle-5 arrived, I noticed Linda had pulled up at the opposite end of the building without lights. "Eagle-5, Lima-2 in position," Linda reported.

I observed the perimeter of the building while Sergeant Dodd and Linda checked doors and windows for signs of a forced entry. Once again, there was, at best, a partial moon adding little to the weak lighting of distant street lights. Then something caught my eye moving on the roof of the building. "Eagle-5, suspect moving on the roof." As I followed the dark shadow, it seemed like it was following Linda's movement as she walked around the building. Suddenly, whomever it was leaped from the roof to land a crushing blow on its prey. I reported what I saw as I ran to her aid.

The marines, who guard the top secret hole on the island, had just completed their shift-change and were driving near the gun club on the way back to their barracks. They always monitor our frequency in case we need backup. Their troop carrier arrived quietly just as Linda and I engaged her assailant.

Her attacker brandished a large ugly hunting knife and savagely slashed at Linda's throat. She was thrown off balance and fell backwards stumbling over something as she avoided the blade. I was about to land my M-79 baton across his slashing arm, when the guy noticed me and instantly changed position, which allowed him to lunge at me.

Things moved in slow-motion as I watched the slight shimmer of the long cold blade come within a fraction of an inch of piercing my unarmored chest. Thinking I was inhaling my last breath, I watched the attacker and his weapon being repelled in the opposite direction from his thrusting move as if he had been tethered and was violently recalled to his master.

My shocked surprise subsided when I saw how Sara had used a kind of energy lasso, wrapped around his torso, to yank the attacker away from me and was placed within reach of a surprised Tiny Masters. Tiny, my huge Marine friend who was part of the crew who had responded to our backup call, had then taken the guy to the ground, twisted his weapon hand and plunged the blade into his chest to neutralize the threat. I had never seen anyone killed like that in my life.

Sergeant Dodd joined us and was checking out the attacker. Then, I heard him announce, "Well, this is interesting. Guess who this is . . . it's Dan Chambers."

Back at headquarters, we had another meeting with OSI agent Meadows. "Chad, good to see you again," Dodd said as he offered him a chair in his office. Linda and I were already seated.

"So, this has taken an interesting twist. Your fellow cop broke into the gun club, but didn't stay long enough to remove any weapons. Why do you suppose he would go to all that trouble and not take anything?" Chad asked.

Given the activity and crime reports for the past month, I suggested, "He must have been trying to get at something in the vault, and we showed up and foiled his robbery."

Dodd looked at me. "Or, he could have used the alarm to setup one or both of you." He turned to focus on the OSI agent.

"If one of those assumptions is accurate, we then have to answer the question, why?" asked Chad.

"Maybe Dom thinks he's closer to establishing himself here than you think," Linda offered.

Dodd chimed in, "Or, maybe the young men he's been recruiting have been motivated by some sort of inducement, something like whoever shows an ability to lead gets a bonus." Dodd's voice trailed off as he apparently thought of something else. "And if that's true, then I can see Linda as being a potential useful target for another reason."

Chad looked at Dodd and asked, "What do you mean?"

"Sergeant Cross is highly effective in everything she does. And, she's doing that in what is still seen as a man's world. For her to be successful, she has to perform equal to or better than most men. You can ask Sergeant Lussier for an example of what I'm talking about. He has firsthand experience."

And with that, Agent Meadows looked at me.

"Uhhh, yeah, my recent experience can be summed up in one short comment: If you think you're going into close, hand-to-hand combat, you'll want Sergeant Cross with you," I said.

"You're kidding, really? Why?" asked the agent as he assessed Linda's slight physical presence.

Linda answered him with quiet confidence. "Because, Agent Meadows, most men look at me and think I'm not a threat. What I am, is a skilled physical neutralizer who can and will rip the ass off my opponent and shove it down his throat if he crosses me." As she said that, Linda leaned over the desk and into Chad's face.

Agent Meadows shifted uncomfortably in his seat as he moved away from Linda's demonstration of inner personal dominance. Relieved that she wasn't going to launch over the desk at him, he told Dodd, "What you do with your people is your business. Something's changed on this island and I don't like it. I've not seen this much activity elsewhere, and then these two recent deaths. It leaves me to believe things are going to get worse." We all nodded our heads in agreement, if I only knew what that entailed.

Chapter 12

OSI agent Chad Meadows wrapped up his investigation and left the island. His warnings continued to play on my mind for several days. Every encounter was important, especially those while on duty. I tried to respond to the same calls to which Linda was dispatched just in case. Eventually, she became irritated with me. She claimed it looked like I was stalking her, which resulted in her demanding I stay in my own patrol sector. But, I just couldn't shake off the darkness that continued to haunt me.

At one point, I recalled one of the lessons that I had learned in life. *Know when to perform well and when not to,* which can be critical. People need to have their space, and I had to accept that I couldn't be everywhere, even if it felt natural, defending those I cared about. Protecting others instead of destroying them was a different focus from what everybody else was doing. But then there was a strong hint that a battle was coming. And protecting Linda was more than just keeping a colleague alive. I loved her and wanted her to survive what was coming.

At the next pre-duty briefing, Sergeant Dodd announced, "All of you have been briefed on the Black September Movement and the series of hijacked airliners they've pulled off. I've been ordered to identify, train, and certify a SWAT Team. This team must operate with great discretion, since the whole world will be watching. Sergeant Lussier, I want to see you in my office before you go on patrol. I'll be calling on a few more troops as I make some additional selections. Dismissed."

He closed the door after everyone left. "David, I know you won't want to do this next assignment. But, I need you to step up and do your part," he said in a serious tone.

"What is it?" I asked cautiously, my curiosity piqued.

"I reviewed your personnel file from your stateside training. Your performance with high-powered weaponry was remarkable, and your instructors wrote highly of your ability in your FitRep. I need you to train as the lead sniper for this SWAT Team."

I looked at him with apprehension. We had grown close since my arrival on the island, and yet his request, which should have been an order, troubled me deeply.

"You want me to become a . . . trained assassin?" I asked in disbelief. I knew this was always a possibility after I completed my training stateside.

"Technically, yes. But let's keep in mind that the odds of the team being called up are slim. The aircraft these assholes are hijacking can easily overfly us, and they operate mostly in the Middle East. But, you know the military; they want to cover their ass, so all we need to do is check the box here."

"Yeah, but Sarge, once you certify me as a lead sniper in my records, that follows me for the rest of my enlistment. What if the receiving command decides they want me to continue in that position?" I asked with increasing concern.

"That could happen if I wasn't going to offer you a deal," he said with a smile.

"Oh really," I said rather sarcastically.

Dodd paused and leaned back as he said, "David, one thing I appreciate about you is that you're not like the majority of the juvenile delinquents, first-time enlistees I have to babysit and force feed. So this is what I'm offering you.

"Do you remember the full bird Colonel that Father Mike introduced us to?" he asked.

"Yes, Colonel Smith, who said I didn't need to worry about my next duty assignment."

"That's right. He's arranged for you to be crossed trained into the 2-7-2 AFSC and assigned to Keesler Air Force Base, where the school is located, when your tour is completed here. All you need to do is complete the weapons training, receive the lead sniper certification, and train your replacement. After you're reassigned, nobody can buck the Colonel's directive."

I thought about that with some relief. "So I'll still be allowed to become an air traffic controller if I help you out?"

"Yes, and you only have to do this for a few months. What do you say?"

With only a few months as a sniper, the odds seemed in my favor to get what I wanted careerwise. "Thanks, Sarge. I'll do it."

The specialized training replaced my patrol duty for the duration. The same marines I had arrested for a variety of things in my first week on Lajes had become good friends and now took me under their wings. One of them, nicknamed Tiny, had become one of those best friends one rarely sees in life.

This nickname was paradoxical. The man was huge at over 6 foot 3 inches with a broad, monstrous upper body, and muscular legs so large that the local tailor had to perform a miracle for him to fit in his uniforms. He was one of few Black African-Americans on the base, and an articulate strategic thinker. We worked double shifts to accelerate my emergence into their dark operational club, which burned me out at times.

Since the focus of a SWAT team is to stabilize a high-risk crime scene, the first order of business was an introduction to long-range sniper shooting. It didn't take long for Tiny to realize I had already mastered that "art." The next step was the silent intruder tactics finishing off combatants with the fine art of delivering silent death. This part of his training was particularly draining because of the personal nature of the attacks.

Once they were done with my SWAT training, I returned to my group as a newly formed leader of professional killers. In the back of my mind, I kept telling myself the odds were very low that I would ever have to take another person's life.

So why, I asked myself, did I have a recurring vivid dream of targeting the same person, a man that I knew to be bad, if not evil? The vision always began the same way: I was waiting for him in an elevated position, and had no problem pulling the trigger when the time arrived. I felt the round depart and watched through the sights of my weapon as the large caliber missile struck his head and exit leaving a gaping hole.

The violence of the images were so intense that I felt I was there in the moment. I saw myself drop the weapon and vomit, as I grasped my shaking torso thinking it might also explode.

Awake and recovering from the trauma of this attack, I desperately focused on what I would actually do if I was ordered to take another person's life. I knew that if the base was put into a difficult situation, they would be required to use the SWAT Team. There was no question that I would have to do my duty and live with the consequences.

After my training Sergeant Dodd gave Linda and me some time off to recuperate from all the ramped-up activity on the base. This was a welcomed change considering Linda wanted to do something different—spend the day at the American Beach near Pria.

"Why don't you spread the blanket out here, and get some rest?" Linda said as she and her friends dropped their stuff, claiming our section of the seaside respite.

Given the condition of my lily white skin, I asked, "If I fall asleep, who's going to roll me over so I don't toast up?"

Linda sat down on the blanket, patting the area next to her. Seeing her for the first time in a bikini was breathtaking. She snapped me back with a smile. "If not me, one of our friends will flip you over, Dave," she said with a girlish smile.

As I stretched out next to her, I could feel the warmth of the morning sun and the soft breeze gently caressing my body. My mind began to drift away to some distant tranquil place and to a time when Linda and I could be alone. I could see us quietly walking hand-in-hand, sitting under an ancient oak towering above us, holding her, kissing her softly, knowing each other . . .

"Dave . . . Dave . . . wake up," a distant voice said. My eyes resisted opening as if they had been glued shut. Then everything came into focus as I looked around. The sun was now on the horizon of the western sky. "Where's Linda?" I asked barely discernible.

Brenda, one of Linda's friends, answered, "Oh, she had to leave several hours ago. She was called back to the base."

"Great." Stretching, my back and legs felt tight as if someone had wrapped them in some sort of thick animal hide. Then it hit me, "SHIT," I screamed. An intense searing pain shot throughout my body as if someone had used a large flame-thrower within inches of my backside. I could barely move without a mass of burning pain.

Brenda was shocked as she noticed the exposed skin of my back was brilliant red and barely flexed to her touch. Good at seeing the humor in things, she commented, "Wow, you certainly look radiant this afternoon."

"Not funny, Brenda. Why didn't somebody turn me over or wake me up?"

Brenda winced. "Sorry. After Linda left, we caught up with some GIs down the beach, and . . . I guess we forgot you."

Our so-called friends delivered me to the base hospital. "Wow, I've never seen burns this bad, Sergeant," said the examining physician. "We'll treat the symptoms, but this is going to take some time to heal."

"Great. How am I going to work like this? I can't bend my legs or change positions. Hell, I can't get to the bathroom," I said in frustration.

"Don't worry; I'll keep you here until you can take care of yourself." And with that, the first application of a topical analgesic was administered, which nearly sent me through the gurney.

"You have a certain glow about you tonight," a sexy, purring voice said pulling me from my dreams. Lying with my backside exposed, I began to move from a deep, chemically induced slumber, to becoming aware of a shapely, smiling image of perfection straddling my body. "Relax, I was just trying to be funny, given what I'm about to do to you," she said with a smirk.

"I've dreamt of this moment, but I don't think it's wise. What's left of my skin may fall off," I said.

"Hold on buckaroo, this isn't what you think," Linda said. She now moved her shapely legs closer to my waist which would allow her to gently apply a hydrating aloe-based cream to my back.

I had been staying with her for the last week after being discharged from the hospital. She and Sergeant Dodd thought it would be better than having me stay in the barracks. She finished her application and stood up. "Let's see if you can get up and walk around."

"Gawd, this hurts like hell," I said, as I twisted myself carefully off the bed and staggered to an upright position.

Once I steadied myself, I began to walk around somewhat stiff-legged looking like a GI version of Frankenstein.

"Nice. I can tell Sergeant Dodd that you'll be able to work dispatch soon," Linda said.

"Oh, that does sound wonderful," I sneered. "Stuck at a desk all day."

"Well, Sergeant Flake, count yourself lucky. You could get a laundry assignment."

"It just gets worse," I said, wincing. "I think I'll lie back down and dream up another me."

After a few more weeks of healing, I was finally able to work. Linda was walking behind me as we made our way to the Security Police building preparing to start the evening shift.

She laughed, "Every time you take a step I see a few flakes of skin drop out of the bottom of your pants. If it were coming out any faster, you could be leaving a trail."

"So much for undercover work," I said.

We were just entering the building when Sergeant Dodd ordered us into his office. "About time you got back to work. Has Sergeant Cross briefed you on the upsurge of criminal activity?"

"No sir," I responded. "But, I could hear the sirens every night."

"Hope we didn't rob you of your beauty sleep, Sergeant," Dodd kidded. And then more seriously, he added,

"This island is changing quickly. Some of the new enlisted types have chosen to engage in trafficking drugs over good honest work. What's interesting is that they've expanded from using the Navy P-3's that shuttle back and forth from Rota, Spain to Jacksonville to anything they can get their hands on."

"Sounds bigger than just our base," I said.

"Yeah, Chad Meadows made that clear. But we'll be doing some additional stakeouts and random searches over the next two months." He reminded us that we're still dealing with a dangerous group of criminals. "So I don't want our troops taking any chances. You'll need to pay close attention and always call for backup. Keep your ears to the ground and let me know if you hear or see anything suspicious," Sergeant Dodd instructed us.

"By the way, there's something else I need to cover that's tied to drug trafficking. Linda, please don't forget the guy you challenged a few weeks ago. He's more than likely heading up the criminal activity. In fact, Chad reminded me that there's a chance he may use you as a trophy."

Linda and I both looked at Sergeant Dodd with renewed interest. She beat me to it. "And what the hell does that mean?"

I was tense now. "Why don't you just put her on dispatch. After all, you're sticking me there because of my tropical tan. Why not put her in there to minimize her risks?"

"I'm not working dispatch and I'm not running away either," she demanded.

"Linda, I'm going to say this just once. If I have to, I will make it an order. If I have a clear indication that you or any other member of my team has been targeted, I will expect your cooperation and accept a TDY assignment. If I don't get that, I will move to have you permanently reassigned someplace where you'll be safe." Linda was noticeably agitated as Sergeant Dodd continued, "I mean it Linda, don't challenge me on this. I'll not lose you or anyone else on my crew just because someone wants to prove something. Now get to work." She stormed out of the room, and I tried to follow as quickly as I could shuffle along.

Nothing unusual happened for several weeks after the meeting with Sergeant Dodd. My body had healed and I was back on patrol.

We were nearing the end of the shift one night when things started taking a turn for the worse.

"Lima-1, Dispatch, fight reported at the Cantina on Militar. Lima-2 will be your backup. Eagle-5 en route."

Linda responded, "Lima-1, Roger."

I was working Lima-2 and was on-scene a few minutes after Linda engaged what she thought were the combatants. I walked into the building just as one of the cretins pulled a knife and the others surrounded her.

Obviously, this was a setup. "Eagle-5, Lima-2, Lima-1 has walked into a trap. We need immediate backup."

As I let go of the mic button, her assailant took his first slicing cut catching a part of her blouse just above her Sam Brown belt. Blood was drawn, first blood, and I discovered that's all it took. I shifted into the unaccustomed role of the aggressor. With baton drawn, I struck the collar bone of one of the assailants who had surrounded Linda and heard a loud crack as he went down. His partner tagged me hard with a crushing blow to the back knocking me off balance. I remember seeing the apparent leader of the group looking a little surprised by my intrusion, yet pleased at the same time. Clearly, he recognized me. As his attention was briefly redirected to me, Linda grabbed the assailant's weapon hand, reversed the direction of the blade with a quick two-handed twist, and firmly inserted the eight-inch steel monster into his chest. The maneuver was quick, decisive, and fatal.

Heart still pounding, I managed to regain my attack position. As I did, I felt a sudden intense burning in my right thigh. The guy who struck me earlier had thrown his knife, which was now protruding from my thigh. The surreal image of the knife's blade buried deep within the muscle to its hilt was hard to process. Had this really happened?

My attention was refocused as I heard a loud, sharp boom. My attacker's face suddenly looked shocked, interrupting the downward thrust of yet another knife aimed at my chest. He fell to the floor in slow motion as I turned to see Linda, standing there, hands still shaking, with her gun aimed at the deceased assailant. Her eyes were stressed out as her face clearly expressed a combination of anger and fear. She knew just how close we both came to death.

She had taken two lives tonight. The assailants were determined to assassinate her, someone they didn't even know. Perhaps they thought she would be an easy kill because, after all, she's just a woman. Or, perhaps Dodd was right, and she was being targeted.

Sergeant Dodd rushed into the Cantina along with Tiny and his crew just after the gunshot.

It was time to slowly breathe and sit down. But, I was losing a lot of blood and my mind fell into a dark hole, my vision and my awareness closed to a finite point, and then I collapsed.

"David, how do you feel?" I heard a familiar voice say. My eyes slowly opened, and I realized that I was in the hospital's ER on the base.

"He'll be fine. We stitched up the bleeders and closed the wound. We'll keep him over night, just to make sure we didn't miss anything," the Doc said.

"Good. I'll keep him company. Is it all right for me to spend the night here?" Linda asked.

"Sure, I'll have the staff slide a recliner in here for you."

The doctor pushed some more pain meds in my IV, and I began to slip away. Instead of just going to sleep, something helped me slip out of my body and I found myself in a tunnel. When I floated out the other end I found myself in a garden with lush, green trees and flowers everywhere. Feeling a presence, I turned and saw Linda. Her smile reassured me this was a place of sanctuary and we were safe. I wondered why we were here.

A soft breeze began to relax me further. Each undulating movement of air brought the scent of spring freshness. Despite this comforting feeling, I could not get past the sense that something was not quite right. I tried to put it out of my mind while trying to enjoy being with the woman who had saved my life, someone I had fallen hopelessly in love with. But, the sense of darkness lurking nearby only increased.

I began looking around and noticed several dark, shadowy figures lurking on the perimeter of the forest. Whoever, whatever they were, they were looking at us and they began to slowly emerge from the forest's edge. Now, my early-warning sense suddenly shifted to imminent danger as the bubbling energy once again began to move up my lower extremities to my chest.

Our unwanted guests slowly came into view. I realized that they looked human, but warped beyond any definition of what that meant. My feeling was that their souls had been totally possessed. It was then that I realized I had seen similar entities in my earlier visions. The only creature missing was their leader who stood taller and was definitely a pure malevolent spirit.

"You miss me?" I heard a deep sarcastic voice say at the edge of the forest to my left. As I turned, I noticed the others separated and allowed him to walk toward us. There was no place for us to run. Just as the dominant hulk reached the front, I saw an intense, blue-white light drop down around us like a protective dome.

The others seemed frightened by the sudden appearance of this light and cowered as they took a step back. One of them tested the dome of energy sticking a finger into it and was repulsed by it. Obviously, the canopy of light was simply for our protection. Although unconcerned about the protective dome, the monstrous hulk knew he could not come closer.

Then, he looked up to see a ball of energy appear and descend toward us. There was no sense of fear in him about this apparition, so Linda and I waited to see what would happen.

This new arrival pulsated with a variety of colors as it positioned itself between us and the leader of these half-human creatures. The ball of light coalesced into the image of a woman dressed in white and blue robes. When fully materialized, she wasted no time engaging the enemy.

"Maridon, are you bored? I thought you would be busy torturing your slaves. Why are you here bothering these two innocent souls?" she asked in a commanding voice.

"You know why I'm here, Mary. Don't be as stupid as some of these lesser creatures you call soldiers," Maridon spit back angrily.

"You have no need to bother these two. They have nothing you want," she retorted. "Why don't you leave where you are unwelcomed?"

"Again, you know why I'm here. I can offer them much more than you and you know that. Leave them to me and take yourself back to that mess you call a colony," Maridon commanded.

"It's their decision, Maridon, not yours." And with that, Mary turned to us and asked, "Would you like to give yourself to Maridon?"

Without hesitation, I responded for both of us, "Absolutely not! Neither of us have any interest in anything he has to offer." I looked directly at him and continued, "Maridon, I know who you are now. And, I'll tell you just as I told your spiritual slave, Steven Bullard, I will never be a part of your work—ever. So, go pursue some other weak-minded person," I said forcefully.

"You fool, believe those spineless guides of yours if you want to. I will show you who's more powerful and I will do it soon. Maybe then you'll realize that you have to be one of mine if you want to survive." He turned and began walking toward the trees where he and his minions vanished.

I turned to Mary and said, "Thanks for helping us. I wonder what he meant by that?"

"One never knows with him. It could mean anything. What I can tell you is that your dreams are accurate, but the timeline has been accelerated. Maridon has done something to change this. We don't know what it is, but we're asking you to be more careful. And, since he is no longer a threat to you right now, I'll let you two have some time to talk," she said in a reassuring voice. Mary then coalesced back into her ball of light and vanished.

Linda had not said anything while all of this was transpiring, so I said to her, "I'm betting you've got questions."

"Ohhhh no, me? Questions? Why would I have questions?" she asked in a bit of daze.

"Okay, so what do you think just happened?" I asked.

The look on her face was priceless. It was if it suddenly occurred to her that we were in a fight for our lives and one that went far beyond a bar on a small island in the Atlantic Ocean. I also wondered what she thought about Maridon and his crew.

She finally said, "I don't understand how we got here."

"I'm not sure why we were brought to this specific spot. But, the mechanism is part of the out-of-body experience or astral traveling I've talked about. All I know is that it's possible to focus our consciousness in different dimensions and experience things there in the same way that we experience things in physical reality."

She thought for a moment and asked, "Do you know why this happens?"

"We need to have these experiences to fortify our spiritual bodies, but we have to be careful, too, and not get egotistic about it. Someone like Maridon will look for an opportunity to convince a person who's too focused on ego-based issues, even spiritual ones. Mostly he looks for things like greed, the lust of power and wealth to give him the opening he needs to seduce people. There's always a price for that, Linda."

"Even though I don't have your history, David, I could tell Maridon was one of those classic bad guys you see in horror stories." She turned to look at me and continued, "I don't care what I have to do. I'm with you. Besides, you're growing on me. I'd like to stay close so I can keep you outta trouble. It's obvious you're not very good in close-up fights," she said half-joking, pulling me toward her.

"Oh, really? You haven't seen what I'm capable of yet."

She smirked. "Well, I've been waiting for that."

I smiled, a bit distracted, but came around. "Let's just keep one thing in mind: maybe we're both being tested for a reason."

"Being tested for what?" Linda asked.

"I dunno, but it feels like being with you is more than just being in love . . . or maybe . . . this is part of what love is all about. You know, it goes beyond just mutual respect. It goes all the way to our willingness to sacrifice anything to protect each other." I regretted saying that as it came out of my mouth.

The implications were unnerving to me. Yes, I had fallen in love with Linda. And it was the kind of love I had been searching for all of my life. I felt I could not only trust her, but that I could easily give my life to protect her without reservation if that was my only choice. What I didn't know was that all of this would soon be tested to the extreme.

Chapter 13

Criminal activity around the base diminished after the last bar brawl. There was a command decision to ship out anyone who was known or suspected to have had any off-duty, non-professional contact with Dominic Rigusso. I had a feeling that something was about to change, but I couldn't put my finger on it to save my life.

"Sergeant Lussier, nice to see you and Sergeant Cross arrive early for the evening shift," said Sergeant Dodd as Linda and I walked down the hall toward the break room. "Why don't you two step into my office . . . again."

"I'm beginning to think we spend more time in your office than anyone else around here. Does that mean we're in trouble?" I asked jokingly.

He smirked as he remarked, "No, but you two do create a lot of work for me. So what do you two do in your off hours, anything fun?"

"Depends," Linda said with a dry tone. "He's not exactly the kind of date a girl is going to lose control of themselves over."

I looked back at her in total surprise. Trying to move on, I asked, "So why did you ask us in here?"

"I've decided to move up your reclassification, David, from our happy little family to your new career in air traffic control. Here's your TDY orders. You'll leave next Monday for Rhein-Main Air Base, Germany. From there, you'll be transported to Wiesbaden Regional Hospital. If you pass your physical and other screenings, you'll be shipped to Keesler AFB, Mississippi in August and begin training. What do you think?"

Knowing what it meant for the two of us, I looked at Linda and asked, "What do you think?" Refusing to look at me, she stood up and walked out slamming the door behind her.

Dodd leaned back in his chair, "I guess it's safe to say she's not happy," he said.

"Yeah, but why? She knew this was coming and never said anything about it. There's gotta be something more to this." I shifted my attention to Dodd's window and watched Linda get into her unit and speed away kicking up dust and stones in her wake. She was obviously an angry woman on a mission.

"You two are close, am I right?" asked Dodd.

"I thought so . . . I mean, I haven't taken any liberties with her, but we have been talking a lot which I thought she preferred."

Dodd stood up and stepped over to the window just in time to see Linda disappear around the corner. He pondered aloud, "Maybe you've been talking too much and not listening to her." He paused as if in deep thought. "Keep in mind, Dave; she's not like most women you meet these days. If she were, I doubt she could survive in our group. But, she's still a woman with feelings, expectations, and a view of the future. And her future vision has been burned before."

He returned to his chair and continued, "How much do you know about her personal history," Dodd asked.

"I know about Brian's death, but not much more. She's got an outer shell that's hard to penetrate."

"All I can tell you is that Linda's life hasn't been easy. She's had a lot of personal challenges growing up as a tomboy, getting her police certification, working with a lot of male jerks, which have given her good reason to build walls. You and Brian have come the closest to breaking those walls down. It's obvious her reaction has to do with you leaving for this pre-screening. You might try getting her to see the difference between Brian's reassignment and your TDY."

"I think you nailed it, Sarge," I said. "And I appreciate you moving this reassignment up. The idea of continually pointing guns at people isn't how I see living my life."

"All right then. You're still going to have to make things right with Linda. I suggest you think about what you're going to say and get it done. You've got three days. I would prefer to see you two work this out and stay together," he said as he came around the desk.

"Yeah, that would be nice," I said, then added. "But how are we going to stay together when I'm shipped out in a few months?"

"I've started to work on that for her. But, it's contingent upon you two working things out."

My heart skipped a beat. "What? A reassignment?"

"I have a friend who runs the cop shop at Keesler and he needs someone like Linda. In fact, a friend of yours from tech school is working for him. You remember Beaux?"

"Beaux Boudreau? Sure I remember that old Cajun dog. He's at Keesler?" I asked excitedly.

"Yeah, and he's almost running the shop. He's an E-5 now and has his own crew," Dodd said.

"This is going to be such a great assignment. Can I tell her what you're working on?" I asked.

"Sure, and let me know how it turns out," said Dodd with his usual fatherly smile.

The swing shift was quiet. Linda had the off-base patrol and I had the flight line. I figured when I saw her after the shift, she might've cooled down enough for us to talk. I was surprised to find that she had already left for home when I rolled up to drop off my unit and report to the armory.

"Hi Tom, slow night?" I asked.

"Yeah, and now I have a few weapons to clean and oil. Whoopee, my life is so exciting. Are you do'n anything tonight?"

"I thought I was, but I don't see Linda anywhere."

"Whoa, be careful if you're plans include her. The look she gave me could've penetrated steel."

"Oh, this is going to be challenging. But I do need to talk with her."

"Well, good luck. If your body's discovered in the morning, I'll know you died trying," he laughed, as he turned to place my handgun on the cleaning rack.

I was walking back to Linda's place when she pulled up in her VW Bug and stopped next to me. The passenger door flew open and an order was issued: "Get in," she demanded.

Linda was driving toward the Pria cliffs. The silence in the car was utterly chilling.

She drove along a small cattle road that led up to the cliffs overlooking Pria Bay and the city. I wondered if she realized that we had parked in the same spot where Julia's husband had murdered her which made me wonder if there was a message in this.

The night sky was clear with a full moon and a soft breeze. A cruise ship sailing in the dark waters caught my attention. Its illumination moved slowly along the horizon. Under different circumstances, this would have been the perfect romantic setting. Given my experience "seeing" people who had been murdered, I expected to see Julia's spirit, but she didn't appear.

The car came to a stop several feet back from the cliff's edge, which provided a panoramic view of the ocean, the bay, and the illuminated city below. But Linda continued to look straight ahead as if the road stretched out over the cliff that we were facing. The silence was almost too much to bear as my thoughts raced on wondering what was going to happen next.

I took a chance and said, "You know I love you. But I can't help with whatever's causing you to self-implode if you don't tell me what's going on," I said, as I touched her hand.

She jerked her hand away and began to cry as she collapsed against the steering wheel. I released our seatbelts and gently held her. "What are you afraid of?" I asked, wet-eyed myself.

She pulled away from me with tears pouring down her cheeks. "I was getting used to being around your cute ass, including the strange way you see things, and now you're leaving. I can't go through that again." She collapsed into my arms. The tearful river flowing down my uniform began withering the well-starched material.

"Honey, you're gonna end up glued to my uniform with all the starch you put in these shirts." I knew immediately that I had said the wrong thing as her crying intensified.

Between the sobs, she added, "I can't lose you like I lost Brian. If you love me, you'd turn down Dodd's offer. You told that Colonel your family was here and that I was part of it. What if something happens to you and you never come back?"

I gently put her at arm's length so I could see her eyes and said, "That's not the core reason you're so upset . . . Hey, wait a minute. If you're concerned about me not loving you or not enough, then that means you love me even though you've never told me. Am I right?" I asked.

"You can be so slow sometimes," she said, shaking her head and sliding back to her side of the vehicle.

"Me? Slow? Well, reading you through the walls of fear you've erected around yourself, makes it difficult," I said.

"Walls? What are you talking about?" she asked impatiently. "What does that have to do with anything?"

"Ever been to Berlin? The Russians thought they could separate the German people by building a big concrete wall and posting guards with guns. But the bonds between people and families are strong, and some will fight to be reunited at any cost and they're not afraid of the consequences of taking the risk. What we're going through right now is kinda like that. You yearn to be with me, but you can't quite breech the walls you've built between us. Your fear is just a ghost from the past. Release it. I'm coming back. Germany isn't Viet Nam, and I'm just going for some pre-screening. There's no one to fight there."

"I'm in love with you and I don't want to lose you too," she said, as her lips trembled trying to regain control of herself.

I smiled knowing what I was going to say and how it would likely turn out. "My dear, sweet teacher and unleashed Wonder Woman, we need to be honest with ourselves about why we're together. And let's not forget that you told me a while back that you wanted me to cool it. I want to make sure that our love has a solid foundation and isn't driven by momentary impulses. I know that seems odd to hear. But Linda, I don't want to find myself alone at the end of the lovefest."

She looked utterly defeated. "So you don't really love me, but you like being with me, is that it?" she asked hesitantly.

"No, that doesn't come close to describing my feelings for you." I paused, and became aware of something moving deep inside me. It was like an ancient door whose rusted, aging seal was abruptly cast open by some unseen force. I heard Sara's voice say, "Just open yourself, David. She's ready for this healing."

A flood of knowledge and emotion erupted from deep within this formerly sealed ancient chamber. I could feel the flood of a spirit-driven mass thrust itself toward the trembling woman who was once again, in my arms.

As it did so, I could feel her soul open and saw the same spirit-driven entity appear from within, merging with what came from me. I felt us becoming a single entity as if we, our souls, were being perfectly joined for eternity. Having never experienced something so pure and complete, I silently pleaded with my Guides to make this moment timeless for us.

Tearfully, I thought I held her close, but what I was holding was *her* as a single life form. The knowing of our spiritual relationship took shape as I whispered into her ear, "We are one together in ways you cannot possibly image, my love. We are far beyond the depth of human feelings. The knowing I have of you is indescribable. We no longer live within the prison of fear. Those walls have crumbled. How could I not utterly love you with all of my being, not just my heart?"

Our lips touched gently and then with increasing hunger as if doing so would cause her tears to vanish and heal her forever. This new eternal life could only have been granted from beyond the veil.

Clothing became suffocating and the small front seat area had become too confining.

We gave ourselves to each other at the altar of our own creation that evening. Her VW bug and the expanse of

Nature held us and allowed our commitment to each other's lives to be expressed completely. This was a wordless commitment that I knew would be shared and last forever. While I was awe-struck at what two human beings can do in the front seats of a small car, another door opened deep within my mind and I saw new images rapidly unfolding before me, again, a foretelling of some sort.

I don't remember the exact sequence, but I remember that my fear increased rapidly and the sense that something deadly, cold, and dark was once again approaching me. Why would I have to deal with this now? The closer it came, the more labored my breathing became. I felt that I could do nothing to protect Linda. Yet I knew I had to try. This was the same nemesis I had sensed in earlier dreams. Was I being attacked yet again?

Perhaps I could escape and take Linda with me if I could only crawl away, but my arms and legs would not move. Was this the warning Maridon had given me? Had he decided to use the moment of the physical expression of my love for Linda to attack? He promised that he would deliver his angel of Death as the consequence for my interference in his master plan. Having no choice but to witness my last breath in this world, I desperately struggled to move. This seemed like it was the last chance to protect the love of my life while freeing myself of this unjust sentence for crimes I had not committed.

"WHAT'S WRONG . . . WAKE UP . . . WAKE UP," Linda shouted in panic as she shook me violently.

"Wha . . . wait . . . .stop. I'm not a pinball machine," I mumbled having difficulty refocusing my attention.

She crawled off of me and fell into the driver's seat. "Oh, that confirms it. You're all right."

"Confirms what? Gawd, my neck hurts." I still felt as if I was drawing my first breath after being forced to swim underwater far too long.

"Your sarcastic humor. If you were dying on me, I doubt you would've been able to complain like that."

I looked puzzled, still in a daze. "What do you mean?"

"Well, you looked like you were having a heart attack. I'd like to think I'm hot, but I don't wanna kill you!" she said with concern.

I almost laughed at the thought. "I wasn't dying," I paused still having difficulty breathing. "Do you remember some of the dreams I've told you about?"

"Yeah," she said.

"Well, I just had another one, but this is the first time I've had one without being asleep."

"You had one of your dreams as you're climaxing?" she said in disbelief.

"I'm not sure of the timing, but let's not lose sight of the fact that up to this point, I was a virgin. I told you that months ago."

"This is a first. I fall for a virgin, we make love, and what does he have: a vision just as he climaxes. I can hardly wait to answer the question that will certainly be asked, 'Oh, and how was he in bed, dear.' Let's see, I guess I could say, 'Well, our sex was so intense that he had visions when he climaxed and it sounded like he was going to die.' That should entertain everyone."

"Very funny, Linda. But I don't share that kind of information. As you might remember, I'm somewhat shy to begin with, and I just don't see that my spiritual life is anyone's business," I said.

Linda began putting her clothes back on as she said, "I believe you, David. But, you looked so stressed. What did you see?" she asked.

"I'd rather not talk about it right now, if you don't mind. I have something else I'd rather share," I said calmly still trying to slow my heart down and clear my mind.

"What?" she asked as she turned her now fully clothed body toward me.

I was exhausted as I laid there naked. I had not returned the passenger seat to its full upright and locked position. My attention was drawn to the distant horizon again as I observed the cruise ship's lights now moving out of sight. How much of what I saw should I share with her? I had no idea what the timing of my OBE or being in this location was supposed to mean, but it evidently applied to both of us.

Reaching for her hand, I said, "Sergeant Dodd arranged for you to be transferred to Kessler if I pass the physical. I'll be in training there for about six months. We just have to work out the details of me being picked up at the Kessler control tower after I graduate."

"What . . . you're kidding . . . we'll stay together?"

"Yeah, it certainly looks that way," I said smiling at her.

"So does this mean we're exclusive?" she asked in an almost comical tone of voice.

"I'd like us to think about building our relationship to one of marriage. That also means that I want all of our dirty laundry out on the table to fix what can be fixed, and get rid of the rest." I leaned my depleted, sweaty, naked body toward her. Gently kissing her for the slightest of moments, I added, "I want our life together to last and be as happy as we can make it."

She smiled, "I guess I can learn to live with your bizarre vision-choking, climax sessions. So where do we begin?"

Chapter 14

As the next few weeks passed Linda and I were always together when we were off-duty. And we were able to back each other up most of the time when we were on patrol. I insisted on that because I was still having dreams that the threat to us would become worse, far worse.

After Julia's murder, Braz Mendoza, my second father figure on the island, had helped me deal with her death. But now, the relationship I had with him and his wife became much deeper. As an interpreter, he was always assigned to the off-base patrol, Lima-1. He was a much older man, father of five children, and had counseled many young people from our security police unit over the years. We all had our challenges becoming full-fledged adults, but the camaraderie Braz and I had seemed to go beyond that. At the time, I had no other way to relate to what I was sensing about him and his intent.

Even though we had not spoken about my relationship with the Other Side, I think he sensed the possibility existed when we first met. But, after Julia's murder, I was invited more often to spend time with his family. And, they introduced me to other members of their church, especially the men. There was something different about them when they were with Braz. I could feel a connection between all of them that was ancient. The conversations we had were quite interesting, but I always felt like they were probing me for some other purpose than just being friendly.

One day, Braz suggested that Linda and I should dine with his family. Since everyone knew about our relationship, it didn't occur to me that Braz might have another purpose for us showing up as a couple.

When the evening arrived, Linda drove us there in her VW Bug. "Braz seemed intense about you coming to dinner. Do you have any idea why?" I asked.

Linda smiled and said, "Yeah, he would. They've known me from when I was with Brian," she said.

"So how close were you and Brian to Braz and his family?" I asked.

She pulled the bug over to a short wall made of volcanic rock covered in colorful island flowers. "Dave, do you know anything about Braz besides being a great interpreter for us?" she asked.

"No, I just know that he's helped me deal with some tough stuff. The locals can be a handful." I said.

"Just curious, but are your instincts, or whatever it's called, telling you anything else?" she asked inquisitively.

"Well, yes, in a way. There's something old about Braz and it's not his age. It's like I've known him before in this kind of role," I said.

"You mean, past life?" she asked.

"Yeah, definitely, and from here."

"Okay, well, if you figure it out, let me know. I'm curious how this story's going to play out," she said with a smile and then pulled the bug back on the road.

We drove along for a minute or two in silence. "Oh, by the way," she said, "why have you been spending so much time with me, besides the obvious," she said with smirk. "I mean, you're my backup on most if not all of my calls?" she asked.

"Well, frankly I can't see living my life without you." The idea of Linda being harmed because of my "other activities" was almost too much to bear. I thought about how I would deal with life without her and I just couldn't see doing it. She was staring intently at me as she stopped outside Braz's home. Now it was my turn to become emotional as I choked out, "Linda, if anything happened to you . . . anything . . ." I couldn't finish the sentence.

Linda put her arms around me and pulled me into her. I couldn't believe that this one thought had completely defeated me. We were hugging each other when I felt a rush of energy sweep through me from head to toe. It was intense, warm, yet it felt so fluid. The energy collected in my chest and began to push its way out as if it wanted to touch or wrap itself around and through Linda. As it did that slowly, tears of joy and love flowed from me. All I could think of was how much I wanted to disappear within her being and hers within mine.

It was then that I noticed she began to respond in the same way. "What's happening to me?" she asked tearfully.

I heard a soft, reassuring voice say, "This is an offering from us to both of you. It's the kind of love two embodied spirits experience when they allow us to show them how." The kiss we shared felt deep and changed everything we had known about each other. This spiritually given gift was one that I felt would continue forever.

Sophia noticed something different about us as she greeted her house guests at the door. She continued to focus on our newfound closeness throughout the evening. But, when Linda and I were about to leave, Braz had an idea.

"I've been thinking," he said. "Linda has been going to the Santa Cruz Cathedral since she's been on the island. And, I know you enjoy history. Would you have an interest in the religious folk lore of our island?"

Something about the question sparked my excitement. "Yes, of course, why do you ask?"

"There are several sites on the island that have historical significance. Would the two of you like to see one?" he asked.

I looked at Linda and she nodded. "You bet we would. What can you tell me about it?" I asked excitedly.

"Our history is centuries old and closely tied to Europe. You know that many of our members can trace their bloodlines back to the 13th century," Braz said.

"No, I didn't know that," I responded.

"My family's history, as are the men you met at church earlier, are tied to the Templars. Many of the cathedrals on the island are here because of them. The Santa Cruz was one of their first."

"I had no idea. Is that what you wanted us to see?" I asked.

"Yes, eventually, but not now. I would like to take you to an unusual cavern that has been used for centuries as a place where powerful rituals have been performed. The cavern was once part of the volcano, which has been extinct for as long as people have inhabited the island," he explained.

"When will we see this place, Braz?" I asked.

"It's just a few miles away. Would you like to go tonight?"

Without hesitation, we both said, "Yes." We thanked Sophia for taking care of us, hugged her tightly, and was ready to go.

Linda and I rode with Braz to the site which was accessed through a small cave opening at the base of a mountain located less than ten miles from his home. The clouds covering the quarter moon made the absence of light that much more noticeable. Braz brought along some lanterns that illuminated our path and the old locked gate at the entrance.

Once inside, we made our way into a tunnel that was just big enough for us to walk upright. This passageway was the lava vent that Braz mentioned earlier. The echo of our footsteps was muted and the shadows cast from our lanterns encouraged the imagination to wander. The rough-carved walls were obviously old, and I wondered what we would see at our destination. As we made our way into the bowels of the old volcano, I noticed a sudden chill as a breath of air pushed past us.

After several minutes, we passed through another rough arch that was the entrance to a huge chamber. "This was a magma chamber for the volcano. We use it for special ceremonies and unusual things are known to happen here," Braz said reflectively.

"What kind of things?" I asked.

"Do you not know, David?" Braz asked facetiously.

As I stood there, I could feel the strong presence of more than one entity surrounding us. This group of spirits made themselves known in a subtle way like some will do. As I felt their presence grow stronger, they pulled me into another unseen room as Braz and Linda followed. It felt like I was having a spontaneous out-of-body experience while out in the world as compared to those who have them while relaxing in a chair or bed. The tugging became even more pronounced as I approached what looked like an altar made of hand-carved wood and marble. The closer I came to this spiritual artwork, the more it became my spiritual focal point.

"Braz, I think I need to sit down for a moment," I heard my voice say, as if I were on the other side of the room. My spirit felt out of sync with my body. I looked down at myself and saw undulating images of my hands and arms separating, and then joining and separating again. And then the entities around me must've become impatient, as I collapsed and felt myself jerked completely from my body.

I stood just a few feet from the altar observing everything. Braz and Linda were trying to hold onto my listless body as they lowered me to the rock-hewn floor. "David, DAVID," Linda shouted obviously frightened for me.

"Don't worry, child," Braz said trying to comfort her. "He's still with us."

As I stood there watching them, I saw the shapeless entities standing around me. A few moved to open a portal, and several more in the form of men passed through the opening from another dimension. It was apparent they were from centuries ago given their appearance. They were dressed in white tunics made of fine material with crosses hanging from silver chains around their necks. All but one were carrying swords in their right hand and a shield braced on their left arm. The swords seem to glisten from a light source that I could not identify.

The one without a sword or shield was their leader and stepped forward as he said in a deep commanding voice, "Are you prepared for what is about to begin?"

"Prepared for what?" I asked.

"You have been given visions showing the battles that are coming and the one who is our enemy. He will not stop until we are all dead or consumed into his darkness."

"Who are you?" I asked.

"I am known as Grand Master de Molay." As he said this, large, red crosses formed on their tunics covering the breast of the men who stood before me.

"I will ask you once more, are you willing to fight for us? There is much at risk and a heavy price to pay if you say no," Molay said.

"Are you threatening me or do you mean something else?" I asked carefully.

"You are one of several who are being drawn into this battle. All who are being approached possess special skills like you. Despite our urgency, though, you have the right to choose. But, if you refuse to help us, the risks of greater harm to everyone, including us, increases terribly. Maridon has discovered new powers and we must stop him. We need your answer now," declared Molay.

I looked back at Linda and Braz. Linda was kneeling next to my motionless body and cradling me in her arms, almost in near panic because she did not know what had happened. Braz, on the other hand, knew what was transpiring and continued to reassure her. Now, I knew why he brought us here.

I turned my attention back to Molay and his crew. "Is Braz part of this?" I asked to confirm my thoughts.

"Yes. He is a devoted follower as are some others on this island. Though they call themselves soldiers of Christ, they are, in fact, Templars by faith and blood."

"Molay, I have been having visions warning of things to come, but I don't understand the threat," I said.

"All I can say is Maridon's threat is to all of us. The visions foretell dark times because it is only one of several possible futures we face. Your choice and those who are like you will set the path that will take all of us into the future that awaits. Maridon will stop at nothing to destroy or consume everyone in his path. You and your kind are needed to defend against his aggression, his heresy."

"What about Linda, is she threatened as well?"

"She is, but what will happen to her will strengthen her. You should not be concerned."

Now I was becoming desperate. Was he telling me the truth or was this a rather artful form of deceit? I knew that certain spirits from the other side were all too willing to use us to get what they want by using fear as a tool. While I tried to tap into my Spirit Guides for help, I felt a hand rest on my shoulder. Startled, I looked to my right and saw a radiant being. It was Sara, but she looked different from how I had previously seen her. She appeared now as being something more than just one of my guides.

"David, you're ready for this, if you want to accept your role and responsibility. Those you see before you are your allies, and they need your help as they need the help of the others who have your same ability," said Sara in a comforting, reassuring tone.

"What role do I play in this conflict?" I asked quietly. "I have never thought violence to be a solution for anything."

"Violence never leads to a lasting solution, David. But, it can create a tiny bit of good that otherwise would not have happened," Sara said. "And that good can multiply many times causing things to happen that are utterly remarkable."

I looked at her in disbelief and said, "You can't be serious. How can any good happen when men are destroying each other and obliterating communities?"

"It's not the violent act that you should focus on; it is the decision to act that the participants make that matter. Do you understand?" she asked.

As she finished speaking, I saw a video, so to speak, of numerous violent incidents that occurred in history as if they were happening in front of me, including the killing of women and children. I heard the wailing of mothers who watched their children die, and others whose bodies were being torn apart.

Near the end, I saw a sequence involving people being starved to death in a concentration camp. Some of them were led into a gas chamber and murdered. Others were deprived of shelter, starved and worked to death.

When I could take no more of this brutality, I saw a man bent over from beatings by his captors. He shuffled over to me and held my hand while wiping the tears from my face. He asked, "Why are you crying?"

"I can't take seeing this kind of cruelty. How can anyone treat another human being like this?" I asked.

"Well, David, had it not been for this, I would have never become a Rabbi. And I have to say, my faith and understanding of everything has only grown from it. Yes, people have free will, but sometimes the ego becomes so controlling that it takes this kind of torture for a person to realize that the ego is their enemy. When that happens, they give themselves into the hands of the purity of love, their soul is released, and they find what was intended for them throughout their life.

"In my case, I had this moment of realization in the midst of being tortured. That's what it took for me to realize the truth of my life. And, as a result, I embraced the love that was shown to me. And with that realization, I became a

Rabbi. It was what allowed me to help many others before I died. And you know, there are others like me here. This is the good that can come from violence. It's not the preferred method, but it works . . . sometimes," he said with a smile. "I hope you choose to help us." And with that, he and the images vanished.

"David, where were you this time?" I heard a tearful voice say as I came back.

"What?" I asked nearly exhausted.

"You were obviously someplace else," Linda pleaded desperately.

I looked at Braz for a moment. I could see he knew why it was important that he bring me here and it had nothing to do with history. Well, there was a little about history involved, but most of it was some needed persuasion. "Why don't you ask Braz. He knows," I said.

"Me? I know what?" Braz asked trying to look humorously innocent.

"You know why you brought me here, and you know that having ties to the Templars is a big part of it," I said with a nod.

"David, everyone knows about Braz's family history. And there's a few more like him on the island," Linda said.

"Really! Well, did he mention he can pass through the veil better than I can?" I asked.

Surprised, Linda stared at Braz. "You do that out-of-body thing like David?"

Braz hesitated before he answered. "Well, it's not quite the same. Yes, I do that occasionally, but the reason I do it is different."

Braz continued talking about what he had been doing and why as we returned to his car. By the time we had driven back to Braz's home, Linda understood more of the why behind my experiences, and I was thankful to Braz for that.

As Linda and I drove back to her apartment, she looked as though something was weighing heavily on her mind. "Hey you," I said half-jokingly from the passenger side. "Are you okay?"

"Uh, yeah, why wouldn't I be?" she said quietly.

"Oh, I dunno, you just look like something's bothering you. Was it all that mystical stuff that Braz and I talked about?" I asked.

"No, well maybe, but I have a question for you and I want a straight answer. Do you understand?" She asked firmly.

"Sure," I said with a smile.

"David, since you see the future, I need to know what you see for us."

"It's clouded and I don't see it clearly. Considering our recent violent encounters on duty and thinking about what might lie ahead, I'm concerned for both of us."

"I've been thinking what you would do if something happened to me?" she asked.

"I really don't know. I love you more than life itself," I said.

"That's what I thought. I feel the same way about you. I've been thinking about asking you to move in with me . . . you know, for us to live together. At least we'd know the other person is okay. How would you feel about that?" she asked inquisitively.

"I...I haven't thought about that," I said nervously.

"David, being together seems like it's part of our destiny," she said with a smile.

"It would be easier and I wouldn't have to worry about you so much," I said.

"And, I find it amazing that even though we've made love, you've never tried to talk me into having sex, just for the sake of it."

"Well, I'm not like most guys. I'm moved by spirit in all things, even this," I said.

Linda pulled the car over abruptly and grabbed me by the face and planted a deep, wet juicy kiss on my lips that took a while to complete. I was gasping for air when she finally let me go. "Gawd, you're such a weirdo. I want you to move in right now," she said impatiently.

"You want me to move in . . . like, right now?" I asked not believing what I just heard.

"Yes. We could get most of your stuff from the barracks tonight. What do you think?"

"I think I've died and gone to heaven, lady."

Living with Linda certainly made life easier. Our relationship strengthened if that was, in fact, possible. The dreams of forewarning continued and we were given the gift of mergence a few more times. Mergence is what I grew to call that intense feeling of our souls touching each other as they did that night in her VW outside Braz's home.

Though our relationship changed dramatically, I'm still at a loss when I try to describe what happened. Some might say, "Oh, all you had was great sex." If Linda were here now, she would disagree. While we were together, our relationship deepened beyond anything we had ever known.

Every time we experienced the gift of mergence that Sara had gifted us, Linda and I began to change from seeing ourselves as individuals to seeing ourselves in some form of oneness, two that had become one to some degree. The more this became real for us, the more of a threat we became to the darker elements around us led by Maridon, and he wasn't shy about letting me know that in the visions that became more involved.

I have thought about this a lot since then, and I have come to the conclusion that the process of joining of two or more individuals is merely a preview of what is coming for all humanity, and what is coming is indescribable. It was for this reason, and others, which we were unaware of at the time, our love for one another would attract far more than just unwanted and dangerous attention—and it would happen very soon.

Chapter 15

"Do you think you can stay out of trouble?" Linda purred seductively in my ear sending a delightful shiver through my body as we held each other in the airport's terminal building.

"I'll try, but you know how bored I get when you're not around," I responded.

The Military Airlift Command (MAC) ran passengers and freight between McGuire Air Force Base, New Jersey and Rhein-Main Air Base which is located at the Frankfurt Flughafen in Germany. The flights would stop in at Lajes Field twice a week to resupply the base and transfer personnel. Today, the passenger terminal for civilian and military passengers was crowded.

Leaving, if only temporarily, a woman I was in love with was the furthest thing from my mind. The sense that she was about to fall into a dark abyss, and I might not be able to protect her, haunted me. If anything was going to happen, I wanted us to go through it together.

"Hey, come back to me," she said, shaking her head. "You've got to board that flying tube if you're going to have a shot at becoming a controller. What's the matter?"

I didn't answer the question out of fear more than anything else. Would I lose her? Was it my own insecurity? I finally caved in and said, "I dunno, maybe it's the idea of not seeing you for a few days. After all, we've been together 24/7 for quite a while now."

"Don't worry, big boy. I'll be here when you get back. Just make sure you keep your eyes and hands t'home. Got it?"

"Oh yeah, I'll have a hard time doing that. Me, the shy, reserved, introvert that sees things no one else does. That'll make me irresistible to every woman in Germany. Hey, maybe the local police will have a straight jacket with 'David' monogrammed on it, just for me."

Linda shook her head. "Come on, I'll take you out to the plane since I'm on duty."

We slid out of her Security Police unit in front of the waiting Starlifter. I was carrying a small duty bag and holding her hand while walking toward the Loadmaster that was boarding the passengers. Linda surprised me with one last hug and kiss. If you've never kissed someone who's in uniform with weapons protruding from their waist, then you haven't lived. I guarantee it will do wonders for your ego. Why? Because it's a true test of one's agility, when you suddenly realize how easy it is to become entangled with a holstered revolver and baton. The challenge is how to become disentangled while still looking like a professional airman. It took a moment but we got free of each other.

"Damn, you can be such a klutz sometimes," Linda said as I smiled, still a bit out of sort. "Why are you so nervous? Something's bothering you. Will you tell me what it is?"

Again, I chose to avoid answering the question. Instead, I chose an easier topic. "There's a lot riding on this trip for us. I'd rather that you were coming along. At least I'd know you were safe."

"Get over it, Mister. You'll be fine and you know I can take care of myself. Just get yourself back here as soon as you can, okay?" She straightened her uniform again and ensured her weapon was still attached and my duty bag was nowhere near her.

I jumped aboard. The door was closed and locked separating me from her. The sounds of that door locking jarred me to the core. It felt as if our fates had been sealed, not just the fuselage of the Starlifter. The plane started taxiing to the runway as I caught the last fleeting glimpse of her waving goodbye through the small porthole of the door.

"Hey, lover boy, I need you buckled up in a seat," said the Loadmaster.

Traveling along the German Autobahn, which has no speed limit, our military bus was slow by comparison to the cars that flew past us. As we lumbered our way down the highway, I began to receive flashbacks from the past. For some reason I was seeing vague images of the warring Germanic tribes who lived here in much earlier times and the brief images of the battles of the World Wars that occurred along this route. I began to think that my Guides were reminding me of the occasional horrific decisions that men made that threatened the lives of many other innocent people and tore families apart.

After an hour of watching the competing imagery on the Autobahn, I was left with the distinct sense that something bad was going to happen. I was still trying to figure it out as the bus arrived at the hotel in town.

"Hi, I'm Sergeant Lussier. My supervisor made reservations for me," I said.

The clerk carefully checked her files and said, "Okay, you're a day early, but I think we can find a place for you." She checked her room log, then looked up. "It's not the Honeymoon Suite, as you Americans say, but it's a bed and a hot shower."

I found my way to the second floor room, and it wasn't much more than she described, but it would do. I put my stuff away, got a hot shower, and went downstairs to the dining room to get something to eat.

The next day, I took a bus to the base and completed the first round of medical tests. It was all pretty standard, and I went back and forth from the hotel to the Wiesbaden Regional Hospital the next couple days. On the final day of testing, I was headed back to the hotel on the bus when an unusual looking guy jumped onboard. He was dressed in casual civilian jeans, shirt, and a jacket, which looked like they had been slept in for weeks. His long brown, unkempt hair, beard, and mustache were that of a person who had been living in the woods rather than the barracks. The assumption that he was active duty was not at all supported by his grungy appearance. But, the medical folder he was carrying corrected that impression.

I could sense that something wasn't right about him. I couldn't put my finger on it, but he seemed to be either an escapee from the psych ward, or worse. We locked eyes and he grinned, which sent a cold shiver up my spine. When he sat down next to me, I knew this was no chance meeting.

"Man, can you believe this? I'm finally out of there. Damn, I never thought I'd be out this soon," he said with a tone of nervous excitement.

"So what are you out from?" I asked, placing my hand over my Security Police badge and removing it, thinking I had to conceal my occupation.

"They thought I might have a screw loose, but I showed'm. I'm out!" He turned to me as if he had a sudden revelation. "Hey, why don't you come with me? I feel like celebrating a little," he said.

As I sat there thinking about his offer, I quickly assessed him. The noticeable tremors in his hands, the dilated pupils, unkempt civilian clothing, all led me to believe something more was afoot. But, I still had no clue. I just knew that I had to ensure that this soldier didn't hurt someone and that's why I said, "Sure, what do you want to do?"

"This bus stops at Ramstein Air Base. I can get us into the O-Club there. I'll introduce you around and then we'll go over to the Flughafen. I know some girls we can pick up and have some fun. What's your name?"

"David Lussier and yours?" I said, as I reached out to shake his hand. As soon as our hands touched, something shot up my arm that was energetically painful, another warning.

"Sam Barton," he said. "Hope you like have'n fun, because we're gonna do it up right tonight!"

Sam's story was amazing. During our bus ride, he told me that he was an Army Staff Sergeant, yet he had access to areas of the base that were reserved exclusively for officers. I was left with more questions than answers the longer he talked. We dropped by the barracks used by visiting non-commissioned officers so he could clean up first, and then headed out.

As we entered the Officers Club, it was apparent that he knew the officer of the day who let us inside unchallenged.

Sam introduced me to full bird colonels, majors, and several junior officers. After having a bite to eat and a few drinks, we were off to the Flughafen Airport in Frankfurt to track down the girls Sam had mentioned. We found his friends at one of the PanAm gates.

"Hey, Kelly, Gretchen . . . look who's here?" he said walking up to them and hugging them both. The ladies seemed surprised to see him and a little cautious.

Kelly was an American on a work exchange program for PanAm Airlines. Tall, lithesome, with brilliant green eyes and shoulder-length brown hair, she had a striking presence. Gretchen looked stressed out. She was a classic Scandinavian with blonde hair, blue eyes, and wearing heels though she was already unbelievably tall.

Introductions were made, and Sam talked them into going out with us. I could tell, though, there was a sense of tension in the air between the girls and Sam. Gretchen turned to me and asked, "What do you do for the Air Force, David?"

Sam answered the question for me, "Oh, he's a cop from a small base in the Azores. He'll be going back soon." My caution meter shot off the scale. How did he know that? I looked at Gretchen and noticed a change in her facial expression to one of near fright. One would think this would allay her suspicions, unless this guy had a reputation of cavorting with "dirty cops."

While Sam went to retrieve a taxi for us, Gretchen tentatively asked, "Do you know anything about Sam?"

"No, I met him on the bus that stopped near the psych ward on the Wiesbaden hospital grounds. Why?" I asked.

"We don't want to be left alone with him. In fact, we'd rather not go anywhere with him by ourselves. Will you stay with us until he leaves?" Gretchen asked almost pleading with me.

"Well, yeah, but why would you go out with Sam in the first place? You seem frightened of him."

Kelly looked around to see if he was coming back, before she added, "Well, he's got money and spends it freely, but a few weeks ago I saw him open a locker in the airport. He had a few guns in there, not to mention there are times he shows up driving a Mercedes with cash jammed in his pockets. He even talks about jobs he's done for 'big shots' that requires him to travel around Europe."

Gretchen added, "And his temper can be explosive. You don't know . . ."

"Wait . . . what trips are you talking about?" I interrupted.

"He takes trips from this airport to other countries then returns. Usually, when he comes back, he has a lot of money on him," Kelly said.

Gretchen's stress level was peaking. She looked as if she wanted to run away but didn't know where to go. "What's the matter, Gretchen?" I asked.

"He also tried to kidnap me once."

"Ladies, you're describing an international criminal," I said. "So why is he still walking around free?"

"Would you believe we tried going to the Polizei, but because he's a U.S. serviceman, they wouldn't listen."

They now began to tell me more about Sam. As Gretchen and Kelly talked, my mind was focused on what to do next. It occurred to me that there was a chance I had been targeted by someone and that tonight was going to end up on the low-end of the entertainment scale. Linda had always been my backup at the fist fests that I attended. But she would miss this one, which added to my discomfort.

We were standing outside the terminal when Sam returned in a taxi. We hit a couple nightclubs in town. Even though I watched how much I was drinking, Sam went on a real bender in celebration of his release from the Wiesbaden psych ward. Gretchen and Kelley were also careful to drink in moderation, despite Sam calling us party poopers. By midnight Sam was sloshed, and we got a taxi to take him back to the base barracks. After dropping him off, the girls and I took a taxi to Kelsterbach, a small bedroom village north of the airport that still held onto some of the old-world charm of the pre-World War II era. Kelly shared a house with other American nationals on work Visas, while Gretchen lived in an efficiency flat not far away. We dropped Kelly off first.

Gretchen asked, "Would you mind staying with me? I'm afraid Sam will show up as he has in the past." I agreed and got back into the taxi.

Still, there were no answers to some of my questions, but I was convinced Sam was using the girls, but for what? I had to figure out a way to do this quickly, because I knew I didn't have much time left in Germany.

My head hurt from all the alarms going off. If Kelly and Gretchen were telling me the truth, then they were in danger and if so, how could I protect them? It was obvious that I had stumbled into a dangerous situation. The on-duty OSI agent at Rhein-Main Air Base was the answer, but that would have to wait. The girls wanted to freshen up before introducing me to their friends, who could shed more light on Sam.

"I'll be just a few minutes. Make yourself comfortable," Gretchen said, as she disappeared into the bathroom for a shower. I settled into one of two micro-sized rooms of Gretchen's small flat. Deep in thought, I was unaware of how intense I must have looked, until she peered around the corner to check on me.

"You look so serious. Is something troubling you?"

"Wha . . . no, I'm fine. Just thinking," I said.

"You remind me of that statue, 'The Thinker'. Why don't you relax? I won't be much longer," Gretchen said.

I smiled, nodded my head, but I was still alarmed about this situation. *I wished Linda was here,* I thought. She had a far more worldly view and would have known what to do. Adding to my concerns was a sense of being confined with no place to escape should something happen while in Gretchen's small home.

The flat was a multipurpose room, which included the kitchen, living room, and bedroom. I had settled on the overstuffed couch, and tried pushing aside my concerns and closing my eyes. My state of exhaustion began to take its toll as Linda's image appeared before me.

A warm, misty vapor flowed from the open shower door enshrouding Linda's image. I saw myself move toward her and then felt us become comfortably wrapped in a warm, loving, cocoon of togetherness. My thoughts of her drew me deeper into a place of safety, acceptance, and healing. I wanted to return to the loving embrace of Linda's spiritual core that we had experienced. She, like everyone else, had a reclusive place of safety, a place where shields of self-protection were not needed.

And, it was where all of the hurt and pain caused by our life experiences were healed when our spirits merged for a moment in loving trust. How do you explain this to anyone without it sounding like some deluded person, or perhaps risking the criticism of others as being "touched?" The knowing I had of her was far beyond normal sensitivity. I didn't really care what anyone thought of us as long as we remained together and she was safe.

A cool, moist, viscous veil settled over me to deepen my focus. I now saw myself lying on Linda's bed next to her.

She laid comfortably atop the feather bedding we had chosen because of its mystical feel. Slowly becoming aware of me in her sleep, she moved onto her side and spread her arms luxuriously across what she thought was her lover.

The open window allowed a soft semi-tropical ocean breeze to gently move the thin curtains back and forth. Their nymph-like dream dance seduced her deeper into a restful sleep still acting as if I was really there.

A soft, almost indistinguishable glow began to emanate from her body as she entered her deepest dream state. It was then, that I was allowed to see beyond her physical being into her center, the very essence of Linda. To lose myself within this place, I knew would allow us to continue our healing journey from life's trials.

My singular focus was to make us whole. We both needed this kind of spiritual healing, but I believed she deserved this more than I did. Trying to move closer to her, I felt unseen hands pull me to one side of the room. This healing was necessary, so why was this being prevented?

Suddenly, I became aware of a dark, ominous figure as it quietly entered her room. I had run into similar creatures, but none of them felt as strong as this one. The others fed on all the beings around them leaving their surroundings frigid cold as if the life had been sucked out of it. These creatures were the relentless vampires of the unseen world, beyond the veil.

In this case, the room instantly became Arctic cold. It occurred to me that I had encountered this specific creature before. Each time it appeared, there was no question that something horribly destructive would happen. The only thing different about this particular inhuman presence was that this large utterly black form was holding something in what looked like a hand. As I concentrated on its appendage, I realized what object it held. The faint moonlight danced languidly across the large, ugly steel blade as it moved slowly. This was the kind of blade that had been used for centuries in dark underworld rituals. It was the tool that was used to viciously extract the last breath from its innocent victims.

As the creature crept closer to its prey, Linda moved to become more comfortable, completely unaware of her unseen assailant and my absence next to her. Standing over her now, the creature appeared to be lusting for her life-blood and her screams of horror. But, it stopped and took a moment to admire the natural beauty of her form. The murderous assailant's breathing became rapid, almost as if it had become sexually aroused anticipating the moment that its deathly satisfaction would be satiated. The demonic creature's blood-lust surged as it reached down to pull the covers from her, revealing what he craved, her sacrificial body.

Realizing what the creature was about to do, my heart began pounding rapidly, ready to explode. I desperately wanted to throw myself over her, protect her from the animalistic slaughter that was about to occur. But, I could not move or scream to warn her. Something or someone had bound and gagged me refusing to let me be anything but an observer. Where love has never existed, only the utter coldness of evil can live. This is where the utter darkness resided within the assailant's core. I, again, violently struggled against my restraints yielding to desperate panic with no regard to physical limits or injury as I struggled to do something, anything.

When I finally realized there was nothing I could do to stop what was about to happen, I closed my eyes. I cried out, tears streamed while I pleaded with God and all of my Spirit Guides to make this monster stop. But, the entreaties failed as I heard the unmistakable thud of the executioner's first strike. The creature's blood-curdling howl bellowed through the night while its image was illuminated by the moonlight. The love and only reason for my life was torn apart.

"Wake up! Are you all right? What happened?"

I opened my eyes and realized Gretchen had been shaking me. Her face was mere inches from mine and looked panicked-stricken. While dealing with the import of what I had just seen, I realized why it was that I was drawn to her and why I had to at least try to help my new friend. I instantly saw the innocence deep within her and how she had been harmed by Sam and all that was associated with him. I knew I had to do what I could to protect her, because that was my purpose here.

Looking concerned, she said, "You were screaming something in your sleep. Are you sure you're all right?"

"I'm . . . okay," I took a deep breath trying to slow my breathing. It was then I noticed that tears had been streaming down my face and my shirt was soaked with sweat.

"Are you sure? You were crying out to someone when I walked in."

"No, no, I'm fine. I must have dozed off and had a nightmare."

"If you're tired, you can sleep here. We don't need to go out with Kelly and the others."

"Oh thanks, Gretchen, but I'm engaged. I wouldn't feel comfortable doing that."

"You wouldn't be comfortable doing what, sleeping here or going out?"

"Sleeping here. The last thing Linda told me before coming on this trip was to keep my eyes pointed at home."

"Ah, so you're engaged to someone in the military?" she asked.

"Yes, we work together as cops."

"Well Sergeant, you are full of surprises. But for now, you're shaking suggests that you had one nasty dream. Do you want to talk about it?"

"No, not really. We need to get back to the base as soon as we can."

"But let's go by Kelly's place first. She'll want to go with us. Besides, her friends all know Sam and they might have some useful information."

"*Guten Abend* Gretchen," Kelly greeted her friend at the door with a hug. "Our new friend looks worn out. What did you two do, have a little fun before coming over here?"

"Kelly, don't embarrass him like that. He's engaged," Gretchen said.

Kelly laughed, "Just your luck." She then took us on a tour around her home while introducing me to everyone. Each had their own stories to tell about Sam and his unusual adventures. Even though they didn't have the actionable details I needed, what they had observed did nothing to quell my concern.

"Thanks for inviting me into your home, Kelly. What bothers me most is how the Polizei is treating this case. I'm limited as an Air Force cop on temporary duty. The only thing I can do is go back to the base and relay this to the OSI agent on duty."

Kelly looked deflated as the truth of their situation began to sink in. Where there was hope, there was now fear.

"Kelly, I'm sorry. I wish I could do more. Why don't you and Gretchen come with me back to the base? Let's see what the OSI can do for you."

"They can't do anything. We've been through that with the Army's Criminal Investigation Division (CID). They're limited to dealing with military matters, and the Polizei won't do anything because he's U.S. military."

"Let's at least try. Sometimes military investigators have good relations with their civilian counterparts. Let's see what happens." After the OBE experience I had at Gretchen's place, I urgently needed to call Sergeant Dodd.

Walking into the building that housed the Rhein-Main Air Base Security Police Division was like walking back in time. The old stone building felt like I had just crossed through a portal to the early 1900s. Surely there would be spiritual apparitions here given the tragic history of this country. I looked for those lingering spirits still dressed in Luftwaffe or Wehrmacht uniforms but none were hanging around.

I checked in with the duty desk and filed a report with the ladies. After explaining why we needed to see the OSI Duty Agent and the concerns I had about Sam, the desk

Sergeant escorted us to an interrogation room. *Hmmm, that's unusual.*

Once Gretchen and Kelly were settled, I asked our escort, "Do you have an Autovon line that I could use to call my supervisor at Lajes Field, Azores?"

"Let me see your orders." After reviewing them, he said, "I don't see a need for you to call him. You're here for medical exams. You're not here as a security policeman."

"Yeah, I know, but I may be delayed getting back and he'll want to know. He's short-staffed. Wouldn't it be a professional courtesy if you let me inform him what's going on?"

"All right, but make it quick."

He dialed and handed me the phone. "1605th Security Police, Sergeant Dodd."

"Hi Sarge. It's David. I'm still in Rhein-Main and could be held up a day or two."

"Okay, and what in the world are you involved in now?" he asked.

"I haven't the foggiest idea. It's complicated and I don't have much time. I'll be visiting with an OSI agent soon. I called to ask a favor."

"I guess Linda was right. We can't send you anywhere without a chaperone to keep you outta trouble. Okay, what do you need?"

"I was wondering if you would keep a close eye on Linda, especially when she's off-duty. Maybe she could stay with your family instead of her place."

"All right, you're not telling me something. What happened?"

"I'd rather not say," I said, as the duty Sergeant looked like he was listening.

"Too many people around?" asked Sergeant Dodd.

"Yes sir," I said.

"You had another one of your dreams?"

"That's right, the weather here is great . . . a little chilly . . . but I hear a bad storm's on the way." I responded hoping he'd catch on to the impromptu code.

"Yeah, Germany in late fall is always preferred to semi-tropical weather. How bad was your dream?"

"Oh, it got my attention," I said. The duty Sergeant next to me was now paying close attention.

"Did you see who attacked her? That's what it is, isn't it? Someone attacked your girlfriend?"

"Yes, but no I haven't tried any of the beer. Besides, who wants to drink by themselves?" I said continuing to cover.

"Your code language sucks, you know that don't you? Okay, I'll try but you know how independent she is."

"That's fine. I'll try to resist the temptation to stay as long as you do your best to ensure everyone is safe there.

You're staffing is good, right?" I asked in hopes the duty Sergeant would stop listening.

"Remind me to never send you to crypto-school. Your code not only sucks, it's bizarre. Get here when you can."

About an hour later, the interrogation room door burst open. Two men who could've doubled as Secret Service investigators entered as if they were on a mission. "Sergeant Lussier, this is Agent Walker and I'm Agent Thornton." They shared their IDs with me to confirm what they said.

"Gentlemen, Kelly and Gretchen," I said introducing them.

A stenographer walked into the room and sat down. Thorton started the interview. "Sam Barton is of major interest to us. We've read your report, Sergeant. What we'd like to do is start from the beginning. Ladies, we would like you to tell us how you met Sam Barton, your relationship with him, people he associates with, and your experience with him."

"Wait a minute," I said, "Before we start, I have one question."

"What's that Sergeant?"

"Why are we doing this in an interrogation room and who's monitoring this interview?" The agents seemed unfazed by the question making it difficult to interpret their true intent. Almost all military interrogation rooms have either audio and/or visual recording capability.

"That's two questions, Sergeant. Do you know anything about Sam Barton?"

"As indicated in my report, the answer is clearly no. I became suspicious of him when he boarded the bus at the Wiesbaden Regional Hospital."

"Well, we think he might be part of a large international group smuggling things like classified documents, drugs, people, and high-value contraband. We're trying to ensure that no one 'accidentally' sees you talking with us about him."

"If you're that concerned about information and witness security, then why are you sending these women back to Kelsterbach? After gathering additional info from Kelly's friends and considering what the ladies have told me, I would say Kelly and Gretchen are in danger. Isn't there anything you can do to at least get the Polizei to extend some level of protection? If not, I'd rather you arm me and I'll drive them back myself."

"You can't, Sergeant. You're not licensed here. If you were armed and returned fire off base and hit anyone, the repercussions would be intense. You ever hear of the phrase, International Incident?" he asked sarcastically.

"Yeah, but how can we let these two go knowing what we think we know?" I asked.

"You tell us. What should the U.S. military do to protect two civilians when they're off base? As for who else is monitoring this interview, the answer is no one," Thornton said.

I took him at his word and looked at Kelly and Gretchen, "You don't have to answer their questions. In fact, I wouldn't blame you if you decided to walk out of here."

Kelly looked at me with the appearance of a person resigned to her fate. "It doesn't matter anymore, David. Let's just get it done."

The next two hours were spent telling the agents what Kelly and Gretchen knew. Then it occurred to me that this would be a good time to ask about the attempted kidnapping of Gretchen, Sam's incarceration at the hospital, and why he was released after committing what would have been a first degree felony in the U.S.

The agents looked at each other. Thorton decided to explain what they knew. "Yeah, good question, Sergeant. When Mr. Barton shoved Gretchen into his car in front of her flat, his left thigh was bleeding profusely. That happened because he was angry when she refused to allow him to enter the building where she lived. He kicked the front door in that was made of re-enforced security glass. Unfortunately, his aim was poor, the glass above the entry point of his leg was large, and fell on his thigh like a guillotine falling on its victim's neck. He's lucky the guillotine didn't sever the descending artery or take his leg off completely.

"Gretchen's apartment mates saw an American pushing her into a car and thought she was being kidnapped so they reported it to the Polizie. The local cops launched a search; the car was located and boxed in an open area near a park. He was arrested and she was released.

"Our agreement with the host country is that they'll transfer all American military arrestees to our custody for investigation and prosecution. In his case, we transported him under guard to Wiesbaden for medical care and later released him for lack of evidence."

I was once again confused . . . *lack of evidence*. Gretchen was turning numerous shades of red, and her fists were shaking in frustration as she began to lose her temper. "No one listens to me, no one, not even the Polizei. He forced his way into my building, forced me out of my home, and into his car. How is this not kidnapping?"

"The report I have here from your people doesn't say anything about force. But, it does say you had been dating him for a few months prior to the incident and why it wasn't treated like a kidnapping."

"They were not dates," Gretchen angrily protested. "Did their fictitious report also say that we were holding hands, kissing like school children?"

I interrupted, trying to calm things down. "Look guys, I don't have your training and expertise. But, these ladies are frightened by this guy and what they've seen him do. I'm particularly concerned that he apparently stores weapons at the Flughafen in a rented locker. No one should have to live their daily lives in fear like this, should they?"

Walker took a deep breath and slowly released it as he settled back in his chair trying to lower his stress level. "Right, well Sergeant, we all have things we . . ." He stood and began to slowly pace as if in deep thought. He seemed to have made a decision as he stopped, leaned across the table and locked eyes with me. "We're limited here. All I can guarantee you is that we'll talk with one of the Polizie inspectors that we work with to see what can be done. When do you go back to the Azores?"

"Ah, you'll see what can be done? This is another point that makes me nervous," I said.

"What's that? You've lost me," Thorton responded.

"Sam knew my background when the girls asked what I did in the Air Force. Why and how would he know that level of detail?"

That raised eyebrows for a moment. "I'm afraid we need to ask the ladies to leave, now."

"Why? They're in this situation too," I said.

"We have things to talk about that they can't be privy to." With that, Walker stood up, opened the door, and waved a colleague into the room. "George, make sure these ladies are not seen leaving the building. Get them into a car and take them home. Make sure no one is waiting for them there that they don't know."

Kelly and Gretchen hugged me. No words were spoken, but I knew they were still in danger. My attention returned to the agents when Walker said, "Stay here Sergeant while we check something."

When they returned, Walker asked, "Do you know an agent by the name of Steven Bullard?"

"Yes, I met him after the death of a Julia Madison at Lajes Field. I understand she worked for him undercover. The interview turned into something more like a threat if I didn't join his happy cadre of troops."

Walker looked concerned as he sat down. "Your friend certainly did work for Bullard. She was an intel operative. What was he recruiting you to do?"

I gave him an overview of my undeveloped ability and what Bullard said he wanted from me. Walker looked at his partner who gave him an affirmative nod.

"Sergeant, have you ever heard of any government projects that deal with clairvoyance or remote viewing?"

"No, but Bullard suggested as much."

Walker took a form out of his valise and laid it on the table. "Well, the U.S. has a highly classified project that deals with the subject. For me to continue, I need you to sign this agreement which clearly explains you're not to talk about this interview with anyone for any reason without prior written approval from us. Do you understand?"

"Yes. But what I do or can do is intended to offer help, not destroy," I said, as I signed the non-disclosure agreement.

"Understood," said Thorton. "We believe that Bullard is a double agent. This entire area of Europe is a hot bed of espionage, filled with spies and double-agents from all over the world. People like you can be a real help because you'd be taking some of the unknown out of what we do. That, in turn, keeps us alive longer because we don't have to take as much risk."

Walker added, "Or, if you're put to work for the other side, it makes what we do all the more dangerous.

"I see. But where does that leave us?" I asked. There are times when questions like this shouldn't be asked. And I was about to find out if this was one of them.

Chapter 16

The situation in which I found myself had become complex. Up to this point, my life had been rather straightforward with the only exception being the dreams I was having. The OSI agents were just trying to do their jobs, and they had this kid sitting in front of them asking questions that no one on their first Air Force duty assignment should be able to ask.

Thornton continued, "Obviously, it's your choice. We need someone who can give us an idea of what Bullard is up to, who his handlers and contacts are, when they're going to meet, and where. It'll give us a better chance of putting them behind bars before they can bargain their guilt away."

While I listened to him, I thought, *Should I do this? I'm not getting the same unnerving sense as I did with Bullard, but it's not the warm and fuzzy feeling I'd like to have.* "Do you know someone by the name of Dominic Rigusso?" I asked.

Again, their interest piqued. "Yes, how do you know him?"

"My partner and I arrested him. Shortly after that, one of your fellow agents, Chad Meadows, interviewed us. He mentioned that we should be careful from that point on because he was pretty sure Rigusso was going to use us as guinea pigs to test his new recruits on Lajes."

Walker stood up and moved to the other side of the room. "Normally, a man like Rigusso doesn't show up until there's a job to do and I can't remember the last time he allowed himself to be arrested for anything. The question is why he would have let that happen." He turned toward me with a sense of urgency. "Have you had any further contact with him?"

"No, he left the island before his hearing, which didn't make sense to me." Walker began pacing, thinking in silence. "Maybe it's just my paranoia, but I would like to know what the connection is between Bullard and Rigusso," I added.

Thornton looked at his partner as Walker slowly sat down. "So what's your decision? Are going to help us or not?"

"I have a personal rule about using this ability. I'll help someone, but I won't do anything that destroys things, especially anything that's alive. And, keep in mind that my ability isn't that great. If it was, I wouldn't be sitting here right now. I would've been able to see all of this was going to happen, and I would have avoided the entire unpleasant mess."

"Great, another idealist. Just what we need right now. After reading your file, Sergeant, it's obvious your exposure to the world is almost nonexistent. Have you ever heard of the phrase, 'fight fire with fire'?"

"Yes, I have. Have you ever heard of a reformed Quaker who has converted to Methodism?"

"No, and what does that have to do with anything?"

"It partly describes how I was brought up and how I live my life. These are my core values."

"So, you're a conscientious objector?"

"No. If I were, I doubt that I would have enlisted. What I'm saying is that I'll help you, but I have no idea how accurate the information will be and I'll stop the first time I suspect the information I give you has been used badly. There is one other condition."

"Great, what is it?"

"You have to agree that Kelly and Gretchen will be protected until this is all over. As I understand it, Kelly is a U.S. citizen here on a work Visa and Gretchen is a German National. I believe you guys could arrange for both of them to work here on base. And, I'd bet if you tried real hard, you could find them comfortable quarters where they can feel secure. Please, tell me I'm right."

They looked at each other and then Walker said, "Wait here. And don't be surprised if the deal includes something more from you than just dealing with Bullard and Rigusso."

With Walker out of the room, Thornton continued, "You do know that both of these men will not hesitate to kill you or others you know to get what they want."

"Understood. I'm still working on that part. Let's not forget that I don't like the kind of encounters your work brings. I have better things to do with my life than being chased by a bunch of maniacs. And, I would prefer it to remain that way."

"Well, Sergeant, in case you haven't figured it out, their part of the real world is a part you inhabit, and with these two, you'll not leave unless they're willing to let you go. So, as long as you have something they want, you're here to stay. At least working with us gives you a better chance to survive."

"See, here's another reason I probably shouldn't get involved. I'm risking my life for what reason, not to mention my partner's life."

"Hey kid, have you been listening? Let me say it again in clearer terms. You are involved already. You've been involved from the first meeting you had with Bullard, and he figured out what you can do."

"Okay, but I'm still a bit confused. You described two men who are greedy and without morals, let alone devoid of any respect for the value of life. They've committed crimes yet they are not in jail. I suspect you know they've murdered people, yet they have not been charged, convicted, and removed from society. This picture seems so . . . I dunno . . . out of balance. I may be ignorant compared to highly educated spy-killers with years of worldly experience, but I'm not stupid."

"You know we're in the middle of a cold war, right?"

"Yes, and . . ."

"Sometimes governments become involved in a little horse-trading. They think what you have is worth more than holding you accountable for a crime you committed, so they trade one for the other. Bullard and Rigusso are excellent horse traders. They not only create skeletons, they know where a few are hidden and put there by some powerful people," Thornton said.

"This is wrong on so many levels. Basically, you're telling me we are all commodities to these jerks in seats of authority. What makes you think that one of them won't trade me or my partner for something they think is more valuable?"

There was a long pause. Obviously, Thornton had said too much, and I had nothing more with which to bargain. His answer would tell me just how far I could trust him. Regardless of his answer, I knew I was going to help them if for no other reason than self-preservation.

"To be honest with you, I can't guarantee you that won't happen, although I think the odds are against it. We'll try to keep your identity off the grid as much as we can. But, in the end, we may not have any choice. Besides, Bullard knows who you are, and if he was captured by the wrong people, he could bargain you away."

Walker returned and said, "Okay, I have your conditions approved. But, keep in mind that we can't force Kelly and Gretchen to do anything. They're civilians."

"Look, all I know is that I was drawn to them and my sense is I need to at least try to protect them. If they choose to remain out there, then there's little else I can do. But I need to get back to Lajes as soon as possible because of warnings that my partner is in jeopardy. I don't know by whom or when anything will happen, I just know she's at risk."

"We can help with that. I'll work on it. By the way, to answer your earlier question, we think Rigusso is the enforcer for Bullard," Walker said.

The deal was done and it was time to move on.

Agent Walker drove me back to Wiesbaden and accompanied me to my hotel. My mind continued to focus on Walker's comment about Rigusso. When I walked into the hotel, the front desk clerk, who had been so helpful, looked up from his book. "You're back late."

"Yeah, sorry, I hope I'm not disturbing anyone. By the way, this is Agent Walker from the Office of Special Investigation."

"Ja, cops helping cops. This is good. By the way, someone dropped by earlier to see you."

"Really, did you get their name?" I asked.

"He didn't leave one. He said he was from the same office as your new friend."

Red flags were frantically waving in front of my eyes along with loud klaxons going off. "Are you sure he left the building?"

"Ja, I think so. I talked with him right here, but I can't see the front door."

"Thanks."

Walker and I quietly took the stairs to the second floor where my room was located. "Let me check out your room before you go in," Walker said.

The second floor hallway had a feel of an unnatural presence. Whatever it was, the creature had brought along its own preferred weather condition in the form of a thin, misty dark fog that only I could see. We approached my room as the fog began to move across my field of vision and became thicker making me think the creature would show itself soon. "There's something very wrong here," I said.

Walker pulled his weapon out from his shoulder holster as we carefully made our way to the end of the hall. The closer we got to my room, the stronger my bad-idea meter rang. Walker looked at the door and noticed nothing unusual. He opened it and cautiously entered. Just as he was about to peer around the edge of the door, something struck Walker across his head. I saw blood burst from his scalp spraying a thick crimson red shower everywhere. I body slammed the door, burst it open, and propelled the assailant backward toward the window opposite the entryway.

The attacker, dressed in the unimaginative dark clothing that cowards of the dark often wear, was unremarkable in build or height. Yet, his ability to recover was incredible. A set of numchucks appeared from nowhere, and I knew I was going to be thumped unmercifully in seconds if I didn't come up with an equalizer fast. I scrambled to find Walker's service revolver, but time was not on my side.

"Hey asshole," the assailant yelled, "someone wants you to know how disturbed he is about your recent conversations."

I looked at him, as my hand searched for the gun. "Really? So you're delivering Christmas messages from evil Santa?" I asked sarcastically.

"I just hate a smart ass."

"Well, you caught me by surprise. All I was doing was trying to enter my room, but then here you are . . . someplace you weren't invited. Had I known you were coming, I would have fixed something for you, like something that goes BOOM," I said, trying to distract him as I moved to block his view of Walker's prone body.

By this time, Walker was coming around well enough to catch the conversation.

"My boss wants you to know, you're going to pay a steep price for what you've done. He might put it off if you do what he wants."

Walker was now sitting up holding his head. "Sorry, my heart belongs to someone else, so I'll have to pass on his kind offer."

"Naw, he said if you don't agree, I'm supposed to take you out and remind you that you're not the only one who'll go down tonight."

Something snapped inside me with that threat. My own life took a distant backseat. "Sounds like a tall order for a bunch of scumbags."

"Hey dead man, do you have any idea who you're screwing around with?" he asked.

"Yeah, I know him, but you're just a janitor, aren't you?"

While I was blocking Walker from the view of our unwanted guest, he carefully recovered his .45 caliber military-issue revolver. He pushed me aside, just as our assailant realized his maneuver. The unimaginative clad intruder moved to attack Walker. One ear-shattering shot was fired—a clean red hole appeared between the eyes of our guest. The bullet instantly tumbled through his brain causing a large portion of gray matter and blood to exit in an explosive imprint on the wall behind him. And again, I became noticeably nauseated.

Though I saw what happened, my mind was desperately focused on getting back to Lajes while trying not to vomit. Becoming nauseated after these brutal attacks re-enforced the idea that I would never do well in combat, but it certainly helped me to remain fit and trim.

I knew that the dreams I had been having about Linda were warnings, and this intruder just reconfirmed the urgency to act that was building within me. Her life was dependent on either me getting back there or Sergeant Dodd protecting her until I returned. Her considerable self-defense skills weren't going to be enough to contend with what was facing her.

"Thought I'd find you here. How are you doing?" Agent Walker asked.

I was sitting in the private waiting area of the Military Airlift Command terminal at Rhein-Main Air Base waiting for the aircraft that would take me back to Lajes. I looked up expecting to see the agent I met last night, but the person standing before me was nearly unrecognizable. Now, his head looked more like a large pumpkin wrapped in white badges. "You look like crap, Walker. I can only image the hangover you're having."

"Ha, the only thing louder than these jungle drums going off in my head might be a bomb exploding." He carefully sat down next to me. "So, you wanna know something about the idiot that was waiting for you?"

"Sure, what did you find out?"

"Your midnight date was new to this gig. The only background we found on him traced back to . . ."

I interrupted, "Let me guess . . . back to either the Army or the Air Force and was recently released from service—a grunt inexperienced at stalking and killing which worked in our favor."

"That's right Spook Guy. And there's no real need to know his name," Walker said.

"I could care less who he was . . . wait a minute, Spook Guy?"

"Oh, Thornton enjoys assigning nicknames to people. He thought Spook Guy was good and used 'Spook' or 'SG' in all of our correspondence about you and in our reports. Besides, the term 'Spook' is also used as a tag for a spy. It makes you sound more like a charter member of our club," Walker said with a smile, as if he were welcoming me aboard.

"Does that come with a 007 license?"

"Definitely not," Walker said more seriously.

"Good, because I have better things to do with my life than play these kinds of bizarre games," I said.

"Well, Okay, but you're still going to help us out, right?"

"Of course, once I give you my word, I always follow through."

"I hear we found you a fast ride home."

"Yeah, a slot on a Boeing EC-135. The PIC told me he was under orders to get me back as quick as physics would allow. He's actually looking forward to the flight because he's been dying to try something new with his equipment."

"Sounds good." Walker paused, "Something new? Like what?"

"Like pushing it closer to Mach 1. Most aircraft of this size generally reach Mach .76. This one is supposed to move along much faster."

Walker laughed. "You're anxious about getting back?"

"Wouldn't you?" I asked.

"Yeah, I guess. I called Chad, the agent that interviewed you last. He's going to check on Linda when he can. But, he reminded me how bullheaded she is about things."

"She's not bullheaded. She's just independent and isn't about to rely on a male to protect her," I said, trying to be supportive but feeling more helpless by the minute.

"Wish I was going with you," Walker said, as he turned to look at the ramp where the EC-135 was parked.

"Why's that?" I asked looking out the same window with him.

"Things can get a little boring around here. It's always the same stuff. People cheat, they spy on everyone and everything, there's the occasional attempted homicide, and every once in a while a body pops up. On the other hand, if I went with you, I might see some real action," Walker said, almost laughing as he looked at me through his pumpkin-head bandages.

"And last night?" I asked.

"Was an aberration."

"Yeah, wasn't he though?"

"No, and his buddies back home won't be either, which reminds me there's something we need to talk about," Walker said in a more serious tone.

"We still have time before my rocket blasts off," I responded, waiting for the next shoe to drop.

"Okay, how much do you know about poisons?"

"Just what I learned at the spy school I never attended," I said with a smirk.

"Well, given your training and background in general, you'll know what to look for if someone tries to take you out by traditional methods. But, you probably don't know anything about binary poisons."

"What the hell is that?" I asked.

"Intel operatives like this method because it's silent, deadly, and they are assured the target has been hit. The poison comes in two parts. The first is applied to drinks most of the time, although it can be put in food. The important thing is that once the first dose is delivered into your body, they'll deliver the second part, hence binary, which interacts with the first causing death within minutes. Typically, depending on the poison used, the tongue and throat swells causing the victim to suffocate to death. What's interesting is that this stuff can be delivered in a bottle of anything. A waiter can pour drinks for everyone. But, no one is affected by the first element as long as they don't receive part two. The victim, who receives the second element, is the only one affected," Walker explained.

"So, if Bullard or Rigusso decides to be a coward and use this method, I should be cautious about eating and drinking anything that I have not prepared myself?" I asked.

"Correct."

"Is there any way to tell if this stuff is in what I drink or eat?" I asked.

"No, well . . . in your case, you might know, but you can't taste or smell it."

A rather tall captain appeared out of nowhere and said, "Pardon me, gentlemen, but it's time for us to leave."

Grabbing my bag, we followed the captain outside. "Don't forget our agreement. I'll be checking up on the ladies," I said, shaking Walker's hand.

"I'll do my part. I still wish I was going with you." Walker said.

As I climbed aboard the small truck that would take us to the military version of the Boeing 707 with its oversized engines idling, I waved at my pumpkin-headed friend.

Inside the plane, I met the pilot. "Welcome aboard, I'm Major Pritchard, Pilot in Command. I see you've met Captain Myers. He'll be checking on you during the flight."

"Thank you, sir, for allowing me onboard," I said saluting him.

"Happy to help. Keep in mind that this is a highly classified environment. You're restricted to this particular seat and the head that's right there. I'm serious about this, so please don't forget."

"Yes sir. I haven't had any sleep lately, so I'm sure I'll pass out as soon as we depart."

"Good, let Myers know if you need anything when he comes to check on you."

With that, I strapped in and a few minutes later we were on the runway accelerating for takeoff. Within seconds, my mind and body began to respond to the rhythmic vibration of the four huge engines that propelled us into the upper atmosphere. Settled in, I began drifting away, thinking about Linda and what lay ahead and then I was out of my body and flying on my own.

The fear and stress that I had recently been experiencing simply evaporated as we were soaring far above the earth. While adjusting myself to this view from above free from physical reality, I noticed something in the distance that looked out of place and decided to check it out. I felt a strong pull to this spot as I approached the object. Then it occurred me, this was the building that Linda and I called home. I felt myself being slowly positioned and held above the building by an unseen entity for some reason. Given what happened the last time I felt this kind of restrictive force, I began to panic.

The same kind of thick haze that I had seen in earlier dreams approached our home from the bay which was a short distance away. The creature that I saw in the earlier dream appeared within the center of the haze that was now a thickening fog. Those restricting me pushed my consciousness downward as if to torment me with another ringside seat to some demented circus of the damned. This ugly unidentifiable mass that I was seeing took on a humanlike form and was about to enter our building. It stopped and looked up in my direction as if it sensed someone was watching him. The creature apparently could not see me hovering overhead, so it continued to search for a way into the building.

It was obvious what was about to happen. I began to struggle, but it was useless. The more I struggled and pleaded, the more I was held back. Then the screams began and I knew what the creature was doing, and what carnage was being left behind. Again, my soul was shredded into a pile of raw nerves. And again, I was left wondering what point was there in doing all of this, why should I continue to live if I cannot protect the one person in my life that I loved.

This time, I saw the creature leave the building still in the throes of its blood lust that all maniacal murderers live for when they execute their victim. But, his departure was different this time. He held in his hand an ancient knife that I, once again, recognized as one used in a different kind of ritual killings. I heard a voice whisper, "He carries the ancient sword of Damocles. You must be careful when dealing with him. Remember what you've learned."

The voice was unknown yet it felt as if it was not just outside of me, but inside as well. I was lifted and turned towards Praia da Victoria so I could see the prominent landmark, the Catholic Church that Linda continually tried to get me to attend. My attention was drawn to the familiar twin bell towers in the distance as the unknown voice began again. "Your allies are of the cross and as ancient as the sword. You will need them and this is where they are to be found, for now."

Suddenly, I felt a jarring, violent shaking that would not relent.

"Hey, Sergeant. Wake up! Wake up!!"

I opened my eyes and realized I was shaking, but it wasn't just the rough turbulence we had encountered. "I'm up, I'm up. What happened?"

"The major wants your shoulder harness secured. We're on extended final and will have to fly through some weather to land. It's gonna be one helluva a ride all the way down. You feel'n all right?"

"Yeah, I'm fine," I said, still drained from what I was shown.

"Hey kid, how was the flight?" asked Sergeant Dodd as he welcomed me back to the island.

"Pretty good until we hit final, which felt like being tossed about in a blender."

"You must be tired," he said.

"Really, and what makes you think that?" I asked trying to smile as a sense of impatience grew.

"Your jokes suck almost as bad as the code talk you used when you called from Rhein-Main," Dodd said with a smile.

"I gotta get home. Why isn't Linda here? Is she okay, who's watching her?"

Braz was walking with us and interrupted, "You're like a son to me and there's no hello? Have you forgotten me already?"

"Oh, Braz, I'm sorry. I'm very worried about Linda. I need to make sure she's okay," I said.

"Ah, Sergeant Dodd says you've been having bad dreams about her," my good friend said.

"Yeah, and I had another one on the plane. This time I wasn't in the same room. I saw it from above. Whoever was guiding the vision turned me toward the Cathedral in Praia as a voice said that the murderer carried the sword of Damocles, and I needed allies."

Braz's face turned from his usual friendly congenial self to one of darkened concern.

"Well, you've got a few allies," Sergeant Dodd said. "Chad can't sit on your doorstep all day, nor can anyone else. But, those who can, when they can, do. In fact, Tiny's been over there a lot. Linda keeps asking him why he's always outside her place when she comes and goes. He just ignores her," Sergeant Dodd said with a smile.

"Great, well no one'll get through that guy," I said with a bit of relief.

"Did this voice say anything else?" Braz asked.

"Yeah, it said something about the allies are ancient too and that they are of the cross. Does that make sense to you?"

"Yes, remember what happened in the cave?" he said, as his face tightened with a deeper concern.

We talked more about the trip and everything that happened in Wiesbaden. Dodd couldn't believe that someone would try to assassinate me and over what?

Dodd was driving, and I could see the building Linda and I lived in barely a block away, now. My heart was pounding with anticipation because I expected to see her at the terminal when I arrived. Panic began to build as we parked in a little-used alley that separated our building from the one next to it.

As I exited the car, something caught my eye in the shadows of the alley. Cautiously, I approached it and realized it was Tiny's body. He was slumped, braced against a wall. The closer I came to his lifeless form, the nauseating aroma of death became obvious. His assailant must have approached him from behind like a coward. It looked like he had turned to meet his attacker, given the presence of a deep angular slash across his torso that forced Tiny to see his entrails burst from his body as he quickly died.

Dodd nor Braz could control me. I remembered hearing Dodd's voice call for help on his radio as I ran for the front door and bolted up the stairs. I kicked the door open to our flat and pressed forward. Bursting into our home pulled the veil of another reality back and forced me to accept what I was about to see. The open door to our bedroom was visible. This was our sanctuary, but it now looked more like the bloody entrance to hell.

Chapter 17

My consciousness became drowned in a sea of
lifelessness and denial as I stood in the doorway to what had
been our bedroom. This had been our refuge from life, a
place where renewing expressions of love of spirit, of mind,
and body were frequently born and nurtured. I questioned
whether the doorway had now become a dimensional portal
to another place, perhaps someone else's nightmare world.
The dark energy in this room was unrelenting, as it seemed
to pull me further into its hellish realm. A more grounded
person would have easily recognized what I was unable to
see . . . the obvious.

My mind refused to process the reality that lay before
me. I attempted to rationalize the situation by telling myself
that for some unknown reason a tear in the fabric of time
allowed me to pass from my home into this depiction of
Dante's Inferno. Was this part of a nightmare that I was
supposed to relive, perhaps to learn something that I had
missed earlier? To simply describe what I saw as being
utterly surreal barely touched the surface of its grisly horror.

There were only a few things that seemed vaguely
familiar. The trail of blood that led from the bed toward the
balcony wasn't one of them. Then I saw dark reddish-black
streaks of nightmarish images, a form of demonic art, using

the walls as its artist's canvas. This was real enough to force my mind to acknowledge more of what surrounded me.

"David, this is a form of demented ritualistic art, and a message to you," Sara said as she appeared beside me.

"Why was I not allowed to stop this from happening, Sara?" I asked, almost pleading.

"There is a reason, David. I know it's hard, but I need you to trust me," she said, placing her arm around my shoulders.

The residue of dark energy that had been left behind in the room had now become oppressive, as if a part of me began to realize that the specter of death was in this place and a reminder of the consequences of my decisions. As I became aware of this utter emptiness, a feeling of desperation and panic stirred deep within me. I could not catch my breath. The foreboding sense of sadness and fear welled up from my legs into my torso and then suffused my mind, threatening to supplant my innate fortitude that might allow me to survive this initial shock. These disturbed feelings rose rapidly like angry lava about to explode from a super-heated subterranean cauldron, trying to further dictate what I would see, feel, and do in its attempt to take over my consciousness.

I knew the shadowy ancient creature that I had seen in my vision while in Gretchen's flat and on the flight back from Germany was the powerful force behind this intrusion.

This ancient presence was utterly devoid of any compassion. And for me, it drew from my inner-most weakness, a fear of complete failure, a loss of someone who held . . . no possessed . . . my heart and soul, which had now become a cold and empty vessel of hope lost.

"Please, she must be here," I pleaded desperately into the emptiness of the room. I frantically looked in all directions; tears blurred my vision as I continued to search the flat for Linda.

"She's here, David. All you must do is choose to see her," Sara said softly.

My mind raced in panic while I continued to deny the truth. I tried to slow my panic-stricken mind as I struggled to look around our bedroom again. I began to see a few articles of blood-soaked clothing, yet these things still did not register as belonging to someone I knew.

Then, I realized our bed had been moved to the center of the room. There, laying peacefully upon the bloody sheets that were pulled back was Linda. Though she still wore her sleeping attire, there was something different about her appearance. I desperately wanted her to be peacefully asleep so that I could wake her from this nightmare.

"David, you need to accept what has happened here. Look at her and know what she has given up for you and what has been taken from you both," Sara said.

Finally, I forced myself to study her body. That's when I knew the monster who had killed Tiny, had also murdered Linda and did so by crudely cutting into her chest and removing her heart. This is why he had brought the sword of Damocles with him. This was the ritual tool he used to pierce my soul and send the message Bullard wanted me to see while feeling his wrath.

But this was far more than just a henchman doing his master's work. This was Maridon speaking directly to me, warning me, as he told me years ago, about the high price I would pay for disobedience. And now, I stood next to the cost of my defiance. Everything that I had lost with Linda's death instantly rushed through my mind. Stealing her heart was an attempt to steal my life force, and now he held it in the cusp of his evil hand never to experience the mergence of our souls again. I could feel that realization becoming clearer as the pain retched through what remained of me. Then I heard Sara say, "He knew you gave yourself to her and by stealing her heart, he wanted you to believe that he was also taking possession of yours."

This place, our sanctuary, was now permeated with her terror-filled cries, pleading for relief from all that had happened. Everything that I now saw and all of my precious memories of this woman's soul filled my consciousness and almost destroyed my sanity.

I sat next to her and held the love of my life in my arms, wishing for the impossible. The room blurred as I began to see everything that had transpired through tear-filled eyes. I saw images of the beast as he attacked her. She took the full brunt of his savagery while fighting back bravely. He overpowered her, forced her to clearly see her executioner, pushing her further into the bed to slowly free his weapon from his first strike. The beast then skillfully opened her chest and cupped her still beating heart with his left hand. He smiled at his victim now in deep shock as he finished her, lancing the arteries and freeing the organ.

Linda was still alive for an excruciating moment before she was finally released, her soul leaving her body. I saw Sara and some others retrieve her, taking her far away to a place I knew as "The Park." A place where all departed souls go in preparation for their recovery from the experiences of life. In Linda's case, I knew she needed help recovering from this terrible experience.

"I should've been here to protect her!" I screamed silently while tightly cradling her. I felt other arms hold me and heard distant whisperings that I couldn't understand. In the midst of my desperation, I tried to find a way to transport myself back in time, to the very first vision of her attack, to protect her from this personal horror. Certainly, my god-given ability could help me protect the one person that meant everything to me. But, it failed me and had now become more like a curse. Why would I want this ability to see into the future if I could not stop her death from happening?

Yet, without this gift, I would have been left guessing what had happened. I knew Linda was a fighter, good in bar brawls, and quick to defend and then attack. She was driven to win these fights because it helped her deal with the brutalities and fear of her past. These kinds of animalistic games played by demented males were no stranger to her. So, to defeat Linda, the beast would have had to destroy her ability to fight back, which he had done somehow.

Again, the images of the one-sided battle were replayed for me as if the beast had won and wanted to torture me further. The thought of surrendering my own life had become my only option if I wanted to free myself from my guilt. Would it not be a blessing to die so that I could be with her? Would it not be justice for the utter failure I had become by not being here when she needed me most? I was desperately lost.

A distant part of my consciousness heard someone yell, "David, where are you?" I was sitting there next to Linda, holding her and not knowing what to do. As this voice came closer, I realized it was Sergeant Dodd and he was doing what I should have done—carefully clearing each room before entering them. With his weapon drawn, he entered the bedroom. While I heard him, he seemed so far away. He carefully searched the entire room. I barely heard him say, "Damn it, what the hell . . ."

I didn't move while others entered the room and expressed their horror at the scene. What was left of my rational mind questioned the only thing that was left to figure out, how Linda's assassin drained her and created the satanic art that filled the room. Was it part of some sort of dark ritual? At the same time, the more these questions continued, the more I felt that part of myself being further destroyed. There were two different David's now, one trying to find some way to detach himself from this reality while the other was beginning to understand.

The detached David looked at her laying in bed again and I saw him reach for her with one hand. As he held her, the look of her eyes staring at him suddenly captured his attention. Her mouth was open and strained as if screaming silently in horror. It was through these beautiful eyes that she allowed him to venture into her soul days earlier and safely rest. Now, she was screaming at him, *Where were you when I needed you?*

He tried to respond but couldn't. With one last attempt, He tried to push myself away from this awful reality and convince himself that this was just another one of those nightmarish dreams.

I have, periodically, seen unnerving acts of violence that humans do to each other. At least in those dreams, I didn't know any of the people involved nor did I know if they even existed. I was always left wondering for whom these dreams were meant.

But now, with both aspects of myself once again merged and unable to move, I simply sat there holding and cradling Linda while I lost what little control I had left.

Eventually, a hand griped my right shoulder from somewhere and tried to pull me out of the bedroom. I held Linda close to my heart while feeling her blood slowly trickle down my arms and soak into my uniform.

I remember someone, maybe Braz, trying to coax me into letting her go. Someone else began talking and doing some things, but nothing made sense. Others began appearing in the flat . . . strangers, people that were never allowed in our private area. All of this activity conspired with my guilt and became a massive landslide of granite brutally hitting and crushing me over and over again. My consciousness suddenly changed, and propelled me from the flat to an old familiar, dark place, a place where most nightmares I had encountered thrived. I knew then that the nightmares of my past were about to begin . . . again.

Chapter 18

Coming to grips with everything that had happened was not easy. The events in Germany coupled with my two visions had exhausted me, even though I didn't want to admit it. Being forced to deal with Linda's mutilated body and the demonic artwork of her executioner finally pushed me over the edge.

I collapsed and finally woke up in the compassionate security of Braz and Sophia's home. During my convalescence, they encouraged me to spend time in the meadows that Linda and I loved. There was an ancient island tree that we often sat under on our long walks together, and this was the tree I now sat beneath overlooking Praia as we had done many times before. The view was enticing and when the wind was light, the flora scents wafting in the air reminded me of her, which was where Father Mike found me deep in thought.

"Well, look who's finally getting out and about," said a soft, kindly voice.

I was drawn back from the reverie of better times by his gentle intrusion.

"You look as if you were in another world, David. Have the walks helped you cope?" Father Mike asked.

The question seemed odd at first. But, then a small part of my mind clicked, and I looked at him and said, "Yes, I've been seeing her every time I come out here. I miss her, Father, and I don't know what to do."

Father Mike sat down next to me and seemed to be considering what to say. "David, I think I know you well enough to say that you're unlike any young man I've ever met. The emotional shock of Linda's assault must be horrible, and I'm surprised that you've refrained from any kind of manic, vengeance-seeking reaction or deeply repressed everything in some hopeless denial."

"I'm not that kind of person, Father. I believe there's a higher order that's working with someone who's gone through these kinds of tragedies. For some reason, I feel like I've been through this before."

Father Mike gave me a kindly look. "Yes, this feels like some kind of ongoing battle." He paused, and then smiled. "Most people think that priests are bible-smart and that's all. But, my son, that's far from the truth with me. I have a sense about you that goes way beyond the physical."

"Really, and what might that be?" I asked.

"It feels like you have been blessed with a spiritual mission. And, if I'm right, that part of your contract with the other side has begun a new cycle," he said as he studied my reaction.

This was the first time I heard him say anything that related to the astral plane as I understood it. Most clergy refuse to go beyond anything that's taught to them at seminary. But here was a priest clearly using his human intuition that bordered on clairvoyance.

"David, trust him," Sara said. "Tell him about the dreams you've had since you were a teenager. It's time and you'll be surprised what will happen as a result."

Still too drained from everything that had happened, I decided not to resist her advice. Father Mike listened intently as I shared with him the dreams involving Maridon, his slaughtering of an ancient village and its occupants, along with his continuous threats to me. "This is another reason I feel so defeated, Father. Linda died because I didn't bow to Maridon's power, and I wasn't there to protect her. Images of her dead body continue to remind me of that failure."

Father Mike said in his typically gentle voice, "It's good that you can remember this traumatic event, my son, and that you can see this connection, but it isn't your failure that caused her death," he said, reaching out and touching my arm to reassure me. "And it's good that your mind isn't repressing the whole nasty affair. You're still dealing with it, and I think you might be getting a bit more help than you know," he said with a smile, standing up. His good energy was contagious, and I couldn't help but soak it up like the love from Braz' family that I had been surviving on.

"You know that Sergeant Dodd will have to bring you back on the schedule soon. But before he does, you'll have to sit with the base psychologist for testing," Father Mike added.

The distant view of Praia da Victoria was eclipsed by the shadows of clouds passing overhead, which drew my thoughts back to the ugly reality I still had to face. "Yeah, I know."

"How do you feel about that?" Father Mike asked, observing my reaction.

"I dunno. I guess I don't give a rat's ass about what others think."

He grabbed both of my shoulders and squarely faced me. "David, you must come back to the fold. As I have already mentioned, you still have work to do on this earth."

I looked away from him to see the birds enjoying their freedom as they soared in the sky playfully chasing each other. The thought of Linda's love, which I was no longer able to feel, and the idea I would never be with her again still haunted me. "If my gift was all that useful, Father, don't you think I would have been allowed to keep her alive?"

"My intuition, David, is telling me that you should place your faith in those who have loved and guided you all your life. I believe you referred to them as Spirit Guides?"

"Yeah."

"Well, the Church would refer to them as Guardian Angels."

"I didn't see any wings on them, Father."

He smiled. "You haven't lost your sense of humor, young man. You're going to be fine. I have no doubt about that." He paused for a moment, apparently thinking about something, and then continued. "Do you know anything about the history of the ancient military order that is associated with the Santa Cruz Cathedral in Praia?"

"Linda mentioned the Knights Templar have a long history on the island," I responded. "And Braz took me to a cavern where they once gathered. It was easy to connect with the energy there. I was drawn out of my body and met Grand Master de Molay, their leader, and spoke with him."

Father Mike nodded. "Braz, didn't tell me about your visit. Did he say anything about their history?"

"I know a little about Crusade History, but the conspiracy to condemn the Templars has never set well with me."

"And so it shouldn't. At one time, the Templars were a wealthy organization and had large land holdings. King Phillip of France was deeply indebted to them for several reasons. Rumors began to surface that the Templars were including paganistic rituals in their order. In fact, some of the rumors mentioned a few of the more experienced knights had also been devoted worshippers of Mithras. Do you know who that was?"

"No, Father, that one's new to me."

"Mithras was the god of war worshipped in secret by higher-ranking Roman soldiers. The secrecy of some aspects of the Templar society drew the attention of those who resented their authority."

"Were any of the accusations true?" I asked, amazed given the Templar history that's broadly known.

"There was never any evidence that proved the allegations. But, King Phillip IV decided to use the rumors to pressure Pope Clement V into issuing a bull allowing Phillip to seize their assets and bring them to trial. Once he did that nasty deed, his debt to the Templars was erased. Many of the Knights were executed while others fled into hiding. Essentially, the order was destroyed by the kingdoms that they had protected."

"So, you're saying they were betrayed and then killed because of a King who didn't want to pay his debt after benefiting from their service?"

"That's right. But, in 1308, Pope Clement absolved the Templars of all charges brought against them and formally disbanded them in 1312. The Vatican's position today is that any wrong-doing was the result of undue influence of King Phillip IV. The Templars were innocent," Father Mike said.

"A little late considering the executions had already taken place, Father." I paused, then added, "I've learned something, Father, but I'm still lost. What does this have to do with anything that's happening today?" I asked.

He turned to me with his usual radiant smile and captured my attention as he said, "Because, my son, the Templars still exist here and now, or a version of them anyway. What I mean is that some of the island residents are direct descendants, and they still practice the old mystic beliefs that underlie many of the world's traditional religions. I think it's time you experience what they do. And, I believe that the Spirit Guide who told you about your allies being here was referring to them. Braz is the only one you know of, but there are more. Would you like to meet them?"

"*Yes, David, say yes!*" Sara silently coaxed.

"I guess, Father, but what good would that do?" I asked.

"Let's wait and see. But, I think you might be surprised. Let me check something out and I'll be back in touch." Before he got up to leave, he blessed and prayed for me and left me wondering what he had in mind.

Sergeant Dodd worked with an Air Force doctor at the base hospital to have me placed on recuperative leave or something like that when I had been removed from the apartment where Linda was murdered. Staying away from the cop shop was the standing order, but he took it one step further by ensuring I remained with Braz' family, which he saw as a safe place. Living with them allowed me to recover, think, and begin to see what to do next.

Father Mike had asked Braz to make sure I came to the Santa Cruz Cathedral by 10 a.m. the next day to meet him. As I walked up the steps to the main entrance, I wondered what the good father had in mind for today's meeting.

"David, nice to see you," said Father Mike as I walked into the sanctuary. This was my first time in the church that Linda loved and tried to convince me unsuccessfully to visit. But, I had lost confidence in organized religion long ago.

"This is an impressive place, Father," I said, looking around at all the ornate carvings, artwork, and stained-glass windows. Obviously, some of the artwork was very old and, at the same time, it felt familiar.

"Yes, this place is very special to all of the people who attend here. Did you know this was the first church built by the Templars who escaped King Phillip's wrath? This massive architectural art was christened in 1456 A.D."

"You're kidding; this place is truly beautiful."

"Yes, this church is filled with history, and the people who worship here knew Linda quite well, especially the children and their families."

"Come with me, I would like to show you something," Father Mike said as he held my arm escorting me to the far end of the large sanctuary to a small gathering of women and children.

"David, these are some of the children Linda helped," Father Mike said, as we sat in a pew near them. They were involved in some kind of Catholic ritual. The women were helping the children light candles that surrounded a small picture on the slightly elevated altar that drew my attention. There was something familiar there and I suddenly felt a need to see what it was.

I slowly stood up and stepped closer. As the children parted, opening a path, I noticed some were looking at me as if they recognized me. Standing within arm's reach, I realized what I was seeing: it was a picture of Linda and me out of uniform in the village. We were so happy when this was taken. The picture triggered a clear memory of us planning our wedding and what we would do once we arrived at our new duty station. I couldn't help myself as I began to cry and collapsed to my knees using the marble altar to steady myself.

One of the women came to me when she realized I was the other person in the photo. As the children surrounded me, I felt little hands touching my shoulders while others held my hands, and a few were wiping the tears from my face. They knew what I was feeling and why, because someone they also loved had been taken from them.

"It's amazing how miracles happen when children are involved," Father Mike said, standing behind everyone.

I turned and sat at the altar facing everyone. A little girl sat in my lap and hugged me. Surprisingly, she said in English, "We miss her, too."

I smiled still crying. I've never experienced a group hug like that one. The heart-felt love of children cannot be equaled. I can only imagine what the adults surrounding us must have thought watching these little angels help a young man deal with his pain.

While in their arms, I closed my eyes and felt myself sinking into their presence. As that happened, I suddenly found myself outside of my body watching what was happening. My body had gone limp scaring the children and a few of the mothers.

"Don't worry, children, he is still with us. He's just on a short journey. He'll be back soon," Father Mike said.

I heard a familiar voice next to me say, "*I think it's time, David.*"

Sara was standing next to me adorned in a shimmering blue robe. As I turned toward her, two arms were thrust underneath my shoulders and lifted me. They, whoever they were, guided me through a parallel dimension. I opened my eyes to see where I was going, but all I saw was black emptiness.

A ball of bluish-white, transparent light surrounded me and my unknown escorts, one male and the other female. They were dressed in simple smocks, and it seemed as if they needed nothing more than basic needs. They glowed within themselves as the light in which we traveled continued to propel us forward. Every time I tried to get their attention, they would smile and encouraged me to look toward a destination in the distance that I still could not see.

I questioned where we were going and one of them said, "Where we are going is unimportant. What you should ask is what will be learned on this journey?"

Where there had been emptiness in front of us, there was now a small, illuminated island with no remarkable attributes. We came to a gliding stop in this place with no recognizable sky or buildings. It felt more like a room without walls or ceiling, yet our immediate surroundings were perfectly lighted.

I turned to see my escorts back away from me as Sara approached. The escorts were smiling with arms outstretched as if silently saying I should be looking forward. I felt so safe in their presence that I didn't want them to leave. But, as they departed, they motioned once more for me to look toward the other end of the space to which they had delivered me.

Sara said, "There's someone here to see you."

I turned to look and saw something or someone walking toward me that I . . . I did not deserve to see again. I fell to my knees and began to cry as I became aware of Linda's presence. She walked quickly and then ran toward me. As Linda approached, she too knelt as we collided into each other's arms. Pressing ourselves together, we devoured each other in a loving embrace and streaming tears in disbelief. Her attempt to hold and comfort the love of her life was not lost on me. Deep within, I desperately asked *how long will this last?*

We held each other for what seemed like hours, refusing to let go. She felt so real to me, so unbelievably real. I could feel the totality of her body, the familiar warmth of her breath, her tears mingled with mine as we kissed each other repeatedly. With some effort, I finally found the strength to ask, "Where have you been? I saw your body . . ." I couldn't finish the sentence as the horrible images flashed once again across my mind and I lost control.

"You can be so slow sometimes," she said softly, whispering in my ear. Yes, this was the Linda I dearly loved and missed.

"I'm slow? You're the one that went on permanent vacation. And you said you wouldn't go anywhere without me. How am I ever going to trust you?"

She pulled away from me and smiled. "We've got to stop using these sarcastic funnies. It wasn't my choice to leave. It was my time, though. And since you know I'm on this side, you need to understand that you still have a life to live."

"I'm not going back," I said desperately between the tears, shaking my head as I held her tight against me.

"Stop being a wimp; you know you have to go back."

"A wimp!" I pushed away slightly and continued, "You expect me to forget you and move on after you make me fall in love with you?"

"I didn't make you do anything. You just fell for the first girl that let you in her bed," she said with a smirky grin.

"I can't believe you're serious. After everything we've been through together. Do you really believe that?"

"No, you love-sick fool. But, somebody's gotta get you off your pity-potty. You've got work to do, places to go, people to help, and things to learn. I'd prefer you spent your life with me, but that's not going to happen now. Besides, I've been assured you'll eventually find someone who will love you more than I could."

I looked at her in disbelief. Linda was my first experience of what I thought love meant.

"Hey, wake up and focus. I don't have much time left," she finally said.

"Wha . . . what do you mean?"

"They're giving us this gift of togetherness to say a proper good-bye, you know, like you and Sara did for me and Brian. And, they wanted you to know that I'm fine."

"Who's they?"

"Come on, Dave, you know who they are. You've been dealing with them all of your life. I actually thought you were cracked when you told me about them. But I've learned that you're not the only one that's got Spirit Guides following them around."

It struck me again how complicated all of these levels were since I became aware of the unseen helpers when I was a little boy. How does a naive child deal with people who think you're crazy, while others go off the deep end thinking that if you have all of this ability, then nothing should surprise you?

The reality of this so-called gift is that it's never enough. At times, I wish I hadn't been given this prescience. The reunion with Linda was quickly becoming too much for me to handle, knowing this was going to be the last time I would ever feel her touch and there was nothing I could do about it. I fell apart holding her desperately and refusing to let go. Then, I realized someone was there encouraging us to separate.

"Linda, it's time for us to go back," a soothing male voice said. She had to push me away because I would not release her. Our eyes desperately yearned for this widening gulf to be reversed, but it continued until she and her escort vanished. I felt Sara's warm, comforting arm around me. The emptiness that filled me earlier had returned, except this time it was far worse.

"You've been given a wonderful gift. Do you know that?" Sara said, trying to sooth the pain of losing her again, for the last time.

"I don't know that, Sara." I turned abruptly to face her and noticed another female entity was standing next to her and continued, "What I know is that much of my life has been filled with pain. Some think I'm insane because of this gift. And now, there's Linda, who risked everything for us and was viciously torn from this life. No, Sara, this is more torture than gift."

I waited for her to say something, but nothing came. "I still don't understand why I would be encouraged to see Linda's murder if I wasn't going to be permitted to protect her."

Sara took my hand trying to calm me and said, "David, this is Agatha. She is considered by the parishioners as the patron saint of Santa Cruz."

Agatha looked concerned, almost saddened. "David, sometimes things like this happen because someone makes a choice but that choice, as wrong as it was, is being converted to something positive. We are preparing you and others for something that is about to happen. If you are successful, those who chose to take innocent life will lose what they are pursuing and be held accountable. Can you see of what I speak?"

I knew within myself she was right, but the pain in losing Linda and how I saw her desecrated was still with me.

"David, I know you miss her. But, you are about to learn something I hope you will find exciting," Agatha said.

"What might that be?" I said, still embracing the idea that what has been taken will never return.

"There is a bit of Linda that remains in you. It's in your memory of her. Don't cling to it desperately. Just let it be, and let it live. You'll find that she will appear to you when you need her most, and she will also guide you on your life-long path of learning. Will you trust me?"

"I don't think having this gift is worth it, Agatha. Perhaps you should give it to someone else."

"If you really don't want this ability, David, you can close the door simply by living your life in anger and seeing everything around you analytically. Your spirit will become closed off and that will block the connection we have with you. But keep something in mind. Though the connection is blocked, it will forever be within your soul and will be an internal conflict for life. Are you sure that's what you want?"

"If I cannot protect anyone, especially those I love, then why should I have this ability?" I asked in frustration.

"If you've decided, just use the analytical part of your mind and tell the fingers of your body to move. You'll sense the physical distraction and be pulled back instantly into physical reality."

I did as she suggested and found myself leaning against the altar surrounded by the children and their mothers. Father Mike said, "Welcome back."

After I recovered from my little adventure, Father Mike and I left the church.

"So tell me, what happened. I'm curious," said Father Mike.

"My Spirit Guide, Sara, and two others took me to a place where I was allowed to be with Linda for a few minutes. Sara said it was a gift. Had I been given a choice, Father, I wouldn't have returned."

"I understand, David. Did anyone explain why Linda's passing had to be?"

"Agatha tried. I guess she's right. But, all of this just feels like it's well out of my ability to understand and cope with. I told her that if I wasn't going to be allowed to protect people, then she should take this gift back and give it to someone else."

"Agatha? Which Agatha did you meet?" Father Mike asked excitedly.

"Oh, Sara mentioned she was the patron saint of Santa Cruz. I hadn't met her before."

"See, David? You are certainly a special soul. You've met and spoken with Saint Agatha. She has quite a history, you know."

"Perhaps, but I still think she should take all of this away. I don't deserve it."

"Now, now ... Listen David, I wasn't going to share this, but I feel I should now. Undoubtedly, you've heard the other side say that something is coming and certain people, such as yourself, need to be prepared. We need you, David, for reasons that I cannot explain right now. Linda would not want you to give up, now would she?"

"No, she'd kick my ass if she were here."

"Well then, it's time to reenergize. Do you remember what happened in the caverns with Braz?"

"Yes, so what?" I asked.

"And you remember what Grand Master de Molay said?"

"Yes, Father."

"Well, perhaps you need to see for yourself that your allies are not only on the other side, they are also around you here as I mentioned earlier."

"I only see children and a few women here, Father. I like them, but I don't see how they can fight anyone who murders others."

"I wasn't referring to them." He paused and thought for a moment. "I need to check something out. I will pick you up at Braz' place tomorrow evening, say around 8 pm. Will you humor me and be ready?"

"Yes Father."

The long walk home was what I needed after all of this otherworldly goings-on. I told Braz and Sophia everything. They were shocked that I spoke to Agatha the way I did. Sophia gave me the history of their patron saint and after hearing all of that, I regretted being so direct with her. In fact, it troubled me so much that I couldn't sleep.

I got up and dressed in the dark at 2 am. After my conversation with Sophia, I needed to go back to the church and make things right with Agatha. Quietly, I left my home away from home, and returned to the privacy of the sanctuary. The question on my mind, *Will I be able to discuss what's made me so discouraged or have I sealed this door forever?*

The church was left unlocked so I quietly entered through the ancient hand-carved wooden doors, thinking I would have to deal with a night watchman. Having seen no one, I quietly made my way to the altar that held Linda's picture. I sat in a pew, closed my eyes, and asked Sara to help me. It didn't take long, and I found myself standing beside the altar with her. She took me through a portal into a room dimly lit with candles on different tables. She pointed to a chair for me to sit. As I did so, Agatha appeared and was apparently happy to see me return.

"You decided to come back," she said.

"I'm sorry about what I said to you earlier."

She smiled and placed her hand on my forehead. Neither of us occupied a physical body, yet I could feel something leave her hand and move through me that was intense yet comfortable. I closed my eyes and opened myself to her. Whatever she was doing, it felt more like being firmly cleansed from head to foot. I couldn't stop myself from crying. Tears streamed down my face, but they were not tears of pain. They were those of a final release. She was sending a kind of energy through me that broke the death grip of guilt and self-loathing that had been strangling me. When I felt her hand withdraw, I opened my tear-soaked eyes and said, "Thank you."

"What you do from this moment on will make a difference in your life and the lives of many others. Or, you can be just like so many other souls you know who live only to satisfy themselves. Which path will you choose?" she asked.

I wiped the tears from my eyes so I could see her clearly and smiled. "If you've been around me as long as Linda, you would already know."

"Yes, I do, but just like you told her so many times when you two made love, 'I like to hear the words,' I would like you to tell me which path," she said gently.

I smiled as I looked down at the floor and away from her. "Okay, I want to make a difference. I want to learn. I want to awaken to who I really am," I said, feeling as if I had finally given up resisting everything in my life.

"You're giving me more than I asked for," Agatha said, while lifting my chin with her finger. "I was the one who gave you the chance to say goodbye to Linda. The love between you was so complete and the sacrifice she made for you was so great that I thought it was needed."

"I'm sorry I reacted so badly. I just wasn't counting on losing her like that," I said.

Looking into her bright eyes was such an incredible experience. It was like connecting with an endless repository of love. As she allowed me to dwell within her, she said, "There is one more thing to keep in mind."

"What's that," I asked.

"The dreams you have been having about Maridon are important. Pay close attention to them. Each lesson, each experience you have henceforth will prepare you to engage him as an equal. If you need inspiration, remember that Bullard and his minions do the bidding of their master, who has enslaved many."

When Agatha said that last part, she hit a cord that instantly created conflict within me. "But Agatha, I dislike violence. I always have. How do I deal with someone whose very existence is based on that kind of dark pain?" I asked, knowing that if given the chance, I would allow my anger to take control and at least try to kill him.

"I know what's in your heart, David. Remember that dark emotions such as anger, hate, and baseless fear are all part of the ego. Let any one or all of these emotions take control of you, and you will ultimately be controlled by Maridon. You, my son, will lose. Promise me you will never forget this," she said and once again lovingly touched my face.

So this scenario had now become serious, which made me wonder how I would manage it.

Agatha held my hands as she continued, "Linda's death was necessary for many reasons that we don't have time to go into right now. I want you to know that her assassin has already been dealt with. And, there is no need for you to do anything that you agreed to while you were in Germany with the government agents, nor should you focus on this event anymore. There is a much bigger crisis looming on the horizon and you'll need to focus on that," Agatha said.

"What do you mean he's been dealt with . . . the guy who killed Linda?" I asked.

"Her death was a matter for the Portuguese. The men, whom Father Mike will introduce you to, found him as he tried to escape on a boat from Angra. Unfortunately, he thought he could fight his way off the island which resulted in his death. Your allies, Linda's friends, have taken care of everything."

"So, what should I do now?"

"Just follow the path you and Linda were on for now. As she said, you will eventually find someone who will love you more than she could. In the meantime, you have a lot to learn, and so much more to prepare for."

And with that, she held me for a long moment then began moving away. She faded into the light of a candle opposite from where we had been talking, and I was left with the most profound spiritual experience of my life.

The following evening, Father Mike picked me at 8 p.m. and took me back to the Santa Cruz Cathedral. We entered the sanctuary illuminated with candlelight that cast undulating shadows throughout the church that seemed to have a life of their own. Father Mike had remained silent until we approached the back of the sanctuary behind the altar. I had not noticed a small door there until he opened it and stepped through.

"Be careful, the first part of this passageway is low," Father Mike said, as he stooped slightly to pass through the doorway.

We descended a long set of stairs into what felt like the bowels of the church. The lighting was, indeed, poor. The only sounds were the slight echo of our footsteps, and the hint of air passing through the steep stair-filled tunnel. The lower we descended, the chillier it became.

We stepped onto a landing that was obviously rough-cut stone. Father Mike led me deeper into the chamber and as we descended, my curiosity grew. *Where was this man of the cloth taking me?* I thought.

I saw an opening ahead that was lit by what I thought was a small flame. As we approached, I began to feel a presence in the chamber that seemed familiar. Father Mike stepped inside and I cautiously followed him.

The chamber looked similar to the cavern Braz had taken Linda and me to weeks earlier. The flame that was small from a distance was actually from several large candles aligned atop an elongated stone. There were several people dressed in long white robes in a circle around the rock that resembled a kind of table, and they were chanting to music that only they could hear.

We stopped just a few feet from them and Father Mike spoke softly, "We'll wait until they're done."

When they finished what they were doing, they all turned to look at the new arrivals. I recognized Braz immediately and two others as being police officers from Angra, the island capitol.

Braz welcomed us to their gathering and said, "Welcome. David, you haven't met most of these men, but they are all your friends. They are the direct descendants of the Templars that I spoke of earlier."

One of the men stepped forward and said, "Father Mike has told us of your issues and our Brother Braz shared with us your vision of Grand Master de Molay in the cavern. We are delighted you're here."

While thanking them and shaking their hands, I noticed the stone that they had been standing around was actually something more like an ornately carved altar. There was a large silver cross standing in its center surrounded by the blazing thick, white candles.

One of them, perhaps their leader, noticed my curiosity and said, "This altar was a gift from a Christian mystic after the first Templars arrived. It is endowed with spiritual energy from earlier centuries. This is where we come to worship, to pass out of our bodies into the astral world and engage our timeless enemy. It is our calling."

"It's good to meet others who have this ability," I said.

Braz continued to introduce me to everyone and then the leader said, "It is time for you to join us. Are you willing to accept what lays ahead for you?"

"Yes, I am, especially with all of you at my side. Our friendship shall not be broken."

The joining of souls' ceremony didn't take long. And, when it was done, I knew this bond would never be broken, but it would be tested by events that would happen in the future. For now, though, the only path I could pursue would take me stateside.

Chapter 19

"Sergeant Lussier, we're ready to board the C-5 now," a young female airman said. I turned to look at Sergeant Dodd, Father Mike, Braz, and Sophia. They were more than friends now; they were my family.

"I'm going to miss all of you." I began to struggle trying to stay in control of myself.

Sophia began to cry, pulled me to her and gave me a mother's hug, like when they know their son is leaving the nest and entering the world. For a short lady, she was strong. A simple kiss on the cheek was never enough. Braz reluctantly pulled her back.

"Sophia, our young man must go. Let him leave with us all smiling and wishing him well," Braz said in his fatherly way, something I had become accustomed to and would miss more than anything else.

Sergeant Dodd shook my hand, but then he too hugged me and said, "Son, we'll miss you, too. When you think of Linda, think of us. We loved her too, just in a different way."

It seemed like I stood there for the longest time, reluctant, maybe even confused. Was this a good idea to pursue a path that would take me away from the people I loved? They helped define my life while anchoring me after Linda's murder. Did I really want to leave them?

Images of what should have been flying through my mind had been replaced by a quick vignette of the life that I might have shared with them: the wedding that would have taken place at Braz and Sophia's home, the first time Linda and I made love as life partners, our eternal pledge to each other—meaningful exchanges that were never going to happen.

As I backed away from Sergeant Dodd, tears began to find their way down his cheeks. That was the one thing I never thought I'd see.

Reluctant to walk out of the terminal building, I said quietly, "All of you have filled an emptiness in my life. You've been the family that I have always wanted to have but never did. Knowing Linda was amazing, being able to say goodbye and hold her once more was incredible, but all of you have given me something that I'll carry with me for the rest of my life."

Father Mike stepped forward and did his best to give me a parting blessing. With these goodbyes completed, I was pulled through the open terminal door onto the tarmac by one of the C-5 crewmembers. That was the last time I would see the family that had gotten me through the most traumatic experience of my life.

"Come on Sergeant, we ain't got all day. This fat pig's finally ready to strut'er stuff," said a large foreboding beast of a man. He had my duffle bag in one hand and me in the other as he accelerated our pace. "If you don't wanna go, you can always stay," he complained as he pulled me along.

"Hey, take it easy," I said trying to keep up. He strong-armed my body up the retractable ramp into the back of the airplane that had just been off-loaded. One of his crew members began securing the aircraft so the Lockheed Galaxy C-5 could finish starting its engines and depart.

The passenger section of the C-5 was located underneath and forward of the vertical stabilizer— essentially its one story up and at the back of the airplane. Passengers and crew have to climb up a ladder to gain access to seating. Today, the seventy-five seats were about half occupied. Since there were no windows in this section of the plane, the five hour trip would be best spent asleep or reading—that is, if I could sleep through all the engine noise, since I had nothing to read.

The Loadmaster stood in front of the seated passengers and began his announcements. "All right ladies, this is my airplane and you're all here by my good graces. Don't piss me off, or you'll have hell to pay. I'm the Loadmaster for this trip. You can walk around up here after we level off, if you can't keep you skinny little asses in your government-provided seats, but only when I tell you. If I tell ya to get it back in those seats, you'll do so immediately without question, or I'll slam you in them. Questions? Good."

One of his crew members did the less-direct safety briefing as the C-5 taxied out. My mind was elsewhere, someplace not that far away, but certainly back in time. It all came back to me as I closed my eyes and saw myself as if I had just arrived in Lajes for the first time.

The flashback began with the C-124 that brought me to Lajes. The old cargo hauler had parked about a half mile down the tarmac from where I boarded the C-5. Losing my grip coming down the ladder, Linda, or Sergeant Cross, caught me, more or less, trying to keep me from landing on my ass. The only thing she accomplished was to soften my unmanly arrival on terra firma. It wouldn't be the last time I'd be looking up at her after landing on the ground. Recalling this encounter, it occurred to me that I fell in love with her when our eyes first met, even if the introduction was a bit clumsy.

I was drawn back to the present as I heard all four of the C-5's huge engines spool up to maximum takeoff power. I could feel the aircraft lunge forward and begin to shudder as it accelerated. The C-5 rotated and in just a few seconds, we were airborne. Essentially, I left my new family, my home behind after making a critical life decision. The faster the aircraft rose, the more I could feel myself torn apart. I was desperately asking my Spirit Guides if this was the right move.

Once the plane leveled-off, the rhythmic vibration of the engines sent an undulating energy through my body that lulled me into a more relaxed state of consciousness. Wherever this would take me, be it into unconscious sleep or spirit dimensions, I had decided not to resist the pull. I wasn't going to fight anything henceforth. I had lost too much and I had nothing left to defend. Given my exhausted state, I slept most of the way back to the States.

We landed some five hours later at McGuire Air Force Base in New Jersey. I had just enough leave to return home for a few days before reporting to Keesler Air Force Base for training. I transferred to Philadelphia International Airport and hopped an airliner to Flint, Michigan where I was born. A long-time friend, Mike Anderson, greeted me at the airport. He told me that my mom had sold the house in 1972 after I went into the Air Force. This was the house where I grew up and had been beaten by my father many times in part because of my so-called "demonic" paranormal experiences.

The man left her in 1970, just before I enlisted. My oldest sister had married a few years earlier, and my older brother had joined the Navy about the same time. Another older sister had left home. So, after I enlisted, mom suddenly found herself with just one person in her life, my younger sister.

Times were hard for mom so she decided to sell the house that she could no longer afford to maintain. My Uncle Carfon invited her to stay at his house while he took off to do other things. He had been married to my mom's sister, Aunt Katie, for many years. She had died of cancer not long before I left home. With no other choice, mom decided to accept Uncle Carfon's offer and took my younger sister with her.

Before I was allowed to see mom, my sister briefed me on her recent illness. No one knew for sure why she was in significant pain, but she wasn't able to leave her bed. This was particularly poignant since it was the same bed in which Aunt Katie had died in years earlier.

When I entered the house, it occurred to me that I had never seen my mother in bed. She felt and looked different to me and appeared to be a shadow of the tall, 160-pound farm girl I knew growing up. I heard Sara's voice deep within me say quietly, "She's coming home, David." I wanted to share something with mom from one of my unseen companions, but for some reason, I couldn't because I was falling apart inside. This was even more painful given that her death followed so close to Linda's.

This was the woman who gave birth to me, the woman who defended me when things deteriorated at school and when her husband beat me. But, she was also the person who refused to accept that her son had unexplainable experiences.

Instead of sharing what was on my mind, I stood there in total silence about the reality that only I could see or hear. I then quietly, lovingly, sat next to her on the bed that had already claimed one life, hugged her and said, "I love you, Mom, with all my heart."

Her parting words said with some intensity were, "You should be in school, not here. You know how important education is." I nodded my head and acknowledged that, as always, she was right and I was going back to school to become an air traffic controller.

I asked my sister on the way out of the house if she knew mom was dying. She refused to accept that possibility. For the second time in the last few weeks, I felt another part of me being set free, and yet knowing my mother, someone who defended me as ardently as Linda had, was going to leave this earth soon drained me further. My situation was changing rapidly, and there was nothing I could do about it. Perhaps what was being released was what was left of my life as it had been. Sometimes change happens because it needs to open the way to growth. But, at the time, it felt more like another landslide of granite was burying a part of me as I left the house.

Keesler Air Force Base was my next stop. Located in Biloxi, Mississippi, my trip required a circuitous route by plane to get there. This was good because I had a lot to think about. There was no one left for me to feel connected with, no one to feel a part of, and nothing was left but to deal with being alone . . . completely alone for the first time in my life.

The flight from Detroit to Memphis on Southern Airways was quiet. I sat by myself staring out the window at all the clouds wondering what it would be like to be a part of them. My thoughts drifted back to the first time I flew a small airplane by myself just a few years earlier. Flying solo was the first time I felt free from all of the painful events that had occurred at home. I was so deep in thought that I didn't notice someone settling in next to me.

"Hi, my name's Sherry Gilbert," an energetic female voice said. I turned and looked at her. She was in her early 20s, neatly trimmed, short, medium light brownish hair, cute, nice smile, and an airman first class. "Oh, sorry, I should've said, 'Hi Sergeant,' or something like that. I'll never adjust to this military stuff," she said with a smile.

"Don't bother. It doesn't really matter. On your way to Keesler?" I asked.

"Yeah, I can hardly wait. This whole training thing has kept me moving around way too much. I'm so tired, and the guys just keep hitting on me," she said with an exhausted voice.

"Isn't that what you want?" I replied, somewhat annoyed. She either didn't catch my tone of voice, or she decided to ignore it.

"Well, yeah, sometimes, but it gets old after a while."

"Don't worry Airman, I won't be hitting on you," I said, as I returned to looking out the window.

"I figured as much! You seem very . . . oh, I dunno . . . settled, maybe? That's why I decided to sit next to you. You've got good vibes," she said, almost flirtatiously.

"Good vibes?" I asked, wondering what she was picking up.

"Yeah, I know if I can trust someone by the energy they send out. You're depressed about something, but you send off good vibes," she added.

That was different—a young lady who's not hiding what she "senses about things." I wondered what other surprises were in store. "You seem tired. Maybe you should sleep now." I said.

"Oh, would you mind? I can only do that on a plane if I have a shoulder to rest my head on. May I?"

"Do you drool?" I asked, kidding her.

"A Sergeant who's funny; I like that. No, I don't drool."

"If you're going to sleep on my shoulder, then you might as well call me David. Deal?"

"Sure, David," she said.

As she relaxed, the feel and warmth of her resting comfortably on my shoulder began to appeal to a part of me that I thought had been completely numbed. Then, the scent of her hair and her gentle breath reawakened what it was like to have someone close, someone who relied on me to comfort them. The pain of my recent history diminished a little as an evolving tide of emotion began to sweep over me. *I can't let this happen again,* I told myself in near-desperation. I didn't know what to do, but I knew that if I'd just stayed quiet, closed my eyes, perhaps my old companion might help.

I felt a hand gently touch mine and move it as if to quietly draw my attention. Only when I opened my eyes did I realize that I had fallen asleep with Sherry. Though my unseen companion was silent this time, the Flight Attendant quietly got my attention so we could prepare for landing.

Upon arriving in Gulfport, Mississippi, Sherry and I said goodbye, thinking we'd be on different buses. The local military coordinator directed me to the bus for non-commissioned officers. I was surprised when I saw Sherry walking down the aisle a few minutes later smiling as if she'd just found a long lost friend. Her eyes never left mine as she sat down carefully next to me. I tried to stop any feelings of recognition or familiarity before they could take root, but it was too late.

"This is so unusual," she said as she moved closer to me.

"What's unusual?" I asked.

"You . . . or that I like being with you. You're so natural, and comfortable." She resumed her earlier position. I thought she would go back to sleep, but she didn't.

"What will you be doing while you're at Keesler?" she asked.

Surprised, I looked at her as she rested against me and asked, "Why?"

"You're just like a guy. If it makes you feel better, you can be the one who asks me out instead of me asking you."

"Why would you want to go out with me? Did you forget that I'm depressed, and depressed guys are no fun to be around unless you like being depressed."

"True, but I think you have a good reason for it, and I think I'm here to help get you back on track. At least that's what it feels like. So, do you want to see me?" she asked.

This was tough. I wasn't over Linda yet. I know what I was told, but it was still too raw. And then there's everything else that seemed to be piling up. "Look, Sherry, I would enjoy going out with you, but you should know that the woman I was going to marry died recently. I still think about her a lot, and I'm not sure you should be around anyone that has his mind on someone else."

"Well, you could let me decide that for myself. Besides, who's asking you to get serious? I'm thinking guy friend."

At first I could feel someone pushing my shoulder, and then Sara began to encourage me, "*Go ahead.*"

"You're going to be too busy once you move in with the other women of your squadron and they'll want you to hang out with them," I said, trying to give her a reason to change her mind.

She raised her head off my shoulder and looked quizzically at me. "Are you trying to brush me off?"

"No," I said, as I looked away trying to think of what to say next. "Besides, you should be with someone who can be more entertaining. Don't you think?"

"I didn't ask you to entertain me. I thought maybe going out a few times would be just what you needed."

"Honestly, I haven't been able to think about anything except what I have to deal with from day to day," I said.

"Well, it's about time you moved on. There's a lot more to life when you can get past the serious stuff. So, why not take a risk? Let me decide for myself who I want to spend time with, and say yes."

"All right, yes, I'd like to see you again," I said finally giving up.

"Since you're the Sergeant, I'll expect you to figure out how to contact me and make it happen. I'm sure we'll have time on the weekends to run around."

With that, she eased herself onto my shoulder again and relaxed. I couldn't believe that someone would find me interesting enough to take this kind of risk, although a part of me continued to question the decision.

After arriving on base, the one thing I really wanted to do was to see an old Cajun friend, Beaux Boudreau. We had done basic and law enforcement training together. He was now a staff Sergeant with his own crew in the Security Police Division. At a minimum, I wanted to ride with him on the swing shifts he worked. If I was lucky, he'd take me home with him and introduce me to his huge family that lived in the Louisiana bayous. He always said that his aunt would probably like to meet me because she'd be the only one who'd understand me. As I closed my eyes thinking about this prospect, I could see Sherry coming along. Evidently, Boudreaux's aunt had a gift of her own, and Sherry might find that interesting, or "entertaining."

Chapter 20

"Ripper one-one flight cleared for the overhead, report break," I said. Students held model airplanes up in the air to emulate aircraft movement around the table-top airport mockup in front of the fake tower cab. It was my turn to pretend I was the local Controller directing these aircraft. This would give us a rough idea how traffic might look flying the traffic pattern around the airport.

"Ripper one-one, roger the break," the student holding the small collection of F-106s answered.

I really wanted to see how this particular student was going to deal with the flight of four F-106's he held. They were going to have to split up into no more than two pairs, but he was limited to two hands. Maneuvering in a tight pattern while trying to land would be difficult for the fast-moving aircraft and landing more than two at the same time on most runways is frowned upon. So, how would he hold four aircraft in two hands while moving them around a small racetrack-shaped pattern.

The day was quickly coming to an end and it was a good thing because I was being distracted by thoughts of Sherry. We had been at the base for a few weeks and had seen a lot of each other off-duty. One of the benefits of continuing this new relationship with Sherry was that she was helping me recover from losing Linda and my Azorean family. But I was also bothered by a growing sense that she was being targeted like Linda, and I didn't want to believe that was possible. At first, I thought maybe my sense of things was due to some kind of guilty feeling for allowing the relationship.

Despite this distraction, I did well in our task of separating simulated air traffic. But I was still trying to figure out a minor point while walking out of the training center to meet Boudreaux. Then it occurred to me: I had missed seeing how my fellow student decided to hold four aircraft so he could simulate two flights of two landings. So much for my entertainment of the day.

"Hey Dave . . . over here," Boudreaux yelled from his squad car.

Beaux Boudreau was a good friend that I had met while in basic training. We then went into Law Enforcement Technical School together at Lackland Air Force Base in San Antonio, Texas. He was average height and build. But, his hair was intense black, almond skin, and a look that made the women around him melt. It was, at times, embarrassing to walk into a bar with him because of the way he attracted the attention of the ladies.

"Wow, you decided to chauffer me while acting as my body guard tonight?" I asked with a chuckle. It was good to see him again after a long day, and I was looking forward to going out on patrol tonight. This was a classic setup for military cops. A Friday night that just happened to be payday with a full moon.

"You, buddy, have got to find something to do with yourself instead of run'n the streets with me and the boys," Boudreaux said, laughing at me as if I were a lost cause.

"What else would I do? I don't get to see you that much, and you're pretty damn good company."

"What about this Sherry girl you've talked about? She sounds nice. And by the way, stop calling me Boudreaux. You know I prefer Beaux."

"All right then, come on Beaux, let's go," I said eagerly, trying to deflect his question.

"You didn't answer the question, buddy. So what about Sherry?" Beaux repeated the question.

"Are you trying to get rid of me?" I asked, then paused. "Okay, she's nice, but I don't need it get'n any more serious than it is," I said.

"Then get yo Yankee-ass in here and let's go. I got some Cajun gumbo wait'n on us and I'm hungry. We'll have some fun tonight one way or another. But, I wanna make sure you understand something. You ain't do'n noth'in outside this car, even if you see me get'n my Cajun-ass whipped. You got it?" Beaux said firmly, like that would have any effect on me.

I got into the patrol unit and smiled. "So, you expect me to just sit here and watch you get nailed. Do you mind if I laugh my ass off too?" I said with a smirk.

"Oh man, you Yankees are all the same. I just know this is a bad idea have'n you along. There are things you just can't leave alone. Ahhh what the hell, if I'm gonna get court-martialed, it might as well be for a good reason. Buckle up asshole!" he said, and we were off.

The night was quiet, too quiet considering what normally happens on a payday with a full moon. But that didn't stop us from having a good time. Beaux was a self-contained entertainment center. He always had something he wanted to talk about and it was usually hilarious. Since he was the senior Sergeant of the watch, he was also the supervisor. This allowed him to go wherever he wanted, when he wanted, tell any joke he wanted, and no one on his shift could tell him otherwise.

The one thing he enjoyed most about his work was being in the right spot, at the right time to stop a crime from going down. It's nearly an impossible task, but it gets easier when someone gives you a heads-up or the crooks developed enough of a pattern that allowed him to figure out the timing and location. But, then there were times, he told me, when he got a feeling something was going to happen.

This was the case tonight. He felt something was about to go down on the flight line. He just didn't know when or where. The base was having problems with crooks breaking into the hangers and stealing tools and equipment. There had been no pattern as of yet, making it difficult for the investigators to anticipate the next break-in. Beaux and the patrol unit responsible for this area had been doing periodic drive-by checks of the hangars, but he decided to do one more slow drive-by of one particular hangar just before the end of his watch.

We came around the corner of the building and saw a station wagon parked out front with the hangar doors open. "Bingo, dude. Not too obvious, Beaux?" I smirked.

He coasted to a stop with the engine off, just behind a fuel truck several feet away from our uninvited visitors. Undoubtedly, they were doing some last minute shopping. This part of the flight line had very little lighting, and with an overcast sky the area was mostly dark. I picked up the microphone ready to call for backup. "Don't call my boys, yet. I wanna see if these assholes are just stupid, or if they're idiots," Beaux said quietly, as he concentrated on the station wagon.

I looked at him not believing what I just heard. "That's not how we were trained," I said.

"Well, we ain't in school anymore. This is live action and I want my share." I shook my head, Classic Beaux. "Oh yeah, lookie-here. They're not just idiots; they're stone-cold idiots. Ohhhh, this is gonna be fun." He slid out of the car quickly without making any noise, then turned back to me. "Okay, call it in while I go have some Cajun-fun and don't forget what I said about stay'n put." I immediately called for back-up.

What made him think they were idiots was what our genius crooks intended to load into their station wagon. He quickly moved up to the opening of the hangar near the car with his revolver drawn. Beaux looked back at me and pointed at our cruiser reminding me to stay put, then he returned his attention to the crooks.

They had moved a couple of tool chests on wheels, called carry-alls, up to the back of their getaway car. The first carry-all was against the tailgate ready to be magically tilted and inserted. One of the brilliant crooks had thought to strap down the upper box to the base so it wouldn't fall off when they tipped it over, perhaps thinking they could forcefully slide it in on its back.

This could've been a good idea, but what about the weight and then the second carry-all? Where was that going to fit, and wouldn't that make the getaway station wagon look more like a tilted wanna-be rocket on wheels? These carry-alls can weigh several hundred pounds.

But that seemed to escape the minds of our genius crooks. I watched Beaux slip into the darkness and wondered what would qualify as "Cajun-fun." While letting my mind imagine some possibilities, I felt an utterly cold, dry shroud fall upon me from nowhere on this hot, humid Mississippi summer night. The chill it sent down my spine was anything but refreshing. My heart beat jumped into a ready-now mode. The question instantly became where the attack would come from, and who or what would be the attacker.

Beaux took the key to the shotgun rack with him, so all I had to work with was a thirty-six inch riot baton. Knowing Beaux, it didn't surprise me that it felt rather heavy for just hardened oak. No doubt he had drilled the center and poured molten lead in the bored hole to strengthen the full length of the baton.

I couldn't let my friend be surprised by uninvited guests, so I made my way into the hanger, alert to paranormal warnings. Then I felt another presence. This entity was ugly but familiar, one that seemed focused on me. All I could think of was whatever or whoever it was had to be either cowardly or highly skilled in strategic planning because it still had not attacked me directly. I was guessing the latter, which meant I had to stay ahead of it. One of the disturbing preferences of my enemy was the targeting of my friends . . . the closer, the better. Hit a close friend, a lover, or a life partner, and the terror it created in the person becomes a kind of sweet nectar that this entity apparently fed on like a kind of dark, spiritual addiction.

As I quietly approached a tall stack of pallets next to one of the C-130s being repaired in the hangar, I saw a familiar, thin, misty-green cloud. The ill-defined mist felt like the same thing that was involved with Linda's murder. I saw it enshroud a rather large man crouched behind large pallets. Beaux didn't notice him. But then, I saw the mist enter into the thief. Obviously, an ambush was in the works.

Beaux was still focused on the two crooks trying to push the last carry-all into the back of their brilliantly selected getaway station wagon. He had no idea what was about to happen. I began calculating strike points to cripple the assailant, when he pulled out a large Bowie knife from underneath his coat. That changed everything instantly removing the luxury of planning.

Since I wasn't that far from him, I launched myself at the possessed culprit and swung the baton with both hands like a medieval battle sword. The unmistakable loud crack of the wrist I struck and shattered could be clearly heard by everyone. Instead of screaming like a normal human being, the possessed assailant turned and glared at me as if happy to see his real prey.

"You finally show up!" he growled.

"Wow, you finally noticed. I thought you were going to ignore me," I said, trying to distract him while I anticipated his next move.

"You want me to kill you now?" he said, licking his lips as if I were the main course.

"Please give me a reason to tear you apart," I said angrily, forgetting that all I had to work with was a baton. There was no way I was going to kill it, or the body it possessed.

"You're less of a challenge than I was told," it said with a barbaric laugh. "But it's not your time. They don't want me to feast on your soul, yet," it growled, sending another brutally cold blast through my body.

Yes, I was getting to know this thing, maybe not by name, but how it liked to kill. And, if I can't kill it, how do I defeat it? This was the same entity that possessed the assassin who took Linda's life.

This exchange had galvanized both Beaux and the crooks, who were frozen in place by this battle.

The possessed human began to move toward me with a strong sense of determination. When I looked into its eyes, I connected with the demon inside and wished I hadn't. What I sensed was unlike anything I had ever experienced. As I struggled to understand its fury, I discovered that I could not move and was controlled by the dark consciousness of this soulless entity. I just didn't know how to fight something like this.

Consciousness? But, if it is without a soul, can it experience consciousness? I asked myself as it moved closer.

The rotten odor of this thing was unique to itself and not of human origin. It was also consuming a part of my energy, sucking the essence of my soul out of my core to at least partially satisfy its addiction. The baton was up and ready to strike, but my energy had rapidly abandoned me and I let the baton fall.

A muted explosion occurred, perhaps in the background, a simple distraction? I then saw the right side of the possessed assailant's head explode as it disappeared in a bloody cloud. What was left of the body fell. Then, the greenish mist gathered slowly over the fallen body and left.

"Damn, I can't leave you in the car without you mess'n up my fun," Beaux said, as he came over to look at the mess he just created. I was still dazed and weakened from this demonic close encounter.

"Oh, my head," I said, as I staggered about blurry-eyed from a massive headache.

"He couldn't have hit you," Beaux said, pointing to where the attacker lay. "What the hell's going on?"

"I dunno," I said, staggering over to one of the pallets and braced myself. I told him what had happened and that I saw a demonic spirit enter the assailant's body, the same one that occupied the assassin who killed Linda.

Beaux stood there and shook his head. "You must have some Cajun blood, 'cause things like that happen to us or our kin folk a lot, or so Auntie tells us."

"Yeah, I kinda had that feeling, Beaux."

"Well, that means you're probably family, and you know what that means," Beaux said with a big grin.

"Ohhhh Gawd, don't tell me I gotta eat crawfish heads or some super-hot gumbo as a test to see if I'll self-combust?" I asked, holding my head.

"For starters, but what it really means is you gotta meet my Auntie. You got problems with spirits attack'n you, she can help. She's a kinda priestess. All my people go to her for everything, including attacking demons," he said with smirk.

My energy had mostly returned. I stood up and looked around knowing that the enemy was still out there. The creature already knows about Beaux, and that was who it targeted this time . . . not me. How long would it take for it to find Sherry?

"Yeah, Beaux, but you remember what I said about Linda? This thing will find Sherry. I need to get her outta the barracks and someplace where she can be defended. You think your Auntie will know how to destroy it?"

"Don't know, but we won't figure it out here. Let's get this cleaned up, file our reports, and make the notifications upline. The shift will be over by then. Good thing its Friday, we're off for the weekend." Beaux had already handcuffed the other crooks, and now the backup team was finishing up here at the crime scene.

We finally closed out the evenings events, collected my small travel bag, and left the base in Beaux's car. It was late when we arrived at his parents' home in the bayou of a small Louisiana county. His mom sent us to bed after we shared what happened back at the base. I was so tired and drained by now that I just wanted to fall asleep.

Drifting off, I found myself walking through a dark forest shrouded in the late evening mist. I could feel moist rivulets making their way down my body yet it was not raining. The late hour should have resulted in total darkness given the thickness of the forest canopy surrounding me. Instead, I noticed a faint shimmer of a greenish-yellow light subtly illuminating my path as if to lure me ahead.

The source was coming from an old, worn-down cottage. As I quietly approached, I saw a wooden front door that was barely hanging on by its hinges. The thatched roof was moldy, and swamp moss was hanging from what would've been the soffit of the roof. The old wood-framed windows were dirty and rotted, covered in cobwebs.

Something told me to be careful, things were not as they seemed. It became more apparent that something was waiting for me inside because the cottage was enshrouded in some sort of unnatural energy—something that didn't belong here.

Quietly, I opened the door just enough to peer inside to see what trap awaited me. As the door opened, I saw a very old woman sitting in a rocking chair crudely carved out of thick wooden branches. A faint greenish aura undulated about her. She appeared thin, ravaged by life's trials and the demands of time. Her hair was long, silver-gray, and draped down about her. A long black cloak covered her body.

As I approached, I studied my surroundings. Seeing nothing alarming, I began to focus on her. For some reason, my yellow flags were all calm. So maybe she wasn't a threat. While that was hard to believe given my recent experiences, my senses were always reliable when interpreting threats. But then, there had always been a link between my enemy and a greenish aura-like energy.

She turned slightly to reveal the profile of her face and then everything changed. Now, I was further confused. She was striking, some would say attractive. Every facial feature was in proportion as if she were perfectly created. Her skin was brilliant white and utterly smooth, again, essentially perfect. And yet her hair, at first glance, was old. I was only feet away as she slowly turned toward me and smiled, revealing fang-like teeth with traces of blood dripping from them as if she had just finished dining on her last victim.

"Your senses are nonexistent here, mortal," she said in a surprisingly aged, but commanding voice. "Do you know why I want you?"

I shook my head no.

"It's what you've done to me and mine that causes me to pursue you. What you've done must be paid for, and you will, indeed, pay for it," she snarled.

"I have done nothing to you, nor do I know you," I said nervously.

"WHAT DID YOU SAY?" she screamed, as she leaned forward in her chair gripping the armrests firmly. "I sit in this chair because of you. You once said you loved me and then you allowed this to happen," she said, as she turned further to face me and ripped her cloak open, revealing a gaping hole in her chest where her heart and lungs should have been. Blood oozed from the opening as if the organs had just been ripped from her body. Shocked, I had to swallow hard to keep from vomiting.

"Don't like what you see, do you? Maybe I should remind you that my breasts were the part of me you lusted for when we were together, and we were together a lot. When you stole my heart, you destroyed what I was," she said with hatred oozing with each word.

As I looked at her, I noticed something began to happen that also seemed familiar. Her eyes began to change. As they opened, I could feel a part of myself being pulled into her . . . deep within her. It was like two massive hands had reached inside me, grabbed hold of my soul and was brutally tearing it from my body, breaking millions of etheric connections, each break creating intense pain like I had never known. As she did this, I knew I would be consumed within her, pulled into her through her eyes, the windows to whatever darkness she now held within her.

The intense pain of separation began to increase rapidly. Then a loud rumbling began from outside the cottage. I could no longer speak or move paralyzed by this spirit's power as she continued to slowly devour me. The rumbling further intensified, shaking the cottage as if an earthquake had begun.

The disturbance increased to such a degree that she could no longer concentrate on her kill. The thatched roof was pulled upward and destroyed, while the walls began to fracture and collapse. Released from her merciless grip, I fell to the floor. Every ounce of energy had been drained from my body. Barely able to breathe, I felt a pair of large hands lift me and carry me away from her tortuous attack which could have ended my life. Now, I rested in a safe place.

I did not see the owner of the hands, but a familiar voice reminded me of something from what seemed like a lifetime ago, "You still don't understand why you should stay away from strange women, do you?"

"Linda? Is that you?" I barely said still trying to breathe.

"I'm shocked that you have to ask," she said.

"I'm not shocked," said another familiar voice.

"What's happening to me? Who is that? Is that Sara?"

"That, my dear friend, is your new gang that's come'n to a haunted house near you."

"Very funny. So you and Sara are ganging up on me. So what's going on?" I said impatiently.

"Well, one way to think of it is Sara's training me. But what's more important is, if you haven't guessed, someone wants to put you where the lights don't shine, which means our work isn't done here yet. And, by the way, they want to make it hurt so bad that you won't know how to ask them to stop."

"But why," I said now at the end of my wits. "I haven't done anything to anyone, and I don't have anything that anyone wants," I said incredulously, then added, "And by the way, are you and Sara a team now?"

"To answer your first question, why do you think you don't have anything the enemy wants? If nothing else, you're a threat to them. You've been told that several times," Linda said. "And to answer your second question: yes, and Sara's a better partner than you ever were," she said, smiling and trying to be cute.

"So you're working together to help me?"

"Yes, but she's also training me to do what she does. But you, my dear, need to focus and get to the real work."

"Doing what? Staying alive?" I asked in frustration. "No one tells me anything until I get ambushed by something trying to suck the life outta me like some sort of modernized energy vampire."

"And your point is?" Linda and Sara asked in unison.

"That's my point. I at least need hints about what's going on. All I get are the chills or a burning sensation if Mr. Blood-bath comes look'n to carve up one of my friends."

"Okay, I'll indulge you. First of all, your Sherry-girl is more than a friend and you know that. And you also know Beaux is more than a friend, too. So stop playing dumb. I can't feed you like a baby. You gotta find the truth yourself and try not to take too long. It's important you figure this out," she said.

"All right, how about a hint about what's coming?"

"Okay, how about rehashing what just happened. There's your hint about what's coming. Close your eyes and do what we used to do when we were together."

Reluctantly, I laid back into the thick grass that surrounded me and closed my eyes, mumbling something about being the last to know about everything and now having two spirit women on my case. I wasn't sure how this would play out, but one thing certain was that there had to be a reason for them both to show up now.

"Hey, little Cajun wanna-be brother, wake up," said Beaux standing near the side of my bed. "My parents ain't gonna like the idea of you sleep'n all day. They wanna introduce you around and be amused by your Yankee-ass blunders."

"Geez, Beaux, how long have I been asleep?"

"You fell in that bed this morning around 2 a.m. And I have to tell ya, buddy, you're a tough roommate to try getting any sleep around."

"Why's that?" I asked as I stretched.

"Because, your dreams get you involved. Damn, I thought you were in another fight or something there for a while. Look, it's 10 a.m. Saturday's a big day for this family. You gotta get up. Come on, let's go," Beaux said as he pulled me up out of bed.

"When are we seeing Auntie?" I asked.

"Tonight maybe, it depends. Why?"

I told him about the dream I had and the impression it left in my mind. I needed to visit Auntie and the sooner the better.

"Ha, one day you gonna admit I'm right. Life is all about relationships and noth'n else."

"Okay, Beaux, you're right. So, when are we going?"

"Come on out here and rub elbows with your new family first. Ya never know when you'll need'm. I'll call Auntie and see when she'll have us stop over."

Beaux's family was huge. All of his brothers and sisters were there. But what surprised me were the extended family members that had gathered outside to prepare for the evening's festivities. This was a close family with lots of friends who loved any excuse to party. If I didn't get talked into eating anything that would el flambo me instantly, I was certain to have a great time. Before any of the entertainment could happen, though, I had to get some answers and I needed them soon.

It didn't take long for Beaux to arrange the meeting with Auntie. He told his parents we'd be back in time for the evening bash. He drove us out of their small town in this Louisiana parish to a nearby swampy bayou to meet his Priestess Auntie. I was doing great until we began walking along a path covered by a thick forest canopy. As we approached where Auntie lived, I noticed her home looked old, if not ancient. Unusual aromas and a familiar yellowish green light seemed to illuminate the darkened area surrounding Auntie's abode. My nerves were instantly on edge. Was the dream I had last night a warning about who I was about to meet? Beaux opened the door and said, "Auntie, dis is da boy I been tell'n you bout. He got da gift."

The woman who turned to look at me as she extended a welcoming hand looked just like I thought she might. "We've already met, haven't we?" I asked.

Chapter 21

Something about Auntie captured my attention the moment she took my hands in hers. We engaged each other as a massive flood of energy began flowing between us. Or, perhaps she was draining my energy—I couldn't tell. I immediately felt as if we had known each other from some earlier time and place. Was this a sense of *knowing* based solely on her touch? Or, was it something about her spirit being expressed through the endless depth of her eyes that drew me completely into her presence? The longer we remained engaged, the more confused I felt; *I couldn't have known her, could I? Her deep, brilliant blue eyes shone . . . a person could fall into forever,* I thought. *A trip into wondrous bliss, perhaps, or is this really a deceptive invitation to hellish regions?* My thoughts quickly raced in an attempt to determine what was happening. *Could this be the same entity that attacked me in the vision last night?*

"Hey you two, mind come'n back to me now?" Beaux asked, putting a hand on my shoulder and breaking the connection between myself and Auntie.

"You're different . . . yes, you're very different," she said in a soft, yet excited voice that resonated deep within me.

"Auntie, this is my friend. He's . . ."

"Beaux, honey," she said, briefly looking at him with the hint of a smile before returning her attention to me. "You don't need to introduce us."

I could still feel her probing deep within me as I said, still trying to understand our connection, "You do seem familiar to me."

Then, a slightly buoyant feeling settled over me, my spirit detached. I had to remind myself that I was actually standing in her living room, looking into those incredible, mysterious eyes. *Stay grounded*, I told myself. But the thought still lingered in my mind, "*Gawd, what is it about her!*"

Then, I felt her draw me deeper into her consciousness . . . not just her presence. Being allowed to enter a part of her consciousness was only the beginning. I decided to just let it happen, and then suddenly I felt myself being moved through her inner space at a rapid pace. Images of things streaked by in a blur, and then our pace sped up and everything became indistinguishable. Suddenly, the images disappeared and I came to a stop in front of a formidable object. The object was large like Hadrian's Wall, and the impression was that I shouldn't cross it.

A wave of energy was generated from the object that shot through me like a mini-tsunami. While trying to remain standing without staggering, I began to feel cleansed from head to toe as a result of the energy wave passing through me. *Did she just do that; cleanse me as a nurse would her patient after a triage assessment?* The object began to move as its surface undulated to some sort of unheard rhythm. It appeared that the rhythmic wave energy from within was beginning to build.

I raised a hand to touch a portion of the object's moving surface to see if anything else had changed. An energetic burst erupted from its now animated facade and wrapped around my arm and then extended itself into my entire body. Whatever it was, it examined me in detail and I could feel myself being tested. As quickly as it started, it was over. A voice brought me back to the small cottage and the experience ended.

It took me a moment to reorient myself, as I heard Auntie speak.

"Beaux usually brings home young men to me who are—how should I say—not as deep as you," she said with a coy, knowing smile. Drained from the test, I remained attached to her striking, deep-blue eyes. Then, she seemed to acquiesce and released me.

Gradually, I became aware of her physical presence as if she had emerged from a thinning fog. She was tall with long, wavy, dark-almond hair draped precariously about her shoulders and falling down her back. It was comparable in length to the evil elderly woman in my dream with her ancient dirty-gray hair. Though there was much to admire about Auntie, I still could not stray too far from her magnetic eyes. *Why am I being pulled back to them?*

Then her lips began to move again. "So, are you going to say anything or just stand there with your mouth open?" she asked softly.

"I . . . Uhhh . . . I'm sorry. It's just that . . . " I hesitated, not sure what to say.

The feeling of having been abandoned overwhelmed me when she released my hands and turned her attention to Beaux. I felt as if I had been abandoned on a distant island.

"Dear nephew, why don't you get us some wine from my collection? I think your friend needs a pick-me-up." While Beaux walked over to the cabinet, Auntie moved us to some comfortable chairs in the same room where I thought I had been attacked in my vision.

"Do you still like ruby Port wines?" Beaux asked. I nodded slowly, while confusing images and feelings were flaring up in my head. I was beginning to think that she short-circuited my wiring just to keep me off-balance.

The nagging feeling of knowing her from an earlier time began to drive me nuts. The knowledge, however, seemed intentionally buried to prevent its discovery. The pressing question remained the same: was she the same entity that appeared in my vision? If so, then she was definitely the enemy.

Auntie leaned forward in her chair with a smile that felt as if it had reached out and attached itself to me. Her consciousness, as she was looking again directly into me— not just *at* me—seemed to be inviting her new guest for another trip but into the depths of something entirely new. She said, apparently sensing my unease, "Darling young man, you seem unnerved by something. What is it?"

I had to think fast . . . no, actually I needed help. But no one was saying anything. When this happened in the past, it was because my guides wanted me to figure it out for myself. But, if this were seriously bad stuff, I was betting they would've said something by now.

Oh yeah, forge ahead, and into what, I thought. Let's see, what are the options? Worst case scenario, Auntie's actually the Welcome Wagon lady from Hell or worse. I decided to ditch the *"run and hide"* option. I've got some big guns on my side too, right? I bet Sara could give her a run for the money. But since no one was attacking or defending anyone here, I decided to take a risk.

"Do you want me to call you Auntie, too?" I finally said with a bit of confidence.

"Seems like there's more on your mind than that, but if it helps you to feel part of the family, okay. Or, if you prefer, you can call me by my name, Amy."

"All right, Amy it is," I said trying to relax a bit more. Beaux delivered the Port. It was just what I needed. A sip of its fruity, aromatic bouquet left a hint of wild cherries on the palette. Hopefully the alcohol would settle my nerves.

"Amy, would you mind if I'm direct?" I asked.

"Please, tell me what's bothering you," she said again with that incredible smile. It wasn't a smile of overconfidence, or *now I've got you*. It was a kind of welcoming, inviting me to be open and connect with her despite the fact that she had already probed my depths, as it were.

"I think you already know everything you want to know about me. Isn't that what you did when our hands touched?" I asked.

"So, what did you experience, David?"

"How did you know his name, Auntie? I didn't introduce you two yet?" Beaux asked excitedly.

"Oh Beaux, honey, sit down and relax. Honestly, I love you dearly, but you need to keep up," Amy said, not looking at her nephew.

"You know what you did, Amy. I'd like to know why," I said with a touch of firmness.

"I thought you'd appreciate someone who shares your talent. Besides, it saves time, and if I'm not mistaken, you don't have a lot of that to waste," she responded.

"I wouldn't call what you did a get-to-know-you probe, and I assure you, I've never done anything like that to anyone," I said.

"So what technique do you use to know the truth of others?" she asked a bit more seriously.

"Well, I still prefer the old fashioned way of asking questions, instead of invading someone like you did," I said, not flinching a bit. "Since you've dispensed with the usual formalities," I continued, "I have two questions. Why do you seem so familiar to me and who are you beyond being Beaux's Auntie whose name is Amy ... really?" I said, keeping my eyes on her, watchful for any further attempt of her mind-melding.

"David, you have so much to learn and so little time. You know it's no accident that you're here."

"Yes, Amy, and I've also learned that people aren't always as they seem. For some, the art of evasion is a critical technique to hide one's intention," I said, keeping my eyes glued to hers.

"The vision you had last night, do you still think it occurred in this house?" Amy asked, taking a sip from her wine glass.

"Yes, I do."

"And do you think I was the old lady in your vision?"

I paused. "I'm not sure; you don't seem to be her."

"I'm not. Let me ask you, do you believe that this is the only life you have ever lived?" she asked rather pointedly.

"I've had visions of myself in ancient lands, but I'm not sure if they were past lives."

"What else could they be?" she asked, drawing me again into those deep blue eyes that seemed to faintly sparkle. *She's trying to explore me again*, I thought to myself.

"Amy, you said that I don't have time to waste. Why not get to your point?"

"Before I do, tell me, do you see me as friend or foe? Maybe then we can move on," she said, leaning toward me.

"How can I figure that out on a first meeting? I don't know you," I said, unable or not wanting to probe her myself.

"I find it so odd that you look and feel all grownup, yet you seem stuck like a child. Yes, you are spiritually gifted. So why don't you use it to 'know me' for god's sake? Why do you suppose it was given to you?" she asked in a frustrated tone.

Beaux stirred uneasily in his chair.

I closed my eyes and thought, *This is pointless.*

"You think so? Why don't you at least try?" said an old familiar voice from deep within me. *"Take a risk for a change and open yourself to her."*

Trusting Sara's voice, I kept my eyes closed and opened myself as I would when going into an altered state of consciousness. Focusing on Amy, I asked myself, *"Who and what are you?"* The image of her that had appeared, when I first began to focus on her, suddenly became extraordinarily clear.

An aura of energy surrounded her as she stood before me. Her blue eyes somehow opened wider than I thought possible while a small sphere of brilliant white light formed in front of her brow. I couldn't decide on which feature to focus: her alluring eyes that continued to draw me deep within her yet again, or the intensifying sphere of light hovering at her brow.

The ball of light seemed to erupt quietly and projected energy toward me. Again, I felt my consciousness pulled from my body. But this time our consciousness merged. As I felt myself joining with her, new images flew past me as if I had become an observer of someone's life experiences in hyper-speed. I had become a sponge absorbing all of the information that was being shared. Suddenly, this high-speed play of one person's life was over. I felt myself gently guided backwards landing softly on something as if someone was pushing—or perhaps guiding me back onto my overstuffed chair. I opened my eyes and knew this exploratory trip was over, and something else was about to begin while in this altered state of consciousness.

The area around me was dimly lit. I wasn't in Amy's cottage now. My hands touched something familiar. Was I in a room? I couldn't see any walls. The creaking of an old door with rusted hinges opened somewhere in front of me in the dark shadows. There was no change in temperature or scent, which are classic indicators of a demonic presence. I looked intently in the direction of the creaking noise when I felt long, bony fingers touch my shoulder which drew my attention to someone standing to my right.

"What have you discovered?" said the deep voice of the old man who now stood before me. He was a tall figure, with long grayish hair, deep-set eyes similar to Amy's, and wearing some sort of cloak or long gown. It was hard to see in the dim light.

"Who are you?"

"What difference does a name make? We've been waiting for you to learn how to *see* the truth of our shared reality. Yet, you seem attached to your physical existence. It's sad, but all human spirits need this lesson to learn how to deal with what is to come." He waved his bony hand through the air and the room was illuminated a bit more to show some antique furniture, artwork hanging on wood-covered walls, and other strange-looking ornaments.

"Come . . . sit here," the old man said.

"Where am I?"

His look was similar to Amy's when his eyes reached for mine. I wondered if they were related. What he did next felt like he had extended his long arms over to my mind and pulled me into him. This time I was able to concentrate, close my eyes, and turn away. "Damn it, stop doing that," I demanded. "You and Amy must've taken the same course,

'How to Creep Out Your Guest in One Easy Lesson.' I want to know what's going on."

He relaxed in his high-backed chair. "We're trying to push your training along," he said patiently.

"Why? Since I've come into this world, everyone has tried to convince me that this vision stuff is all demonic. A maniac tried to get me to work for him and when he couldn't, he viciously murdered the one person I loved most in this world. And now, you come along and want to accelerate my training as if I've been pursuing a degree in Spookology for years."

"That's because you have been . . . well, not Spookology, but you know what I mean. Everyone who is born into an embodied life is there to learn. It's unfortunate that your learning curve must be accelerated because of a new challenge that has occurred."

"What challenge is that? If I may be so bold to ask."

"Do you recall the conversation you had with Saint Agatha? She mentioned that the man, who had tried to enlist you to work for him, was linked to a powerful dark entity that we know as Maridon."

"And what am I supposed to do with someone like that?" I asked.

"The gift you have is not demonic, as your uncle called it. It is very natural. Some are better able to handle it than others. But, there is a demonic element on this side of the veil, and you have been pursued by a rather powerful group since Lajes. They know what you and others like you are capable of, and they're trying to lure you to work for them."

"Well, whoever they are, they're doing a poor job of convincing me. I don't believe in harming others."

"I understand, but history shows that some of you will choose the other side. How else do you think the demonic clan was created? Ego isn't limited to just embodied spirits. It is what we all train to overcome. While you, David, are making progress, there is still work to be done."

"So, let's try this again. Where am I and why am I here?"

"You are sharing an inner dimension, another form of reality, with the one you know as Amy. She is trying to help you accelerate your training at our request. And, her family is here to offer assistance that you will eventually need if you are to succeed."

"And why should I trust you? You've refused to tell me who you are." As I said that, a small, but brilliant ball of light formed behind him and grew quickly. I saw an image begin to emerge from the ball as it walked toward us. Then I realized who it was.

"I told you he'd be hard-headed, paranoid, and difficult," Sara said, then turned to me. "I thought you would know how to recognize a spiritual mentor given everything we've been through." Motioning to our ancient relic with her long fingers, she continued, "He's right. A name means nothing. You need to learn how to recognize us by the energy we hold. It's unique like the fingerprints of the human body. This one isn't a guide, though. He's more like a commander, if we were talking about the military. The only reason he's here is because we need to kick your ass into gear. Are your eyes open yet?"

"Okay, I got it. So come on, share . . . what am I supposed to be doing?" I asked, a bit more desperately.

"You need to start using what's been given to you and start fighting back. We can't control the affairs of humans," she said. "But, we can help those who are embodied deal with situations like the one that's about to happen."

"See, here we go again, Sara. You communicate like the rest of this so-called highly evolved crowd. You guys tease me with tiny bits of information, and then you get a little testy when I don't guess the right answers," I said impatiently.

"You don't have to guess, Dave. You already know the answer . . . at least some of them," Sara responded.

"Okay, so why not give me a hint about what's going to happen next and why I don't have time to waste."

"Gawd, Dave, a snail crawls faster in dripping molasses in an Arctic storm than your thinking. Okay, so what do you sense about your—our—enemy?"

"Since he couldn't convince me to switch sides, he took Linda away from me as the price of my decision," I said.

"Correct, and do you have any other emerging relationships that he could use for an encore performance?" she asked.

I felt my heart and my breath freeze. The answer was what drove me to meet Amy. "Sherry. You said it would be okay if I opened myself to her. Why?" I asked in sudden panic.

"Grow up. You're the only one that can stop what's about to happen, but you've gotta get back there to do it."

My eyes opened to find Amy still sitting in the chair across from me. This time she was leaning back and relaxing with her long, shapely legs crossed. I hadn't noticed them before. She had the look of a person who's thinking, "*I told you so.*" Beaux was standing next to her with the inevitable look of *"What the hell's going on?"*

"So how do you think you'll engage the enemy?" she asked, as if she already knew the answer.

"I don't know. The only thing I do know is that someone's got it in for me and is doing everything they can to make it hurt, and they'll harm anyone close to me the longer I resist their will," I said with a sense of urgency.

Amy smiled as if her new student was beginning to wake up. "Well, you're getting closer. So, do you want to know what happened and how it's possible?" she asked.

"Gee, let me think about that for a moment . . . would that be crucial?" I asked sarcastically.

"You know there's nothing helpful about sarcasm," she said.

"All right, but I've got to go. Besides, I can't believe you'd ask such an obvious question."

She stood up and walked to the window looking as if she was studying her wine glass as she walked. "Okay, now that you know a bit more, there's something you also need to know about the enemy you're facing. Your vision the other night wasn't taking you here. The entity lured you into a place that looked like this cottage. And, the old woman you saw wasn't me. This was done to dissuade you from trusting my counsel."

"I've come to understand that. So, how do I defend myself against such illusions?"

"This entity has many talents, one of which is shape-shifting. This is why what you and I did just now, our mergence of energy, is important," Amy said.

"So, you're saying for me to know what's in front of me is real, I'll have to engage the enemy by entering their mind. That doesn't sound smart to me," I said in disbelief.

"If you can enter a person's mind just as you did with me, then that person is real."

"So what happens if it's a demonic servant of Maridon?" I asked.

"You'll have only a few seconds to intuit what it is. But, the one thing he will do to lure you into his trap is offering something that entices you, but it's really just the store front to hell," Amy insisted.

"Oh that helps . . . what about the place the entity took me to, then. What can you tell me about that?"

"He created a kind of holographic environment to make it seem as real as what surrounds you now. He was able to do this because your skills are not refined enough. But, had you had time, you would've been able to figure it out."

"Amy, I really need to go," I said getting up and moving toward the door. Beaux followed.

She walked with me and said, "There's one more thing. You need to release your intuitive skills and allow them to work for you. To detect any of Maridon's soldiers, you'll have to be sensitive to their energy. Remember, this thing can attack you directly but, for some reason, doesn't want to. So, it's going after anyone who's close to you."

"I think I know who it's going after now and it's what I've been afraid of since I got here. But, I'm curious. If this thing is going after anyone I'm close to, will it go after Beaux?"

"No, at least I don't think so. If it did, the entity would have his entire family after it. And this family isn't something to toy with," Amy said with a note of pride in her voice.

"Really, and why's that?" I asked.

"There is more than one way to battle your enemies. You can do what's obvious, hitting them in the physical, or you can attack them on their home turf. Some see this as a kind of black magic using curses and potions, it's not. That's an amateur's view of the whole thing. Spiritual confrontations are often quite unusual to observe and unbelievable to be a part of. You're not going to understand if you haven't experienced it," said Amy.

"Are you telling me Beaux's family leads a double life?" I asked.

"That's one way to think of it, I suppose. If something attacks one of us, we don't bother with physical reality; we go right to the source which is always found in the world of spirits."

My attention slowly turned to Beaux as I began to realize he understood more than he had let on and was the reason he had introduced me to his family. I was being accepted into a gathering of Spiritual Warriors. "Beaux, is this why we're here, with your family?" I asked.

He looked at Amy as if silently asking permission to answer. "He already knows the answer, nephew," she said.

"I think I know, but I would like another opinion. Do you think Sherry is being targeted?" I asked.

Those remarkably beautiful eyes locked on me once again as Amy said, "Again, you already know the answer, David, don't you?"

This realization hit me hard, as if I had been standing on the railroad tracks and a speeding freight train had crushed my body. My nerves tightened, sweat began pouring out of me, and the sense of urgency finally bolted me out of the cottage yelling over my shoulder to Beaux, "I have to get back to the base . . . NOW!"

Chapter 22

"Damn it, this is all my fault. If anything happens to Sherry . . ." I was deeply conflicted and Beaux knew it given that I was talking to myself. No doubt he was used to members of his family going inward, but as I caught myself revealing what troubled me the most, I wondered if his family would have handled this differently.

After a while, he added, "We'll be back on base in a couple of hours. Try to relax and let my guys do what they do." If there had been any doubt in his mind, he was now well aware of my anxiety concerning Sherry given that Linda was murdered by these "people." I had gone along to meet Beaux's aunt hoping she would know more about who and what I was up against, but the time for an in-depth exchange vanished when she confirmed the imminent danger that I had sensed all along.

After leaving the cottage, we rushed back to his family gathering to thank them and say our goodbyes. I wasn't surprised to find that they had relatives and friends in the Louisiana State Highway Patrol, along with most of the parish sheriff departments on the way back to our base. With Beaux driving at breakneck speed, we weren't pulled over and in fact had a friendly police escort to the Mississippi border.

We stopped for gas after crossing the state line. While I was filling up the car, Beaux checked in with his shop at Kessler. "No luck. None of my guys have been able to locate her," he said as we got back into the car.

"Do they know if she's still on base?" I asked with a sense of desperation.

"Nope. One of my guys stopped by her barracks and checked with the house matron. She said that Sherry went out for the night, hoping her boyfriend would be back soon and that he would catch up with her at the NCO Club."

Damn it. I've got to find her. She's in danger and again I'm not around to do what I'm supposed to do, I thought to myself. There was something excessive about feeling a strong responsibility as a protector that had been bothering me since Linda's murder and now again with Sherry. I had to put this out of my mind and think. For now, there were no real options except being patient. But patience wasn't one of my virtues, if I had any at all, especially when the safety of people I cared for was involved. Beaux could see I was about to burst out of my skin.

"Dave . . . look at me . . . come on . . . look at me." I turned to him. "I know this is tough. But, you can't be everywhere right now. You need to rely on others. And in this case, you need to trust that my crew's out there doing everything they can to find her," he said, his voice full of sincerity.

I took a deep breath. "I know, Beaux. It's just that this can't be happening again. Who am I that these . . . evil entities are focusing their hatred on me by hurting the people I care most about?"

"Buddy, you've got to stay focused on things you can influence right now. And, when this is over, you need to spend more time with Auntie. She's your mentor in all things spiritual from now on—you know that, don't you?"

I closed my eyes to get a sense of it, and it felt right, or at least in regard to physical reality, but again, something seemed incomplete. Regardless, I still had Sara on the other side of the veil.

"Thanks for introducing me, but I can't help but wonder: does she really need this kind of trouble in her life?" I asked.

"Well, if you weren't part of the 'Big Picture,' I'm sure she would've sent you on your way. But, right now, don't blow up in my car; I just had it cleaned," he said with a smirky grin.

I tried to smile but couldn't. "Beaux, one of the many things I don't understand is that while I was flying back to Lajes from Germany, I tranced out and saw what was about to happen to Linda. I'd never had an experience like that before." I paused for a moment to collect myself. "But this time, there's been nothing. I can't get a hint of anything. Whoever's controlling what I can see from the other side is holding back, and I just don't understand why. How's that helpful? Hell, it's not even fair!" I said angrily.

"Auntie told me a long time ago, Dave, that these gifts always work much better when you're relaxed and not trying to force things. Right now, you're super-tense, not to mention you always prefer doing things yourself rather than relying on anyone. Maybe the test here is realizing you're part of a family now, my family, which includes my guys at work." I nodded my head knowing he was right, but I still couldn't slow down my mind. Beaux continued, "You know there's no accidents in life, so whatever is supposed to be . . . will be."

"Okay, I get some of that, but don't tell me I can't change anything. Sherry's only crime was getting mixed up with me. Sitting back and accepting her death as inevitable isn't an option, Beaux. You know me better than that."

I never felt so helpless, but Beaux was right in one regard: I'd been told by teachers from the other side how visions can be blocked when a person is pressing too hard. But wasn't this different? What purpose did another person's death serve? The evil ones got the message: nothing will bend me to their will. And why wouldn't my guides help her or let me protect her?

We had about an hour before arriving on base. I leaned back in the seat, closed my eyes, and did what I could to lower the near-panic state that was tearing me apart. The car's vibrations and the music Beaux was playing helped. I closed my eyes, and my mind began to slow down and focus on Sherry. But, the intensity of my desire to be with her, to keep her safe, only grew.

Our last time together replayed in my head. I saw us walking in the park on base, and then began to smell a strong aroma of newly blossomed wild flora. Everything shifted to images of blue and yellow flowers in a field surrounded by thick evergreens and hardwood trees swaying gently in the breeze. I could still feel her hand holding mine, her head resting on my shoulder as we enjoyed the nature that surrounded us.

"Open yourself, child, and relax," a soothing voice said. As I did so, Sherry drifted away from me and a familiar set of hands grabbed me underneath my shoulders and propelled me upward, giving me a friendly version of a "bum's rush." We flew gracefully through the air and soared over the trees then circled the meadow where I had just been standing with Sherry. It felt so relaxing that all of the panic and tension of the current situation vanished. My unseen escorts took me up higher into the sky toward the only visible clouds around us. As we approached them, I could see numerous thin tendrils of spiraling energy being drawn into their center as if something was hiding behind them. The energy seemed to disappear inside their core and then the clouds parted as a portal opened. It was through this portal that my escorts took me.

On the other side, I found myself hovering over Kessler Air Force Base. We watched a car followed by a pickup truck approach the intersection below us. With both stopped, the driver of the truck walked to the driver's side of the car and leaned on the door.

Suddenly, without provocation, the man pulled the driver partially out of the driver's-side window and began slashing the person with a knife. I sensed that the knife had been used in ceremonies or sacrifices from ancient times. It was then I recognized this weapon as the same one that had been used on Linda. The assailant appeared to be experiencing some kind of demonic pleasure from slowly taking this person's life while causing them intense fear. When he was done with the now-lifeless innocent driver, he turned and held the body up so I could see what was left of the person's face. It was Sherry.

A vengeance-driven anger exploded within me as I tried to attack her assailant who was more beast than human. My escorts held me back. A deep, reassuring voice said, "Vengeance is not yours to take. A time is coming, friend, when this wrong will be repaid. Be patient. We are showing you this to help you cope now and to know it's not in vain."

"But, she doesn't deserve this! I can't fail her, too," I screamed in utter helpless desperation.

"You have not failed her as you did not fail Linda. What you see this entity destroying is just the vessel. The soul is a part of us and she will live on forever. No one can change that . . . do you understand?"

I felt someone shaking me as I was jolted back into my present awareness inside Beaux's car. He had pulled over when I began to scream and shook me back into this reality.

"What the hell happened? Are you all right?" he asked.

After telling him what I saw, Beaux asked if I could describe the pickup truck, the psychopath, or the traffic intersection. My visions seem fairly clear when I'm in them, but when I'm back in this reality, the details can sometimes be very difficult to recall. I did the best I could to answer his questions; Beaux made another stop and phoned his dispatcher to share what little information I was able to provide.

We were back on base well after sunset. The evening entertainment available to the base occupants was already in full swing. Beaux's first stop was the cop shop to swap out his personal vehicle for his police unit, to put on his uniform, and to share some ideas of what to do next with a couple of his officers who met us there. While doing so, he seemed preoccupied with something else.

"Beaux, if you're worried about what to do with me, I promise not to do anything crazy," I said, trying to reassure him.

"Yeah, right. I can just see you not doing anything crazy like scouring the base looking for her and then stumbling into her assailant. Yep, noth'in stupid," he said sarcastically.

"Beaux, you can't expect me to just wait around for someone to call and say, hey, we found'm," I said.

"Okay, that's it. I can't trust you by yourself. So, you're coming with me. At least I can keep an eye on you while everyone else is doing their job," he said.

His crew had checked the NCO and Airmen's Clubs, the theater, and other businesses on base, but didn't find her. That was unnerving because if she was attacked off base, there was nothing we could do. I was about to leave Beaux's unit and look for Sherry in town on my own when the dispatcher called.

"Blue Five, dispatch."

"Dispatch, Blue Five, go ahead."

"Possible 10-187 at G and 3rd. Unit on-scene, request you proceed immediately. OSI advised."

"10-4, any other info available?"

"Blue 5, the unit believes this is your target. It appears to have just occurred."

"Dispatch, roger, lock the base down immediately, inform the upline NOW!"

Beaux had gone lights-and-siren when he heard 10-187, which was the code for a felony assault. We weren't that far away, and I was desperately hoping that Beaux's troops had arrived in time and she would pull through.

"Listen to me clearly, Sergeant Lussier," Beaux said. I knew when I heard this form of address that he was serious. "When we arrive on scene, you are to stay in this vehicle. Do you understand? And, while we're en route, if you see a pickup truck that looks like the one in your vision, you tell me, got it?"

"Yes, Beaux, I got it."

"I mean it David; you stay in this vehicle when we roll up on-scene. And don't give me any problems," he said sternly.

We pulled up behind a police unit used by one of Beaux's crew which was parked behind Sherry's car. An ambulance was in the street blocking the intersection. I couldn't see much detail because of all the flashing lights and the people walking around.

Beaux was about to exit our unit when he slapped a handcuff on my left wrist and then applied the other cuff to a steel bracket that held the radio. "David, I can't take any chances. You've got to stay here. I'll take these off when I come back." And with that said, Beaux was out of the car.

My mind was racing with all sorts of possibilities, and yet there was this tiny bit of hope that just maybe she was still alive. That sliver of hope drove me to struggle with the handcuffs, trying to free myself and leave Beaux's unit. I was shaking, almost nauseous. Could I handle seeing her knowing what had probably transpired? I couldn't get out of Beaux's restraints, so I gave up struggling and sat back in the seat.

I tried to relax, thinking I would leave my body and go to her. But, I was too hyped-up to make the connection and nothing would work. Sometimes the mind will create what feels like an alternative reality, so it doesn't have to deal with painful circumstances. But this time, instead of wanting to escape from the hell of this moment, I desperately wanted to be within the reality of it.

I felt a hand rest upon my shoulder surprising me. Then, I felt myself leave my body and exit the car. Someone gently pulled me toward them as they stood outside the unit. The image of the person in front of me was blurred by my streaming tears that I could no longer contain; I heard a familiar voice whisper in my ear, "I love you, David. I love you so much and now you know without any doubt."

While I tried to listen to the person's voice, what was happening in the street seemed like an illusion. Had time retreated to allow me to enjoy one last moment with Sherry? Perhaps this was an alternate outcome rather than what I was going to have to live with for the rest of my life. Or, was

Sherry really standing next to me, holding me, and saying these sweet words . . . something I wanted to hear but couldn't allow.

My vision finally cleared enough to see Sherry standing next to me in a translucent form. I saw her smiling face, as her open, loving soul pulled me into her heart, and that was the last thing I remembered.

"I should've known you wouldn't follow instructions," I heard a voice say, as I came back into my body. "Your wrist should heal in a few days. How do you feel?" Beaux said.

"I'm okay," I said, as I sat with my back against the ambulance rubbing my right wrist. I told him what I remembered, that I felt someone pull my spirit out of my body to see Sherry one last time. "How long have I been gone?"

"Not long, your wrist looks like you would've cut off your hand if you could have."

"I don't remember that part, Beaux."

"Wanna know what we got so far?" Beaux asked.

"Yeah, let's get on with it."

"We found a witness that saw the whole thing. And, we got a description of Sherry's assailant and the truck. He doesn't seem too smart or just doesn't care about being caught."

"Beaux, the guy who murdered Linda wasn't concerned about that either. When the Portuguese police caught up with him, it was obvious he couldn't get away, yet he didn't hesitate to fight them to the death. So, if your guys find him, make sure they know," I said emphatically.

"Don't worry about my crew, Dave. They'll take care of business. Besides, I doubt we'll find him on base. It's more likely the civilian cops will take him down."

"So, what kind of shape was she in?" I asked with a shaken voice.

Beaux turned away and took a deep breath as if he needed to think how to answer. "She was in rough shape. And, she didn't die right away. That asshole cut her up pretty good and just left her hang'n outta the car window to bleed out." He took a long breath to find the strength to continue. "The unit that found her was only a few minutes away when she was attacked. They stumbled onto the scene by accident. When they got to her, the truck was gone, but she was still breathing."

"Did she say anything?"

"Not right away, she was in shock. You know the hospital's only three blocks from this intersection. My guys called for an ambulance and they were here pretty quick. We arrived right after them."

"Beaux, I need to know what she said," I pleaded.

"Something about she didn't understand, and she was just trying to help. But then the EMTs figured she knew she was going to die, and she told them to make sure you knew that she loved you, that she loved you more than life itself."

My mind tripped back to all the moments that Sherry had helped me cope with everything that had happened since Linda's death. The feeling of her arm around my waist pulling me toward her—reminding me of her gentle playful tugs when we were out on dates—was a kind of confirmation that it was her. I shared the memory with Beaux and that was the first time I saw him lose it.

As we went back to the cop shop, Beaux told me that he had no intention of leaving me alone for the next few days. He decided to take me back to his home after he completed some paperwork. Before we could leave his office, though, the situation changed.

"Hey Sarge, an OSI investigator's here to talk with you guys. He says he wants to speak with your buddy, and he doesn't seem real happy," the dispatcher said, sticking his head in Beaux's office.

"Great, that's all we need right now. Does the old man know?"

"Yeah, he showed up just before the suit did."

"Okay, tell'm what's going on, and see if he can get us outta talk'n with the guy for a day or two."

"Will do, sir." The dispatcher hurried down the hall to deliver the request. Just as he disappeared, a short man dressed in the stereotypical government black suit and tie slid around the corner like a deadly serpent slithering into position to finish its prey. He displayed a hungry smile as if he knew dinner was being served. I whispered to Beaux, "I don't like the look or feel of this guy. Don't forget who got me into this mess. If they're connected, this could get dangerous real fast."

"So, you must be Sergeant Lussier," the salivating serpent said, "who sees things that aren't there, but leaves a mess everywhere he goes." The guy couldn't have been taller than 5 and a half feet, perhaps thinking he could make up for his lack of stature with brashness.

"And you would know because you do the same?" I asked with a sarcastic sneer.

"Sergeant, are you being disrespectful?" he asked, as if to remind me of our difference in rank.

Beaux stepped in between us and asked, "And you are who? Keep in mind you're in my building and in a secure area. Either present some ID right now, or I'll have you in a cell."

The predatory smile tightened as if he enjoyed the stare-down. He slowly pulled out his credentials and presented them for Beaux to examine. Then, he pushed past him and continued his verbal assault. "Word has it, one of our recruiters was interested in you, and her interest got her killed a few months ago."

"Really? Sounds like you need a more reliable source of information. If you are who you say you are, that shouldn't be hard to find," I rejoined, questioning his authority over me.

This had the desired effect. "I could have you placed in protective custody until I'm through interviewing your ass about what just happened," said the miniature secret agent wanna-be.

"It would be nice to know who the hell you are. Do you mind introducing yourself? I believe that's part of the mandated protocol," I said.

"He's Captain Randall Chandler," Beaux said.

"My file shows you have had quite an adventure in Germany and then found that your girlfriend was murdered in the apartment you two shared at Lajes," he said, trying to provoke me.

"And what does that have to do with this . . . incident?" I asked, barely keeping myself under control.

The guy poked a finger into my chest. "I decide what's relevant and what's not, Airman, not you."

That was all I could take, and I pushed the guy back. Beaux instantly thrust himself between us, restraining me with a barrel grip around my chest, which kept my arms at my side. Had I actually struck Chandler, as I wanted to, I would've played into his game.

"Now gentlemen, we need to calm this down. I don't know about you, Captain Chandler, but we've had a very stressful day. Sergeant Lussier isn't an Airman, he's earned his stripes and has done nothing wrong, so why are you acting as if he's the culprit here?" Beaux asked, still restraining me.

Chandler stayed back but stared intently up at me and asked, "How much interaction did you have with Steven Bullard? I believe he contacted you on Lajes after the death of our agent."

"Yeah, Bullard tried to get me to work for him . . . just him, not the Air Force or any other government agency. And, he's the one who's been ordering the deaths of . . ." I was yelling at Chandler, when Beaux cut me off and pushed me back further.

"Look Chandler, the woman murdered today was a friend of the Sergeant, and he's pretty stressed out. Let's . . ." Beaux was interrupted by Major Canton bursting into the room. He was a good six foot three inches tall and black as the ace of spades.

He stood between us, further widening the gap. "All right, who the hell are you and what's going on in here?" the Major demanded.

Chandler produced his ID and introduced himself again. Then he insisted on clearing the room so he would have me to himself under his authority as the OSI investigating agent. The Major didn't buy it.

"Yeah right. Look Captain Chandler, I'm ordering you to leave this building and have your Commander call me. You have not been identified as the agent in charge of this homicide. Until I get clearance from up the line, no one has permission to interview anyone without my express permission. Beyond the violation of standard protocol, you have no probable cause to interrogate this Sergeant since he's not a person of interest in this case. His time and whereabouts have been confirmed. So essentially, he's of no use to this investigation," the major said firmly, just inches away from Chandler's face, though he did have to bend down to deliver his message eye to eye.

After stammering for a moment, Chandler began to retreat. But as he did so, he said over his shoulder, "I'll see you soon, Sergeant Lussier. You can bet on that."

After Chandler left, the dispatcher hurried back into the room. "Sir, is that OSI guy still here?"

"No, why do you ask, Airman?" the Major asked.

"I don't think he was from our OSI group because their office just called. Their investigating officer will be delayed."

Chapter 23

"Welcome to Louisiana, again," Beaux smirked as we drove across the Mississippi border. The road trip had been quiet so far. After the incident with Chandler at the cop shop, it became apparent that certain members of the OSI had hidden agendas that the Security Police knew nothing about. Everyone thought that my reassignment back to the U.S. would end any involvement with whomever, or whatever was creating the havoc around me.

The goal of this splinter group was more than likely control and dominance for purposes not yet known. And, it was obvious that those within this rogue group were willing to sell their souls to gain access to a path of dark power, if that's what it took to obtain what they lusted for most. Even though I knew some of them, I still didn't know with certainty who they were really working for in this reality. All I knew was they were controlled by a dark, powerful entity. Their total disregard for the value of life was beyond imagination. Whoever they were, they were about as close to a real life definition of "Evil" as any I could image.

What to do next was anyone's guess. It was the Thanksgiving holiday, and the Air Traffic Control School at Kessler Air Force Base was closed. A decision was made to remove me from my class and temporarily assign me to

Beaux's unit until this situation was resolved. So, I was back in "the game" that I had wanted to avoid after Linda's death. The evil ones continued to pursue me, and this wasn't going to stop until one of us, or all of us, were dead.

The thing about people who have limited life experiences or are unaware of the existence of the astral plane is that they are oblivious to the ugliest realities humans can create. The downside is that if they're drawn into one or more of those realities, they may not know what to do. For those who knew about my "events," often commented, "Gee, can't you see when these things are about to happen?" Or, "Surely you can see who's actually behind all of this, can't you?" The answer was generally, no.

I had always thought my unseen teacher/guides controlled what I was able to see, but I was beginning to learn that's not always true. When they used my exposure as a teaching tool, there was a good reason. But others, like Maridon, could intrude. And, as a result, I began to view the scope of my ability as being limited, like a child learning to ride a bike. You have to start with training wheels or limited sight. This can become a crutch if you question your competence in dealing with paranormal issues. But back then, there was no one in this reality who could teach this material to others like you can teach math, history, or any of the "how to" professions that everyone relies upon. So I had to accept the risks, trust myself, and know that my guides were always with me.

We rolled up and parked at the path that led to Auntie's cottage. Though Beaux and his family liked to refer to her as Auntie, she was Amy to me. This was the name her mother gave her, and one that seemed more appealing given her youthful appearance. Besides, this name and its personage, once again, resonated deep within me and I didn't know why.

Amy was a few years older than me, but she looked and felt more like someone who could interact with anyone. In fact, she seemed ageless in a way, like I had known her from different lifetimes.

Her lithesome appearance, long full brownish-red hair was rather lush, and I wondered how her loosely grouped strands would feel moving slowly through my fingers. Her eyes were a deep blue with the most unusual thin gold band around the iris, making them come alive in a mysterious way that grabbed my attention every time I saw her.

As Beaux and I walked up the path to her cottage, I began to feel safe again . . . almost relaxed. There was a presence that surrounded her home that was palpable and protective. Beaux knew this, too, which was his reason for me staying with her.

"Beaux!" Amy said as she blew through the front door to greet us. She kissed him on the cheek, and then turned and once again focused her attention solely on me. She never looked "at" me, but always looked deep within me and linked up with whatever she touched. I could feel her pull me into her heart, or at least that's what it felt like.

Our connection felt more like our energy touching and briefly merging at times as if it had been done many times before, and we both knew it, or I did at some level. Whatever she was initiating, we had begun a kind of rekindling—a work from long ago that needed to be finished, or so it seemed.

"Come in, both of you. We need to talk," she said rather urgently.

Her home had a different feel from when I was there last. Did I really belong here and just didn't know it? Did I have roots here, deep roots? When we were seated in the living room, she sat across from me and said, "You have, you know; you just can't remember."

"I have what?" I said curiously just to verify what she meant.

"Roots here. You were just thinking that," she said with a smile.

"Why is that?" I asked, wondering about the reach of her mind-reading.

"It's part of the contract. No one is allowed to remember all of their previous lifetimes for good reason. How would we learn anything if we could remember our history back to the very beginning? If we make good decisions, we evolve and move on to higher forms of learning," she said. "And, if we don't . . . but let's not dwell on that."

"That's great, but what am I supposed to be learning now? This struggle feels more like I'm in way over my head."

She leaned toward me and took my hands in hers as she said, "Darl'n, you are in over your head. These kinds of lessons normally occur over an entire lifetime. You, on the other hand, do not have that luxury. Your life-lessons had to be accelerated and condensed to months not years. You can't stop now, even if you want to, because our enemy has focused on you. You're going to have to deal with it if you want to survive. And believe me, it's not just you who's threatened. There are many others like you who have been accelerated. And, just to confirm what you sense: things are start'n to get a little out of hand."

"Really? And why's that?" I asked.

"Because we have a growing problem. You know that the embodied soul has free will. Well, as you've sensed, those souls who have never been embodied and who are part of the world of dark energy can influence their targets—get them to deceive and, if need be, murder others to accomplish their goals."

"My visions have never spoken to anything that would appear to affect anyone but me and those that I'm related to in some way," I said in an irritated tone.

Amy looked away, as if she had suddenly shifted her focus to someplace else or perhaps some unseen audience who was telling her what to say next. She finally added, "Well, this is your lucky day. You've occasionally asked for face-time with those who guide your guides over the years, but they have refused for good reason. These master teachers guide everything, the master plan, so to speak, who embodied souls rarely ever see or have become involved in this level of . . . operation.

"But now, they think it's best that we let you observe what we're talking about. You're going to be introduced to the enemy on his home turf. Are you in?"

"I thought I already met him on the island. What would you be showing me that's different?"

She leaned forward as she crossed her long gorgeous legs and allowed the hint of a knowing smile to appear on her ageless face as she said, "Oh honey, you didn't meet the enemy. You met someone who was in league with him, a dupe who believes he's on a winning team, when in fact he's just being used. You need to see exactly what you're up against to understand. So, are you ready?"

I wasn't sure I wanted to go on this guided tour with her. Any foray to the other side in search of who knows what would be filled with risk. But, then again, what choice did I have? I could feel my heart begin to beat in near panic as I asked, "How long will we be gone?"

"Where we're go'in, darl'n, there's no relationship between time that passes here and what passes there," she said.

"I don't understand."

She leaned back in her chair and looked more thoughtful as she decided what to say. "Time is relative and unique to each dimension, and if you haven't figured it out yet, there's far more dimensions, or realities than just the one we're in."

"Yeah, I got that. But, I thought time was universal."

"It's universal in the sense that it exists, but no, it's anything but consistent when you move between realities. Your visions haven't demonstrated that yet because up to now, you haven't had a need to understand this concept. Besides, it's only one reference we have within the reality dimension that we're in currently. So, where we're going, you'll think a day has gone by. When we return here, you may think that only a few minutes have elapsed. It just depends, and don't ask me what it depends on because I don't know. All I know is what's happened each time I've gone there."

And with that, she stood up and looked at Beaux. "I need you to hang out here and make sure we don't have any surprises when we return. You know what happened the last time."

"Got it. I'll call Dad and ask if we can get some of the family to drop over just in case," he said with a smile.

"Surprises? What happened last time you did this?" I asked, as Beaux was going to leave the room to call home.

"Ohhh, noth'in much. We were just trying to help someone out and ended up with a few unwanted visitors here that had to be smacked around a little," Beaux said with a mischievous grin.

"Well, don't put out the welcome mat," I said, figuring we'd have our hands full on the other side.

Amy impatiently added, "Okay, here's a little advice. We might run into someone you don't wanna be friends with and these will be the kind that are gonna wanna hurt us real bad. This is where it gets entertaining. If we're attacked, we can be hurt, but we can't be killed because we're in our energy bodies. But, if they figure out where our physical bodies are, then they can make it impossible for us to come back. Get my mean'n?"

"Got it, so let's prevent that," I said wearily.

"Okay, for sure," she said as she reached for my hand. "Come with me." Amy escorted me into her bedroom and asked, "Which side of the bed do you want?"

"Uh, wait a minute . . . the bed?" I asked.

"I want you near me all the time here and there. Beaux will protect our bodies while we're gone. And, for us to do what we gotta do, it helps to be relaxed as we trip-out. So, pick a side and plant it, big boy."

As we laid next to each other, Amy held my hand. Moving into a relaxed state, we began the process of exiting the body. Feeling her close to me felt natural for some reason and it accelerated the transition. I moved through the physical veil and exited this dimension as I've done so many times in the past. But this time, I had a partner and tour guide. When we exited and stood next to the bed, our astral energy bodies looked just like our physical bodies. Beaux didn't see us as he sat in the living room getting comfortable while waiting for reinforcements.

A rushing sound behind me caught my attention, and I turned to see a portal open in the bedroom wall that emitted an abundance of radiant light. I could feel us being drawn toward it as if being inhaled by some sort of large vortex. As the rate of our movement accelerated, the feeling of a large unseen hand grabbed us and began pulling us aggressively through the now- swirling mass of brilliant energy.

Once through the portal, we entered the hallway of an ancient castle with tall, dark walls that looked familiar. This was a place I had been to several times in earlier travels throughout my life. Obviously, this was some sort of way station to the other side.

My attention was drawn to the same paintings of people on the walls from different periods. We continued moving, but instead of stopping or turning a corner, we accelerated even more and I braced for impact at the end of the hallway as I had each time in the past.

We transitioned through the wooden wall easily as if it didn't exist. On the other side, we ended up in another environment that looked and felt odd. There was something unnatural about this pastoral setting. It had the feeling of having been ravaged in some way yet it was not obvious. We were surrounded by grass and trees that covered rolling terrain while mountains completed the picture in the distance. Yet this all seemed unnatural, like parts of it didn't belong here or it had been manipulated in some way.

As we flew low across the tree tops and lush meadows, Amy looked at me smiling and said, "We have to stay low. The group we're trying to avoid will know someone came through the portal, but they won't know who we are. Once we crossed into their world, we'll be seen as threats." Her smile was comforting, but I had no idea what we were about to see or do.

We passed a tree line as she led me into a particularly lush green meadow. Again, as natural and clean as it looked, there was something missing. Then I felt as if a colony of ants were trying to climb my spine. I always had this sensation when something dark was about to happen. "Who would be looking for us?" I asked Amy as my scan intensified.

"Those who live here. Have you noticed how nice this place looks? I've discovered it's all fake in a way . . . or not complete. You can feel that, right?" Amy was looking around us intently as we landed in what looked like tall green grass. Then, I began to feel something rumbling from deep within me. The disturbance quickly transitioned into pain that was changing rapidly. It was as if something had come to life within me and was now forcibly pushing itself out of my body, more like giving birth than expunging something alien. One way or another, it was coming out. I dropped to my knees and braced myself.

Amy turned to look at me and smiled. "I see the ancient warrior in you has returned."

"What are you . . ." I stammered, as I began to feel like this thing was trying to burst from me . . . or perhaps through me? It became impossible to tolerate any longer. I looked down at myself to see what was happening. I was shocked to find what looked like two bodies trying to occupy the same space but were slightly out of sync. The other body competing for my bodily space was far more physically developed, wearing some kind of tunic covered in a steel mesh and it wore heavy, hob-nailed sandals. My new arrival began to move more aggressively to displace me, or separate itself from me.

As I became more unnerved by the bizarre experience, I focused on Amy. "What's happening to ... " Then, I noticed something similar happening to her. "Amy!"

She smiled and said, "Stop resisting him, David. Just let him come." She leaned her head back as if she were looking at the sky in relief, held her arms up, and just stood there. Whatever was in her slipped out and seemed to further pull the warrior out of me as well. The shapes of the two entities became recognizable as human forms, one female, the other male. This transformation was something new, and I wanted to observe it more closely, but it was quickly over. My curiosity now held me captive as I wanted to know more about these two despite my exhaustion.

Their appearances revealed well-developed physiques. But, despite the hardness of their bodies, there was an allure about them of being open, attractive, and connected with each other. Their apparel looked as if they were part of a fighting force that frequently savaged their enemy in the shield walls of ancient times. The female's body was equally muscled as the male. Her long dark hair enhanced her appearance with a complicated braid. A tunic and wire mesh adorned her body similar to her male companion, but had added protection for her adequately shaped breasts.

He, on the other hand, had blonde shoulder-length hair, thick and wavy. Interestingly, he stood equal to her not just in height, but in every other observable aspect.

Their scabbards held swords that looked like the spatha used by the soldiers of the Roman Empire. But, the hilts were far more ornate and longer, similar to the Celtic tribes of the post-Roman period. I had the sense that these swords were more ritualistic than battle-hardened. I also sensed that by being patient, the truth of it all would be revealed soon.

While I assessed these new arrivals, the two embraced as if they had not seen each other for centuries. Finally, the female warrior separated from her lover, and said to him softly, "We are here, now." She continued with a commanding tone over her shoulder to us, "You have nothing to be worried about."

"Who are you?" I asked dumfounded.

"We are . . .you. Can you not see that?" she asked in disbelief. Now she had my attention. The science of what she claimed made no sense. How can I be looking at myself? Then, an awareness grew within me that changed my perspective—a broadening of my limited viewpoint might be one way of describing it. What if a soul is, in fact, embodied more than once as claimed by Eastern religions? Would it be possible to meet another version of yourself during an out-of body-experience such as this? If this was the case, neither of them looked like us, but they just seemed all too familiar in a way that could not be explained otherwise.

"Uhhh . . . no . . . sorry, I don't see that. You two don't look anything like us."

Amy began laughing, obviously, at me. "You're gonna be such a handful. We've been embodied many times down through the ages. These two are us from an ancient era," she said, then paused. "So, what stands out to you about them?"

"What stands out, besides the lack of a physical resemblance, is that I don't like fighting at all. In fact, I avoid it because like begets like and just causes more of the same. And, since I value life, why would I kill someone?" I said incredulously. The mere thought of such an act was repulsive to me.

"Darlin', these two only fight when they must . . . especially the entities that will find us eventually. Remember, they come from a different time. That's the first thing I hoped you'd see. The other thing, which is just too noticeable, is that . . . they love each other. Aren't you get'n a sense of familiarity from any of this?"

As Amy said that, it felt like an old door to a hidden closet in the back of a room slowly opened. There was a sudden rush of wind carrying endless streams of history that had long been forgotten, and it filled me with the life experiences of these two and the spiritual bloodline of my existence.

"Try not to be too upset, darl'n. You—he—were good at everything you did, especially when you fought."

"Amy, this is a bit overwhelming . . . all this ancient information."

"Look at it this way, each time we live, we learn and grow, adding another layer of knowledge to the onionskin of our lives. If we're successful over time, and we keep build'n new layers, what we're do'n is evolving ourselves. So, it's no wonder, David, your reaction isn't unusual. You're becoming aware of what you were long ago. It's the very reason why we aren't permitted to remember our past."

"Thanks Amy, I needed that. But when do the major alarms going off inside me all go away? Something's about to happen and it ain't gonna be fun."

The male warrior's attention was drawn to the tree line behind Amy.

"We should move . . . now," he said firmly.

The female warrior took off toward an opening in the trees while the male warrior pushed us along. As we ran, I had to ask Amy, "Just curious, but what do we call these two? Certainly not Ancient Amy and Ancient Dave."

"You need not concern yourself with names. You won't be here that long," the male warrior interjected in a deep commanding voice.

We passed through the opening in the forest and entered a valley surrounded by another ridge of mountains.

Within this valley, I saw a stone structure ahead surrounded on three sides by a smaller forest. The structure looked imposing and dark, and was built as if it were always ready to defend itself against any intruder who would dare come too close. Odd, one would think there would be an army of defenders on the ramparts, and in the towers. And yet, I could see no one. A palpable energy, though, was present that seemed ready to explode in violent hatred at us should we continue toward its walls.

As we stood there in the broad area in front of the foreboding structure, I wondered why this place seemed so dark yet we were surrounded by the light of day. A feeling of darkness pervaded it, as if residing within was a kind of deadly creature starving for its next meal. I tried to ignore what I felt so I could study what I was seeing. But the more I tried, the worse this distraction became. Whatever was inside did not want us nearby and it was ready to deal with us. The sense of an impending battle began to build as if whatever resided here was about to explode from within and destroy everything, including us.

We moved to a small knoll opposite the structure, which placed us farther away from the gates and there we waited. The female warrior drew her sword abruptly and said to us, "You are here to see this, and then you will go and leave us to our work."

My attention was pulled back to their unusual weapons. The swords they held now gave off a kind of glow, as if they had come to life. I had to ask, "Are you two holding a Roman spatha?"

They looked at me, as if surprised that I would know anything about ancient steel weapons. "No, these are known as the Kult of Athena. Our weapons are empowered to fight the darkness that will be here soon," the male warrior said grimly.

We had felt their presence first and then we saw them. As if on cue, the castle's hoard of defenders appeared and began to swarm over the top of the fortress walls. As they moved closer, I realized these were the same beings I had seen in my earlier death dreams. These had to have been the lost souls of those who had given themselves over to the ego-driven darkness of greed and lust for power, which is always Maridon's bait.

Looking briefly at Amy, I could tell she was having the same reaction to this new enemy even though she had seen this before. It occurred to me that it would be difficult to become accustomed to witnessing something this hideous. There was no consistency in their shapes. Some appeared to have been soulless while others were from physical reality. They had appendages that varied in size and length as one would expect to see with various people. Their skin appeared to be thick and dirty, an ample site for endless pestilence to reside. As the enemy swarmed toward us, their growling, guttural sounds and the rhythmic thumping of swords against shields were something that, again, sent dire warnings through my entire being.

They continued to pour over the walls and filled the area in front of the castle, which I now realized had been used as a battlefield many times. The evil beings filled their side of the line of engagement and formed a shield wall. The sounds of the vociferous growling and hissing of demonic threats grew while they attempted to send fear into the souls of their future victims. I recognized this as being the ritual of combat from centuries ago. The shield wall of combatants was where the courage and skill of delivering death to an enemy would be tested.

Then it occurred to me that the intense warnings I had been feeling all over my body was an indication that pure evil was nearby, and it was something other than what I saw standing before me. Some of the demonic beings on the shield wall had never been and would never be embodied as I understood it. If what Amy described earlier was true, then all I was seeing was nothing more than the energy bodies of the lost souls and those soulless creatures created by Maridon. I could not reconcile this separation because I did not understand how anyone could fight something that is not in physical form.

The one difference I could understand was their sole purpose in this dimension. They were here to create fear while ultimately delivering death, not life, to their victims. And once fear destroyed any semblance of love that was present, the attackers would ensure the death that was freely given was slow and torturous. They lived to hear their victims beg for mercy before they would consider dispatching them. It was this final delivery that would partially satisfy their endless blood lust.

Yet, I knew delaying that final step as long as possible would be the only hope of fighting against these creatures, for now. It would cause them pain, which made me wonder how long they would continue if they were unable to satisfy their lust for fear, pain, and death. Somehow, I knew the answer would be forthcoming, and my rationality and its conflicts with which I struggled would end.

While I considered all of these possibilities, I saw our two protectors suddenly raise their shields and swords toward the heavens and make a deep-throated howling call. They struck their swords against their raised shields once, yelled once more, and then struck their shields a second time followed yet by a third. Each time they struck sword to shield, the sound echoed throughout the battlefield as if it came from thousands of warriors doing the same simultaneously. After the echo began to subside, the heavens above and behind us exploded as if a massive thunderstorm had just been created.

The newly formed clouds opened and revealed the arrival of an army of warriors thundering to our side of the shield wall. Their physical appearance mirrored that of the two who stood before us, if not more so. Their shields, swords, helmets, and chain mail all appeared new and well-polished. As they rushed to align themselves with our two "love" warriors, I saw that the line of engagement, our own shield wall, stretched across the entire battlefield as far as I could see in either direction.

The new arrivals were so numerous that they formed three waves. Our duo pushed behind the third row of newly arrived soldiers towards us. "See that small hill behind us?" The female warrior said grimly.

"Yes," I replied.

"Go there and watch." She pointed to Amy. "She'll know when you must leave. Don't hesitate when she says it's time. Do you understand?"

"Yes, but why are you going into battle now? No one's going to die here today, right?" I asked.

"Everything is possible here. Death is as present as anywhere else. But, it's a different kind of death than what you know. Watch carefully and learn. This is what we all have been preparing for, defeating the darkness that hatred brings is crucial. And, with this battle, it begins. What you do not understand, she will explain," she said, pointing to Amy again. She turned to her warrior lover, and they pressed their way back to the front line to lead their troops against this horrendous enemy.

As we stood on the hill behind the line of engagement, Amy was obviously taken by what was happening in front of us. "Amazing, isn't it?" Then, I heard some ancient horns cast their deep-pitched voice to fill the battlefield air with a sound that was like a thousand bulls wailing in agony. The gates of the ancient castle opened, and I saw a familiar tall, foreboding creature, almost human in appearance, emerge. It wasn't walking; it simply floated to a command position in front of the horde of dark defenders. It was then I realized that this is where these human-like entities derived their authority to exist and to destroy. "Yes, it feels very unnatural, yet there's something familiar about it all," I said to Amy.

"That's because when one of the original crowd decided he was just as powerful as God, he wanted to prove he could do everything God could do. So, he created some of what you see here, but he couldn't create the core element that gives life to everything . . . love. He has no interest in such things. His desires focus solely on absolute power. He temps his minions with wealth and prestige, and uses fear and death to grow his power. These are the things that corrupt our egos if we let it," Amy said as she looked around and then continued, "We'll have to go soon."

As he moved closer, I could clearly see him and said, "I remember seeing him the first time when I was fourteen." That particular precognitive vision had never left my consciousness. "How long can we stay?" I asked.

"Just long enough to show you what we're up against. Once you see, you'll understand, and we'll leave. Believe me, this experience will change everything inside you. It did for me when I went through this initiation," she said with a tone of concern.

Amy had my attention now, and my spirit went on high alert. I now felt a sudden need for a weapon of some kind. An urge that felt at once deeply unnatural, yet quite equally familiar. Something was changing within my consciousness. Possibilities that I thought were foreign to me began to feel acceptable. I wanted to feel the hilt of the Kult of Athena in the grip of my right hand. I longed to engage the murderers on the opposing side as if I were avenging the wrong they committed over and over throughout the centuries, the wrong I had witnessed in many of my visions. I was, in fact, connecting with another part of myself that stood on this battlefield as a leader of those who believed in the same values throughout my life.

I had been told by spiritual mentors that souls like mine come equipped with all sorts of sensors that will warn us when danger approaches. I just had to open my mind and be willing to accept these warnings. Sounds easy, doesn't it? Well, it's anything but easy.

Suddenly, we were hit by a wave of energy. Amy asked in a sharp voice, "Did you feel that?"

"Gawd, yes . . . what the hell was that?" I asked, unnerved by this energy that had just pushed violently through me. What I had sensed was a strong vibrational movement throughout my body. It felt angry, almost as if it wanted to a rip me apart. It came again and as it continued, the pain it created could not be denied.

Finally, I knew what was causing it. A small number of the enemy was looking directly at us. They had a look on their faces that sent a deathly chill to my core. Their eyes were penetrating us with a singular focus as they drooled relentlessly. They appeared anxious to sate their bloodlust, suggesting that their last feeding was perhaps two or three centuries ago. Dinner had finally arrived, and it was us.

Chapter 24

Blaring horns filled the air once more. The maniacal soldiers facing us became nearly uncontrollable as the battle was about to begin, and their deepest desire to feast upon this mayhem would be granted. Our warriors on the shield wall stood ready to fight. Then, without any obvious reason, the animalistic sounds of our opponents were silenced.

The foreboding humanlike creature that had emerged from the castle earlier moved ahead of their line and stopped. I recognized him as Maridon from my earlier visions, but now that he could be seen better, it was obvious that this demonic spirit stood out among his death-hungry line. Their leader's power was well evidenced by his heavily muscled body and the fear his underlings exhibited as he walked amongst them. He wore a tunic beneath what appeared to be newly polished mail, which oddly stood out, but allowed his body to move easily. The dull sounds of its rustling metal could be heard subtly announcing his arrival as he approached our warrior leaders. The closer he came to us, the more his ornate helmet demanded my attention. Though it was incredible to see, his armament served another purpose that went far beyond just being a tool of war. It was symbolic of his power and dominion over those he chose to enslave, and it was meant to create a deep fear of impending doom in his adversaries.

He carried a shield that was far more prominent than those of our troops and as equally ornate as his helmet. The angry images that decorated its surface glowed a sickening greenish-brown color while it pulsed subtly. Would it not seem reasonable that his chosen weapon would have been a sword? He had, instead, a battle ax with an enormous war head that only someone of his strength could wield in battle.

He stopped close enough to our line so I could see his mail in greater detail. The defensive metal clothing covered him as any other warrior. But the metal appeared to be polished red steel, which gave me the impression that it had been dyed in the blood of the living—perhaps his victims from earlier battles. A sudden flash of imagery appeared, and I saw him slaughtering soldiers and innocent villagers in earlier battles. Some were begging for mercy as his huge battle ax sliced the air at blinding speed, easily cutting through more than one body at a time before moving onto others. For some reason, I recalled the recurring visions that began when I was fourteen. It occurred to me that this was a reminder to show his longtime solicitation of me and how much I should fear him if I didn't accede to his threats. Yes, this was obviously the leader of these dark creatures and the realm they claimed, suggesting he did not come by this position lightly.

As I stood there, all of this was feeling increasingly familiar as the visions of a lifetime suddenly became my reality. Countering this unnerving realization, I thought of how our troops would defeat him as they had done many times before, which bolstered my confidence. Maridon wasted no time claiming his authority as the monster aggressively stepped forward and spoke.

"You dare bring these two onto my lands? What reason do you have to invade me again in this manner?" he growled in a loud, deep tone that carried easily across the battlefield. We could hear him as if he was standing only a few feet away, even though he stood atop a small rise in front of our troops.

Our female warrior leader stepped forward and responded aggressively, "This is NOT your land and we are here by right. You and your ilk are imposters claiming to be greater than He who created everything we all know and have known for eons. Why do you show yourselves in this manner, insulting and threatening us as you do?"

"Imposter? Insult? You are the ones that bring these two creatures from the other side into our midst only to show them what? How we will rip your bodies apart and devour what's left of your carcasses before them? Is that why you're here, to show them how and why you fear us?" the leader growled in retort.

"We do not fear you or your egregiously bloated ego, Maridon. You have not and will never change. These two see what you really are. You show yourself in visions as being superior and unconquerable, which denies all that can be plainly seen. You are a menace to all living creatures here and on the other side. You have no respect for our Lord or that which He has created."

"Your so-called Lord is weak," he snarled in utter disrespect. "He sends a woman to do a man's job. So take me, Ariel, destroy me, if you feel you can. Do you have the balls to do something you think is easy? Ha, how stupid of me, of course you don't. You're nothing more than an ignorant bitch who thinks she's a man. Remind yourself, Ariel, reach between your legs and discover what's missing. As for the so-called men that you call an army, they must be suckled to your tits. Why else would they allow a weakling woman to speak for them? I will do them a service today and put them out of their deluded misery where they stand," he said scowling at her.

Thrusting her sword suddenly at him in righteous anger, her muscles flexed intensely as she retorted, "Your people have tasted my steel before in combat and many did not survive. You'll taste it again today if you do not return to your castle and leave us be."

As she held her weapon skyward, it began to glow, then surged with a brilliant blue-white radiance as if it were breathing and filling with justice-seeking authority. The creatures on the line, who could see her and the sword she brandished, appeared to know what she meant, as some began to turn away from her and cower. The Sergeants, who controlled their line, began flogging those who trembled in fear to ensure they understood what was required of them and what would happen if they failed. Despite the brutal flogging, those punished knew what was to come in this battle and that it would not be pleasant.

"You're nothing but a worthless bitch on this battlefield. Things have changed, Ariel. You and your army of ball-less men are about to find out. And, I might add, your guests on the hill will be my evening meal. I will not let them return from whence they came. They are mine now," he said forcefully. And with that, he turned and confidently walked back to a command position, pushing his creatures out of his path with a sweep of his shield arm.

Ariel returned to stand next to Ancient Dave and prepared for what was about to happen. She stood facing him and they appeared to draw strength from each other. Suddenly, they raised their shields and slammed them against each other with vigorous determination. Then, they raised them higher with a war cry to encourage the entire line and our warriors joined in the cry for victory over their deranged enemy.

"Amy, what was he talking about when he said things have changed?" I asked, while keeping my eyes on the line of engagement.

"I didn't know anything could change," she said, while still looking at the shield walls.

I considered her response and what it implied and then said quietly, "I hope you're right, but just in case I think we should have a plan. If we can't get back to the portal, where would we go?" I asked.

Amy thought for a while before answering, "I've never had a need for an escape plan before. You know, Maridon likes to imply that things are worse than they are. What we just saw was bluster. They always do that before a fight. It must be a kind of mind-game. Let's not worry about it," she said reassuringly.

Something told me to pay attention to everything happening and specifically to the small group of creatures that were closest to us. They may have been several hundred feet away, but the warnings I felt made me think that they had the task of getting to us regardless of the cost. And even though I was told death was not possible on this side, I realized then that I needed confirmation.

Death, as we know it, is really nothing more than the death of our body, a vessel that allows the soul to experience physical reality, the laboratory of learning. On this side of the veil, I had always been told that I would experience everything as an energy body. I would appear the same as if I was in my physical body, but I would not experience the same tactile sensations all the time.

So why not do some simple tests? I could feel the ground underneath my feet. I could smell the gut-retching odors of the barbaric creatures near us. The heat and breeze was something that I also felt as if I were in a physical body. Since there was a soldier next to us, I borrowed his knife. Drawing the blade across the back of my arm, I saw blood begin to trickle from the stinging wound.

"Amy, I've got a question. Are we or are we not in an energy body?"

"Our energy bodies, Dave, you know that," she responded still focused on the shield wall.

"Well, I hate to burst your bubble, but maybe that's changed. I held my forearm out so she could see the slowly dripping blood. Her eyes widened as she stuttered to say something that wasn't coming out. She knew what this meant and it apparently hit her hard. She looked up at me and said in a near-panic tone, "What do we do? I don't want to be stuck here."

Just as she said that, the horns of war sounded again and both sides ran at each other. I've never seen or heard anyone charge each other and collide as they did here. The deep thudding sound of shield hitting shield in combat is unlike anything you could imagine. Now, adding to that an entire line of combatants that was as long as the eye could see. When these shields hit at the same time, the resounding, deep vibrational thud echoed through me and across the entire battlefield like a shock wave. The loud rhythmic grunting of the combatants pushing against each other began and grew rapidly. The chaos of battle had been unleashed.

Swords and spears began seeking purchase deep within their adversaries as combatants slashed across the shield line. Occasionally one would find its mark and the screams of living creatures fighting to the death were replaced by the wailing of a person or a creature who sustained a mortal blow, and then they appeared to die. Warriors and creatures in their respective second lines would replace those who had fallen. A grueling battle like this would prove to be a slow process of determining who was stronger and more capable of outmaneuvering and outlasting the other.

I had no idea what to do if this went poorly, but apparently the idea that death actually existed here continued to grow as each new combatant fell. Ariel left us a small number of guards who were close and ready to defend us if needed. My only thought was how to escape behind the line with them, work our way back to the forest's edge, and get to the portal. But, I was almost certain that getting back to this gateway was too obvious and easily understood by the opposition. I knew I had to have another option if this failed.

My attention was drawn back to the line where our adversary was executing a carnage that would give nightmares to a normal person. Our side of the line looked like it was beginning to weaken in a spot close to us. If there was now death on this side of the veil, there was also the certainly of injury. And the injuries to our soldiers were disabling to the point that our uncontained opponents looked like they were going to breach our part of the line. With each advance, there was more success. They pushed slowly into and then through the first line of warriors. Our next two defensive lines swarmed in to slow them down as they tried to push the garish creatures back.

I could not help but again think what if the enemy breached the remaining lines? They could capture us, not to mention defeat Ariel. It became obvious that something needed to be done.

"You," I called out to one of our protectors and motioned him over to us. "What is your name, trooper?" I asked.

"I am Ninian."

"Ninian, we need to get to a safer place. Will you and your companions come with us to the forest?"

"Yes, Ariel wants us to stay with you."

"Good, if Ariel loses this battle, is there someplace we can go if we can't get back to the portal?"

"You could come with us. Our village is not close and while it isn't in this dimension, it can be reached from here. We'll have to move fast and stay under the cover of the forest if we are to survive. Maridon can now see things that he was unable to in the past, and we don't know how he does it."

"Has Maridon ever won a battle against Ariel?" I asked. And as I said this, I heard a loud roar of victory behind me. I turned to see a large number of creatures break through our lines and pour in behind our troops attempting to cut them off from the others. The army was now split into two groups, a general's dream come true for Maridon.

Our warriors were regrouping and trying to avoid being encircled. The battle raged at a higher pitch as Maridon came into the line where Ariel and her mate were fighting. He swung his battle ax through our troops as if he were slicing cheese. I was appalled by the appearance of body parts leaping from their host as if they had been blown from their mount. With each swing of the ax, Maridon came closer and closer to Ariel, the prize he obviously wanted badly.

"We need to go now," I said to Ninian urgently.

He agreed and quickly led the way behind our lines toward the trees with his fellow troopers surrounding us. As we approached the edge of the battlefield, a squad of creatures began to pursue us.

"Run," Ninian screamed over his shoulder as he drew his sword.

We had not quite reached the forest's edge when Ninian and his troopers stopped. He chose to provide a defensive line to slow the advancing creatures while Amy and I continued into the forest. Before he released us, he looked at me as if he knew how this would end for him and held out a sturdy long-bow and a large quiver of heavy, metal-tipped battle arrows. Though I didn't believe I had used this kind of weapon before, it felt familiar somehow. I accepted the offering from a man who had prepared himself for sacrifice.

"Go now, hurry into the woods. Protect our Amy. She is obviously frightened. Our people know and care for her as if she were one of us. If we survive, we will find you. If we do not and the portal is closed, there is a river near the forest edge. Follow it toward the sun. In three days, you will come to something that will look vaguely odd. Trust your senses and cross through it to my village. Tell them what happened. They will know what to do. Now go," he told us.

Both of us were frightened as my mind raced through all sorts of possible outcomes. How should I deal with this? We ran as fast as we could and left our protectors behind. Amy kept looking back at them nearly crying as if she were leaving family in the hands of a barbaric murderer. I thought to myself, *If they don't survive, what could I do to protect us from Maridon's creatures, let alone Maridon himself?* I thought about the tool Ninian gave me. The bow was huge and durable; the arrows were long and heavy. But, how could I effectively use such a thing without any training? As I held the weapon, it began to feel even more familiar as if I had used this particular bow many times in the past.

We finally reached the forest's edge and moved into the tree line for cover. I turned to keep sight of Ninian and his troopers, while moving the two of us to an area where we could not be seen by the enemy. The deep-pitched thudding and noises of sword striking sword in combat had accelerated. The nightmarish growling of Maridon's creatures were the only sounds that could be heard.

We stopped inside a ravine near a tree line that looked secure. I turned to find Ninian again. Just as I did so, the battle reached a fevered pitch.

His group was obviously well-trained and seasoned. They had taken down several of our pursuers. Slowly, but surely, they defeated all of them and then quickly moved into the trees to follow us. Just as they approached our hiding place, I saw one of them suddenly propelled forward with a look of shock. A long, heavy arrow with a savage-looking head had penetrated his torso and protruded from his chest. When he fell, he fell as a dead man, and so I was convinced of this change. Death was here and this was one thing that had changed from earlier contests.

"Into the forest . . . GO," Ninian yelled to us and to his troopers as more arrows flew past them.

We ran hard for what seemed like miles trying to avoid striking tree and limb until we could run no farther. We finally stopped too exhausted to continue. That's when I noticed the sounds of birds singing in the trees and wind gently moving through the canopy above us. All of this had replaced the screams of the battle and arrows flying into the bodies of our warriors.

It was time to rest and make plans. If Amy and I were to return home, we had to find a way to get back to the portal. My guess was Maridon had already foreseen this and would be waiting with a plan of his own.

Chapter 25

"How far are we from the portal, Ninian?" I asked our protector.

"Not far. It is in the valley on the other side of that pass," he said pointing the way.

Something about leaving them behind kept nagging at me. "Ninian, I thank you and your troopers for protecting us. I do not have the skills to fight beside you, my friend."

"Ha, Ma'el and Ariel have told me about the mysteries behind you two. You may think you don't, but you do," he said with a grin.

"Ma'el? That's the other warrior's name? Ariel's partner?" I asked.

"Yes. They have been together for a long time. But, you should know that. Aren't you him?" Ninian said, somewhat confused that I wouldn't know that.

"Sorry Ninian, I'm still a little lost as to what's going on here. While watching our troopers battle those creatures, I felt a sense of familiarity with the fighting, the planning, and all that goes with it," I said.

"Yes, you should," he said as he studied me. "Do you have any idea where you are?" he asked.

"Not really. All I know is that I came here to learn something because of a new danger in my world, which has cost the lives of two friends, one of which I loved dearly," I said.

We had to stop and rest. Once we were settled down, Ninian seemed to be deep in thought as he took a moment while leaning against an old tree.

"I don't know what I should say. Perhaps I should begin by telling you about us. We are known as *The Guardians.* Our purpose is to protect you and this realm as we protect our king and his clan," he said.

"The Guardians. That says a lot."

"We are the king's best troopers, and we all come from the same village and the same bloodline."

"Your King. Who is he?" I asked.

"His name is Ma'ele Ruanaid, Ma'el Sechnail is his son," Ninian said.

"Who is Ma'el Sechnail?" I asked, trying to keep up.

Ninian smiled. "I guess you wouldn't know your father since you didn't know your own name," he said.

"No. Ma'el didn't think he and I needed to be introduced, since I would only be here for a short time."

Ninian leaned forward with a sense of excitement. "Well, Ariel and Ma'el are formidable warriors on and off the battlefield. They have never been defeated on the shield wall, never. And, Ma'el has learned that having Ariel do his talking rattles the enemy. They're not accustomed to being confronted by a woman, and are particularly deflated when she defeats them in battle. It's just unheard of over here, my strange friend."

I could see that the idea of fighting behind a woman, who wields a sword and shield as she does, was heartening to him. "So, what are they like off the battlefield? Do they get along?" I asked.

"They do, but they also are not shy about arguing if they are so inclined. When that happens, they step outside and close the door," he said with a smirk.

"Aren't you concerned that an argument might go too far," I asked.

He laughed, "Oh no, we never see them make up, but they always do. And when they resolve their issues, you can hear them making-up for hours in their chamber," he said with a typical male grin.

After resting for a while, we were back on the trail headed toward the valley that held the portal. As we approached the pass, a dire feeling of impending disaster was bearing down on me, almost collapsing my body. I staggered, losing my balance, and then stopped on the path. I bent over trying to support myself.

"What's wrong?" Ninian asked.

"Amy, come here," I struggled to say.

"What's wrong, are you okay?" she asked.

"Can't you feel that," I asked in disbelief. After all, she was far more psychic than me. "No, what are you talking about?" she asked.

"Gawd Amy, it feels like a ton of bricks just landed on my shoulders. I can hardly stand upright, and it's difficult to breathe. It's like someone's trying to keep us from going any further."

Amy looked down the path while Ninian looked ahead as well. "You might want to send a scout ahead and see if there's anything we need to prepare for," she said to Ninian.

"Scouts were sent ahead after our last stop," he said and then thought a moment longer. "Perhaps you two should stay here. Normally they report back, even if there's no problem," he said, as he waved his fellow Guardians forward.

While they moved ahead, I had to sit down and close my eyes. The weight was draining me and I needed to rest. "Amy, I've gotta take a break. Let me know when they come back, or if you hear anything abnormal."

And with that, I had no choice but to slip into a trance state. Immediately I had the sensation of being pushed forcefully along our path and then past Ninian and his Guardians. As I approached the pass, I was pushed upward and had a view of everything from just above the mountain crest on either side of the pass. That's when I saw that Maridon's creatures had taken positions along the ridge and were armed with long bows and spears. There were also a few on the other side of the pass waiting in case any of us pushed through their gauntlet of death.

I realized that whoever was pushing me along was trying to help me and it was urgent. "Trust your skills. You know how to use the long bow. Now go use it. Deliver our justice to these cretins," the unseen guides instructed me.

My eyes opened abruptly and I grabbed the long-bow and large quiver that Ninian had given me earlier. Amy joined me as I rushed off to catch up to Ninian and our friends. "Where are we going?" Amy asked, startled by my sudden movement.

"It's a trap, Amy. I saw it. We've got to catch up to Ninian and warn him." I said.

We saw them ahead of us and ran harder to warn them before they entered the small clearing that led to the pass, but they had already reached the entrance.

"Ninian," I yelled. "Stop. It's a trap." The echoed warning bounced between the hillsides that held our enemy.

Ninian turned around and saw us with a look of surprise. "You should not be here," he shouted.

The first round of arrows began thudding the ground around us as we all took cover. Remembering what I was told during my vision, I left Amy with Ninian and made my way up the face of the hill to one side of the pass careful to maintain cover. My hand held the long bow while the other reached for an arrow. Seeing my first target up higher and ahead, I mounted the arrow and tried to pull back. The strength required to release the arrow with authority was tremendous. Suddenly, energy flowed into me, as if I had done this many times, and I pulled the bow string back and released the arrow without any effort. I watched the warhead streak through the air and thud into the distant creature's chest causing him to stagger and tumble down the cliff.

I found my next target and did the same. As quickly as I could, I dispatched yet another. My relentless attack encouraged Ninian and his Guardians to press through the pass slowly to ensure that there were no additional surprises. Other barbaric combatants tried to surge forward and kill us, but they fell to the Guardian's swords and my battle arrows.

It didn't take long for us to dispatch them all. I joined Ninian and his troops in the pass feeling jubilant about our success, but then I noticed Amy was not with him.

"Where's Amy?" I asked desperately.

"I left a trooper with her where you caught up with us," he said.

I rushed back to find her because I felt something was wrong. The unseen pressure was returning and I knew what that meant this time. As we approached the area where we had emerged, we saw that the trooper who was protecting

Amy had been slaughtered and Amy was nowhere to be found.

As I looked around trying to see where she and her kidnappers might be, we heard someone shout from above us followed by a ghastly laugh that echoed through the pass.

"Did you lose something? Come through the pass to the other side. I think you'll see her there," the deep voice shouted.

We took off cautiously on the run in case it was another trap. When we exited the pass, everything changed. I saw the portal ahead, but in between myself and the portal stood Maridon, with a heavily armed squad of his creatures and Amy. They had her on her knees bound tightly. I could tell she was in pain by the way her arms were pulled viciously behind her.

Ninian angrily responded to Maridon's insult. "Let her go, Maridon. She has no value to you. You cannot threaten her family here and receive a ransom. Let her go."

"No value? Are you daft?" He paused, then added, "Ah, I keep forgetting. You are one of Ariel's tit-suckled males who lets a ball-less woman do his talking. I'll not let her go, boy. She's mine to do with as I wish and I have many wicked wishes for her tonight. And that's her value to me. This will be a special treat given she comes from the other side of the veil. How often does a powerful King such as myself have that kind of treat here?" Maridon said sarcastically.

How could we get her away from him? We were outnumbered and Amy would not be so easily rescued or bargained for. As Maridon and Ninian insulted each other, I began to slowly work my way around to a position that would allow me a better shot of Maridon's creatures.

I moved off to one side and took a position on a small rise hidden by trees that allowed me to see my targets clearly. I positioned a handful of heavy arrows in front of me sticking them in the dirt. It felt natural having them there and would allow me to fire several quickly. If successful, I would be able to keep the creatures at bay while Ninian and his crew moved to attack.

I let loose the first volley and all but one hit its mark. The arrows hit so fast, one after the other, that Maridon and his creatures were kept confused. This surprise attack allowed Ninian and his crew to advance on them.

Once Maridon realized he was exposed and his troops were almost completely decimated, he decided to withdraw from the battlefield. He made his way to a thick grove of trees to take cover, savagely dragging Amy with him. I could see her wincing face while imaging the screams of pain twisting through her tortured body.

As he made his way toward the trees, I saw why he headed to this particular location. He evidently had the power to open his own portals, and as he commanded one to appear, it opened a passage that led back to the interior of his fortress.

I had only seconds to act if I wanted to save Amy's life. This was the longest shot that I had taken, but I had to take the chance. The arrows I launched flew for what seemed like forever, and then I saw the first one strike the shoulder of Maridon's arm dragging Amy. Just as that arrow struck, a second one missed him, but another struck the same arm that caused him to release his captive.

Amy pulled herself away, stumbled, and then regained her balance and began running clumsily back to Ninian while Maridon continued through his portal. The door to his fortress abruptly closed behind him protecting him from any further assault. That's when I noticed there were others that had joined us in the battle.

As I looked toward the portal, Amy and I needed to go through, I saw Beaux and a few others who had apparently seen what was happening and rushed through the gateway to help us. The joy of seeing my friend propelled me down the hill as I rushed up to him and greeted his party.

"Beaux, you're here! How did you know to come?" I asked excitedly.

"Hey, didn't you know we could see into a portal and watch what's going on? We saw that monster grab my Auntie and I wasn't have'n any of that!" he said excitedly.

Amy hugged him after Ninian released her bonds. "Thanks, Nephew," she said.

"So, are you two ready to come home, now? This place doesn't look that friendly," Beaux smirked.

While I was thankful for Beaux and his family's help, part of me was still assessing what to do next. If we returned to our time, I'd still have to deal with Maridon's influence. He had already proven to be dangerous and difficult to defend against. That was especially true since I was pressed to figure this out and come up with a plan.

If I stayed to deal with Maridon, I would be addressing the threat he posed on his own territory and perhaps with far more allies than I would have in physical reality. The question was how would we defeat him and how long would this take?

"Ninian, do you think Maridon will leave us alone for a while? Perhaps long enough for us to talk this out?" I asked.

"You hurt him badly, David. He'll not forget you. And, he'll want far more than just a pound of flesh or your head on a stake. No one has ever done that to him before," Ninian said with some pride.

"They haven't? That's odd. He's such a huge target. How could anyone miss that?" I asked in disbelief.

"Remember, Maridon himself said things have changed. Maybe he wasn't counting on that change affecting him, too. If I'm correct, he's now just as susceptible to injury and physical death as any of his creatures or us. I wonder how long it will take him to heal and then what will he do to seek vengeance against you, David."

"We have to decide whether I should stay here to fight him or go back to the other side and fight from there. Any thoughts?" I asked, looking at everyone.

There was silence, but I had a nagging feeling where this discussion was heading. Beaux finally said, "If you're staying, then so am I. I'll send one of my guys back to let Mom and Dad know. The rest of the family can decide what they want to do."

"And don't think you're going to send me home like a lost little girl. If you two stay, I'm staying, too," Amy said.

"What if Maridon captures you again? You almost ended up being his personal treat. I can't go through losing someone I care about yet a third time, Amy. You have to go back," I said with a firm tone.

"Oh that makes perfect sense. Send me back to protect me. Well guess what, Maridon can just as easily find me on the other side. You're growing on me, David, and I don't think being separated is a brilliant move now. Besides, Beaux should go back with the rest of our family. What happens if Maridon sends someone to attack them?" Amy asked.

"Hey, anyone who's foolish enough to attack us is going to get their asses kicked by a lot of crazy Cajun guys.

And we don't take captives when we fight such evil," Beaux said with pride.

Amy looked at me and asked, "We should strike at the heart together, don't you agree?"

Having thought about everything that had happened up to this point, I had to agree. There was no way to deal with this situation any more effectively than doing it right here. But, if we stayed we would be doing so at great risk because we still didn't understand the total scope of what we were dealing with here, and it was Maridon's turf, not ours.

"Amy, normally I would agree, but I don't see us knowing enough to defeat Maridon. I think it would be a better idea for us to go with Ninian to his village and find out what happened to Ariel and Ma'el. Then, we should return to our own turf and plan our next assault from there. I'm beginning to feel something's happening back there that needs our intervention, but I don't know what it is yet."

She laughed at me and said, "Dave, this started as your fight. But, it affects me just as much as you. Besides, I'm involved now. The decision has to be yours. The nice thing about it is that if you stay, you've got a lot of support."

She was right as I would learn repeatedly in the future. She was always going to be right no matter what I said or thought. Beyond that, I was still trying to get my mind around the implications of our relationship as it seemed to be evolving. Obviously, we were together in earlier lives.

"Okay," I said as I looked at Ninian and Beaux. "It looks like we're going with you, Ninian." It was anyone's guess where this would lead or what would happen next. One thing was certain. We needed to find out what happened to Ariel and Ma'el as soon as we could. Maridon was going to be one unhappy camper and I wanted to hit him soon and hard somewhere, somehow.

www.ingramcontent.com/pod-product-compliance
Lightning Source LLC
Chambersburg PA
CBHW050901250626
47155CB00001B/55